A Novel By

Fergus Hinely

Copyright ©2025 Line By Lion Publications
www.pixelandpen.studio
ISBN 9781948807708
Cover Design by Joshua Biren
Editing by Dani J. Caile

For more information, email www.linebylionpublications.com

*This book is dedicated to my fellow teachers in Okinawa, Japan,
who helped me when I was alone in a strange place.*

Part One: The Beginning

Chapter One

Fred Windsley

HE was digging a crumpled box of teriyaki Slim Jims out of a sand-filled snack aisle of a Texaco gas station when he heard a low purring sound. Fred Windsley, already jumpy from three energy drinks he'd downed twenty minutes ago and a large wad of loose Copenhagen burning through his bottom lip, whipped around in the dim gas station so fast he heard his neck pop.

"Ah – oh, o – shit – that hurt."

His surprise was quickly forgotten, replaced by a throbbing in his already red and peeling neck. He rolled his head and loosened his jaw to try and alleviate some of the swelling pain. From behind one of the little dips and dunes of sand inside the gas station sauntered a silky looking black cat. The cat flicked his unusually long tail against the top part of a shelf and blinked green eyes at Fred, as if prompting him to explain his intrusion. Fred looked back at the cat for a few moments in the silence and the stillness, then returned to his Slim Jim excavation.

"Meow."

Fred paused and turned back to look at the cat. "Shoo." Fred waved his hands ineffectually, like 'go away.'

The cat let out another, "Meow," and this time, it somehow sounded a little contemptuous.

"I got nothin for ya' pal. Best just keep on munching on whatever you got here. Must be something good ta last you this long, eh? Just… move along now. No room for pets with ol' Freddy."

Fred had come into the cliché post-apocalyptic habit of talking to himself quite easily, so talking to a cat was easy work. He hadn't been an especially popular kid, *or adult for that matter,* and had often found himself alone with his thoughts, with no place to vent them other than the air. *Before*, of course, if he had really needed to, he could've talked to his sister, or maybe his mom, but — *Not no mo*, as Fred would often say to himself. *Not no mo*. It was slowly becoming his mantra. If he could read or write, he might've found great release in those activities, but alas…

The past eight months had found Fred almost completely alone. He hadn't seen another human being since El Paso, four months ago. And that hadn't exactly been a golden opportunity for conversation. The nightmares still plagued his shit freezing nights.

Freddy, having thought his shooing would be enough to discourage the cat, turned his back and resumed digging. The black cat regarded Freddy for a moment with those glistening green eyes, then made his way over to him with a very purposeful strut. Each step sent the cat's shoulder blades shooting up from his lean muscled back in folds of inky black fur, like pistons in a perfectly oiled engine. The feel of another living creature nudging against his lower back made Fred freeze in his tracks. It was a strange thing. And not something he'd allowed himself to believe he would experience again in his life. In fact, in the last week, Fred had become almost entirely convinced that he was the last living person in all of east Texas. Maybe the whole god damned southern United States. Though, somewhere deep down, he knew that wasn't true.

There were certainly some people to the west. He knew that much. Though how many were left, he couldn't say. As far as north, south and east went. Fred had no reason to believe they would be anything different than where he was now. That is to say, *completely fucking buried* in sand.

Fred reckoned he was somewhere just west of Fort Worth, though he had no real way of knowing. If he was lucky, the desert might allow him a glimpse of a road sign, or a building header. He'd been trying to follow the highways, but the first day into his eastward journey, Fred had known that was going to be impossible. Where once had lain the great horizontal monuments of American civilization, the great expanses of hot, black, yellow-striped freedom — *the highways of America, the veins* — now sloshed an ocean of fine, golden sand. Completely unreadable, and constantly changing.

Fred could feel the warmth of the little black cat through his canvas cargo pants. It seemed... *wrong* for some reason. *Too hot.* Strangely hot. But also good. *Really good.* Like hugging your parents after your first day of public school, or the warm handshake and embrace of a good friend after a long time apart. The cat weaved around Fred's body like a snake around a log, smooth and silent and powerful. Fred looked down between his crouched legs to find those green eyes gazing up at him, startlingly green against the dull brown of the shaded sand. Slowly, Fred reached down and slid his hand over the ears of the cat. He started to purr.

"Well... would you look at that. Knew I was good for somethin'. I'm a doggone cat whisperer," Fred chuckled quietly. He hated the sound of his voice in the dead silence of this new world. It made him feel even crazier than he already was. And he *was* crazy.

The biggest irony of this moment for Fred, was the fact that he hated cats. Always had. Maybe some neighborhood tom had bitten him in childhood. He didn't think so, but he couldn't say for sure. Ever since he could remember, he had despised cats. In his high school years, he'd even gone as far as going out of his way to hurt them. Well, at the very least scare them. Throw a rock, honk the horn, swerve the car a little bit towards one on the side of the road, that kind of stuff. And in this vast new wasteland, the first and only living creature he'd seen in months, besides the vultures of course, was a cat.

"Well... I suppose you're not all that bad, eh? Ain't much goin' on around here is there. You feel like taking a little ride?"

*   *   *

FRED and the black cat with the green eyes, who he had decided to call Jerry, sailed through the desert on a Triumph motorcycle. The turquoise gas tank and red racing stripes were long faded even before Fred *liberated* the bike from an antique automobile dealer in San Francisco. Lots of people had been liberating shiny things from their glass prisons there. Word had gotten around that shit was going to hit the fan very soon, and so, the people had gotten ahead of the curve and thrown the shit themselves. Fred had ridden that Triumph motorcycle through what felt like the nine rings of hell. Burning buildings, murder, gunfights, gang war... violence on display like those animatronics at Disneyland you pass while coasting gently along train tracks disguised as a little stream.

The bike wasn't particularly suited to desert travel, but Fred had fitted some chains to the wheels that helped tremendously. Still, the bike did best when this new American desert was merciful and provided a flat plane upon which to ride. Which, unfortunately, wasn't all that often. Some of the dunes in west Texas Fred had crossed had been taller than four hundred feet. He couldn't decide which was worse: staring up at that wall of sand and hoping to god the little bike could make it up, or, *once he made it to the top*, staring down that terrible steepness and struggling to keep the front wheel straight.

Now, the going was easy. Since the Texaco station where he'd found Jerry, the sand was only about ten feet deep, and level. *Thank Christ*. Fred could almost see where the highway might've been. Almost.

Jerry was a very strange cat. He'd — Fred thought it was a he — followed Fred out of the dark gas station and into the blazing sun without hesitation, and jumped right up on the bike. No schmoozing necessary. Now, he sat between Fred's legs with his front paws propped up the handlebars, ears quivering in the breeze, green eyes gazing ahead like headlights.

Fred had been able to outfit himself rather nicely back in California, but a series of misfortunes on his way east (east, always east) had left him looking more and more ragged. The desert wasn't helping. Every inch of Fred's exposed skin was a red and white field of cracked and dried agony. Underneath the shade of his worn out tan fisherman's hat, his face was a sunken shriveled thing. Like kangaroo jerky. He licked his lips. The hot dry air rushing against his face hurt like lemon juice on a thousand tiny cuts.

Fred had run out of sunscreen weeks ago, not that it helped all that much. The gas station where he'd found Jerry had had a bottle of Banana Boat fifteen. *Funny*. Like trying to put out a house fire with a thimble. Except the thimble was actually full of gasoline. He'd been lucky enough to find a pack of bottled water at the Texaco, but he was still banking on being able to find more in Fort Worth or Dallas. *That's right. Yes. Dallas*. He'd stop there and have a good rest. *A good, long rest.*

Fred wasn't exactly sure why he was going east, other than to run from the people back west. It wasn't the sand he minded.

It was what the sand did to the people that really scared him. Made them act like lunatics. And Fred ought to know a few things about lunatics, being one himself. But there was... *something else* pulling him east. Maybe not a *calling*, but something like when the bathtub starts to empty and all the water circles the drain. *Just natural.*

Consciously, Fred thought about seeing the Atlantic Ocean. He wanted to know if what he'd heard was true — that the oceans were drying up. Or dried up already. He had watched the Pacific start receding back in January, right at the beginning of all this. *Well…* at the beginning of the worst of it anyway. This hell had been in the making for a good long while. Still, he hadn't wanted to believe it. Folks had braced for a tsunami, but the water just kept getting farther and farther away from shore, never to return, like God sipping up the last remains of his pacific milkshake through some mighty straw. But Fred still couldn't wrap his head around the idea that *all* the oceans were going or gone. In his mind, he thought that if he made it to the east coast, he'd find those beautiful blue Atlantic waves lapping at the shores of Corpus Christi and Surfside. And Mark Cuban would be there, sipping a Landshark and beckoning Fred underneath his many colored beach umbrella.

The handlebars twisted violently under Fred's grip. Suddenly he was in the air, flipping in eternity. Then the ground was there, scraping off his skin like forty-grit sandpaper. The same sand that felt like warm silk in a still hand, turned hard as asphalt when it came flying at you at thirty miles an hour. A couple more rolls, then everything came to a stop. Fred could hear the sound of the wind racing across the barren dunes. And the low hum of the Triumph motor that finally stalled when Fred did not rise to feed it.

He lay on his back, staring straight up into that terrible, terrible sunshine. He let out a small groan and pulled his right arm out from underneath him. His hand was facing the wrong way, and his pointer finger was *pointing*, but in a direction that made Fred want to hurl. And then he did. He could feel hot blood and spit running down his cheek and onto his neck. Then the gritty, but pleasant feel of a tongue across his temple. Fred slowly turned his head left to find Jerry sitting primly, licking his paw. His fur wasn't even ruffled. His green eyes seemed to laugh. *Laughing at me*.

"What... the fuck," said Fred.

"Meow," said Jerry.

After some time just lying there, Freddy finally managed to sit up. It was the sun on his face that made him do it. It was like pouring hot oil on his already badly burned face. His bucket hat was still strapped to his head, but his high-speed love affair with mother earth had taken half the brim off. After overcoming his nausea, Fred got shakily to his feet, cradling his mangled arm. He limped over to the thoroughly murdered Triumph. The chain on the front wheel that he'd fixed there to help with traction in the sand had come loose and all at once caught on the frame of the bike. The sudden break had ripped the front wheel clean in half and nearly taken off the whole front steering system.

Fred gazed down at the wreckage plaintively. Jerry pulled up beside him, sat down and looked at the bike. After a moment, Fred let out a big sigh.

"Well, shit."

He turned and started walking.

Chapter Two

Stu Black

"AND – and, what – what was it *again,* that compelled you to do something so… so… *inadvisable* as to try and take one of my bikes? Hmm? Mr. Black?"

"Last I checked, no one person owned all of Phoenix, *Mr. Flemm.* And certainly not everything in it."

The fat man in the strange, half torn, but clean tuxedo let out a laugh. A sound somewhere between a snort, a cough and good howl. His smile widened into a watermelon slice. His brown eyes glittered on either side of his beaked nose like polished deer shit.

"Well, Stu – seems you haven't been paying attention. Phoenix *is* mine. What's left of it, anyway."

The man, who had taken to referring to himself as The Gambler, let a touch of anger and fear cross his face. *The sand scares him. Scares him bad.* Though he had tried to make his self-imposed nickname stick, Stu had overheard nearly all his goons, as well as most of the remaining citizenship of Phoenix, Arizona, refer to him as The Penguin — purely due to his resemblance to the Batman villain. His real name was Hugh Flemm. And with a name as unfortunate as that, Stu could hardly blame him for trying to change it.

"And who decided that?"

The Penguin let out another chuckle. "I did."

Stu Black sat with his hands tied behind the back of a wooden chair facing The Penguin. The thin nylon rope they'd used to bind his hands three days ago had dug deep rivets into the skin of his wrists. They were in quite the agony now, especially after being forced around the wide back of a chair. But Stu gave nothing away. His face remained calm. As did the tone of his voice. When he'd been dragged out of his cell of the Phoenix county jail for an audience with Mr. Flemm, he'd fully expected to break down and beg for mercy, to cry or scream or just die… but none of that had happened. Finally, sitting there in front of the sadistic bastard, he couldn't let go of whatever that *thing* was in him. *Maybe just a spine.* He supposed he'd come too far to abandon the camaraderie he'd found in jail over the past few days. *Ironic.* He couldn't let Jim or Sarah down, couldn't bring himself to submit to this meatball.

"What do you want from us?" Asked Stu.

The Penguin looked at Stu silently for a few moments, gently massaging the loose fatty skin under his chin before replying.

"*Us,* Is it? You know your friend – what was his name? The one you came into town with – Carl? God, what a boring name. Well you know, Carl gave you up like a sack of potatoes, my good man. He was so eager to join our splendid republic, he agreed to kill you and that pregnant bitch himself. With…" The Penguin choked on a little laugh. "'With an axe' I believe he said. 'Like the Shining'."

This did have an effect on Stu. The mention of Carl, and this subsequent bullshit twisted Stu's face into one of pure disgust, as if a bucket of raw sewage were being held just below his nose.

"You don't believe me. Understandable. But I'm telling' ya true, no lie, scout's honor. And all that was even before I let Oslo go to work. I do think he was being sincere, dear Carl. I think he would have actually gone through with his proposal, but I like my employees loyal from the beginning. And, just recently, we were in desperate need of a fresh example of what kind of punishment *treason* begets. Begets? Yeah, begets."

"You are a sick one, ain'tcha. Mommy not give you enough hugs and kisses as a child? I reckon not. Fuckin' ugly ass baby, I'm sure. Wait… let me guess, adopted. She pick you up at the pound?"

Stu raised his eyebrows in a comical look, as if the question had been posed by a well-meaning friend. The Penguin smiled and leaned back in his squeaky beige office chair.

"I like a fighter. You certainly don't lack for balls, Mr. Black." He let out a big sigh, like a father getting ready to lay out plans for the following week – *first we've got soccer practice at five thirty on Monday, then piano lessons for Katy on Tuesday, etc, etc...* "First, I'm going to hang that old fuck with the weird eyes right in the center of town. It'll be a *good* show for my *good* citizens."

*   *   *

STU clenched his teeth hard and tried not to betray any emotion. The Gambler — The Penguin — Hugh Flemm, was referring to Jim Quail, Stu's cell mate, and, rather surprisingly, his new friend — new apocalypse buddies are hard to come by. Though he supposed hardship often brought people together – puts things in a different perspective, as it were. The more intense, the stronger the bond, *potentially*. And the new Phoenix county jail certainly was intense. The "weird eyes" was a reference to Jim having been born with complete heterochromia. Or two different color eyes. In Jim's case, a striking mix of blue and brown.

Jim had been the first to find himself at the mercy of the psychopath Hugh Flemm. For nearly 5 months he'd been confined to a six by eight concrete cell and forced to perform all the clerical and mathematical tasks that The Penguin required for the maintenance of 'his' city. Which was a shocking awful lot, it turned out. Jim was an older man, going on sixty-four, but still spry for his age. He'd had quite a while to adjust to his new circumstances, having been a tenured professor not too long ago, so by the time Stu had arrived three days ago, he had a whole yoga routine and exercise schedule all worked out. Though now that they had stopped distributing food so *generously*, he'd decided conserving his energy might be a better idea.

As for his '*treason*,' he'd been confined to a cell simply for being himself. A decent, democracy loving, American. Or, "Just a regular goddamn person," as Jim would say. Unlike many of the people here, Jim was a Phoenix native. He'd watched his town's slow, steady descent into madness. A few wrong words at the wrong time, and he'd found out that his enthusiasm for freedom of speech was not shared by all the new residents of Phoenix. He'd managed to narrowly escape death by The Penguin because of his above average talent for logistical management. A skill Mr. Flemm lacked for dearly in both himself, and his appointed goons.

Sarah Bracken, the other resident of their little jail community, had come a month ago, picked up outside a drugstore on the outskirts of town by one of Hugh's patrols. She was attempting to take a few aspirin, a pack of wet wipes, and... a bottle of water. She hadn't known, of course, about Hugh Flemm's claim to every droplet of water in the greater Phoenix area. Sarah had promptly been delivered to The Penguin for judgement. At first he'd taken a slimy kind of liking to her. Like a slug trying to mate with a falcon.

Sarah Bracken was quite beautiful – long blonde hair, a tall figure and striking blue eyes. She had come in from out of the northern desert on a Honda CB350, looking like some kind of Mad Maxian goddess. But The Penguin soon found Sarah was not a thing to be claimed like some lost dog. She said not a word to anyone for two months after her capture. The Penguin tried everything his exceedingly pubescent mind could conceive of to win her over, or really just get a word out of her. She gave him nothing. Only at the threat of violence had she let loose the words, "I'm Pregnant."

This admission had prompted a bit of an internal conflict for Hugh Flemm, who had at first refused to believe it. He hadn't quite gotten bored of tormenting Sarah, as freshly appointed dictators do in their spare time, the idea that she was 'soiled,' frustrated him. He couldn't reconcile these two — equally repulsive — halves. And so, Sarah found herself locked up in a jail cell next to Jim Quail. Another one of Hugh's toys in his big, concrete toy box. And three days after that, Stu had crashed the party, being dragged in bloody to his cell across the hall.

All this ran through Stu's mind and as he looked into the many rolls of clammy white skin that functioned as The Penguin's neck. For a moment, he felt deep empathy for this man. This slimy living meatball. Stu was pretty sure, under normal circumstances, he wouldn't have liked Hugh Flemm. But at least they could have been civilized, could have shaken hands and talked like *people. Now… this. This insanity.* Stu wondered, not for the first time, how it had all come down to this shit. *How did we let this happen? To the world. To America, god dammit.* It wasn't like they hadn't seen it all coming. There had been time to stop it, *delay, find a solution… **work together.***

There it was. The real problem. Working together.

*　　　*　　　*

THE desertification of America was slow at first. But it spread like wildfire. More sand, more wind. More wind, more sand. And on and on, until the whole midwest was playfully being referred to as, 'the sandbox.' Only by people who hadn't seen it, of course. Who saw it on their phones in-between five second videos of sixteen-year-old girls dancing to Korean pop songs and fatal automobile accidents, and who gave it about as much attention as they gave the other two. But then the sand had come for them too.

Just a little dust in the air one day. Then a little pile of fine, golden sand piled up by the doorstep. A cup's worth. Sweep it away. But the next morning, the little pile was back. And it wasn't such a little pile. And then a few aisles at the grocery store go empty. "A supply issue." And finally the sand gets so bad they have to shut down that one intersection in town. Some of the plows aren't working, so it may be a while before they can clear the road. "Just a bit of sand in the engine oil." Then one day, the front door won't open, and the TV isn't working. Next, the wind comes. And people's cars start flipping on the highway and on the back roads and in driveways. The air is an all mighty piece of sand paper, scraping and tearing and blinding. "Where is the fucking Army?", "Why isn't anyone helping us?"

Stu shuddered involuntarily. The Penguin noticed Stu's quiver and smiled.

"You didn't answer my question," said The Penguin, through moist purple lips.

"What?" replied Stu.

The Penguin rolled his eyes, annoyed. "Why were you trying to take one of my motorcycles?" he asked.

"...Well, for starters, I didn't know it was yours–"

"We've been through this, man. Where were you going? What of California? More people are turning up out of the desert everyday. Our little oasis here is starting to feel a little crowded. Tell me what you *know*."

"I know we're fucked. That's beyond any doubt at this point, I feel confident in saying. And I didn't come from California."

"Where then?"

"Denver."

"Does the Colorado still have flowing water?"

"I watched the last fuckin' drop melt into the ground at the bottom of Lake Havasu."

Stu remembered watching it go. He stood at the bottom of a crater in the earth. Not made by an asteroid, but by many years of erosion. And now it was empty of its gorgeous, precious water. *Fresh water*. The sand had already begun to move in. All around the edges of the crater, the golden sand flowed like lava in slow moving dunes, an ocean of molten gold, sloshing in to fill the void left by the Colorado river. A younger man had looked up into Stu's eyes then- looking desperately for an answer. Stu hadn't had one. And now that man was dead. *Carl. Oh, Carl.*

The Penguin got that frightened look again. A little bead of sweat popped up on his left temple, and he suddenly looked very uncomfortable in his heavily modified tuxedo.

"Shame." The Penguin sat back in his chair and pretended calm control. "What made you come this way? To strike out east into the desert was suicidal. Surely, the logical choice would've been to head to the coast, no? Did someone tell you about Phoenix?"

"Logic had nothing to do with it. And you wouldn't believe me if I told you."

"You'll tell me all the same, or Oslo will pull it out of you like shit outta Calamari."

Stu was quiet for a moment.

"There was a bird."

"A bird," said The Penguin flatly.

"Not one of those god-forsaken-fuckin' vultures that always seem to be around. A Bluejay. I think. Or maybe a bluebird? I don't know."

"A Bluejay made you walk into the desert?" asked the Penguin, incredulous. "I saw plenty of fackin' bluejays back when there were still trees growing, and it didn't fill me with any urges to go traversing The Sahara."

"It wasn't like we had many other options."

"We?"

Stu stiffened and after a moment, looked away from the Penguin's snake eyes down into the infinity of the floor. Just when The Penguin was about to prod him, Stu began to speak again.

"The river was gone. The sand had already filled in the basin, so you could hardly see where it'd been. Coulda gone west... but we'd heard stories that made us think we wouldn't be finding any big welcome party there. I was traveling with a young boy named Sam... as well as Carl. Sam... he – he was in really bad shape. He'd broken his leg..."

"Oh, okay, okay – Jesus. I don't need a fuckin' novel. What happened with this bird?"

Stu looked up at Hugh Flemm with murder in his eyes, but kept his voice low and steady.

"Sam was laying there in the sun. Dyin'. When this bluebird comes skipping along, happy as you please. It flies right over to Sam and lands on his forehead. It's tweeting and turning in circles like it's got some exciting news or something. It's all Sam can do to up to look at it. He smiled at that bird – and then – right there... he... just died. Died with a smile on his face. And this bird looks at me, tweets and flies off east into the desert. I mean, you could almost hear it saying… *this way*."

Silence between the two men. Stu gazed into the brown beads of The Penguin's eyes.

"So you decided to follow it into the desert? Christ, you are a fuckin' head case, aren't you."

"At the time... it seemed rather divine."

"Oh, I'm sure it did, fucknut."

*   *   *

THE Penguin took a deep breath and let it out, like preparing to end a phone conversation. "Okay then. Well, at least nobody told you about us. That's good news. Very good. We're trying to keep it that way."

"The water won't last. You know that," Stu said, very matter of factly.

"Come again?" said The Penguin.

"The ground water. It's drying up. That's why we had to leave Denver. It'll happen here too. I expect it's already started. Eh? I know you're taking measurements."

The Penguin began to sweat again. Rather profusely.

"Our ground water is just fuckin' dandy, cowboy. Don't you worry your pretty little head about it. Speaking of which, your execution is scheduled in two days. Tuesday, I believe. You'll be last on the docket. Since you've made such good friends with sweet Jim and Sarah, I thought you'd like to bid them farewell as they… boogie on into the next life."

"…. Might be kind, killing us."

"I'm so glad you see it that way."

At this, The Penguin snapped his fingers and waived at the man named Oslo, two hundred pounds and seven feet of blonde, half-blind, Swedish muscle. He looked like some kind of Nazi experiment gone wrong. And as far as Stu knew, he couldn't speak. Though he could certainly understand The Penguin's instructions. He came in and lifted Stu out of the chair like a stuffed animal. The binding on Stu's wrists twisted and bit into the already deep red cuts there. He grimaced. The Penguin shooed them out of his office in the back room of the Best Western hotel on Van Buren street. Stu had thought it a curious place for someone as narcissistic and materialistic as The Penguin to make his headquarters, but somehow, it seemed right. *Just tacky enough.*

The walk from The Best Western to the *Arizona Department of Corrections, Rehabilitation and Reentry facility*, also on Van Buren street, was a short one, though quite full of interesting things to look at.

The world was changed from the days before the sand. And thus, the people had changed with it, or were changing. *Those who go on surviving anyway.* The desertification of America, and as far as anyone could say, the rest of the world, had been swift in the end. Just like one of those exponential graphs they used to show in school and on the news — a rollercoaster gone out of control. But true and total collapse had come at last with the arrival of the solar flare. The largest ever recorded, and the last. Just before the world lost power, Stu had seen a news report warning people of the effects of radiation and the potential death of all GPS systems, etc. etc. And then the power had gone out. Just. Like. That.

That had really done it.

People were different without electricity. Without the internet or phone service. Some people had given up then. They could see the new reality forming and understood it would be too much, too different. Their eyes had gone grey. Many had chosen easier ways out, rather than face the desert. Stu's wife had been one.

But then there were the others. Those who hadn't given up, but rather glimpsed opportunities in this new crudeness. People like Hugh Flemm. Some kind of primal fire had been lit in their souls. They felt it, and they liked it.

The main strip of what remained unburied in Phoenix, Arizona was brimming with this kind of frantic, nervous hunger.

Trash can fires burned in the early evening like liquid orange obelisks, each placed just close enough to one another to connect their spheres of light. Around these pillars of flame stood black shadows, murmuring and shuffling, some standing completely silent and still in the night. The fires cast warm yellow and orange light, giving Stu flickering glimpses of unshaved faces and hard eyes. Some of those eyes followed as Oslo dragged him down the street in, somehow, unkind silence. The real danger was away from the fires. In the deep darkness. The night without fire or electricity.

The trash can fires were the closest thing to street lights left in Phoenix. They sat on Van Buren like a line of fireflies in an ocean of night. And away from the fire, in that blue blackness, people were still killing each other for food and water, still dying of untreated illness and injuries. Still raping and stealing and running.

Better than 200,000 people remained in Phoenix. Quite a drop from its pre-flare, pre-desertification population. But still a lot of damn people. Stu thought, bitterly, that there was at least some sense to The Penguin's feelings of claustrophobia. *This is unsustainable.* Stu had been stunned at the crowds when he'd first arrived in Phoenix. He hadn't thought so many people would remain together – *could* remain together in a place like this. But apparently the big guy upstairs had decided to make Phoenix an exception.

An older man, nearly blind with whiskey, stumbled his way into Oslo's path. "Say – *hic-cup* – JAck. You got any SMokes on –" The tower of Swedish muscle simply crumpled him. One punch to the stomach and the drunk man fell to the ground. A foot to the face and the man's front teeth went flying. He lay still on the pavement. Oslo didn't even stop walking. Stu grimaced at the sound of Oslo's foot connecting with the man's face.

When they finally made it to the jail, Stu was shoved back in his concrete hole like rat in a box. Oslo spit through the bars, turned and left without a word. Stu drew himself up against the wall, in ragged pain from the worsening wounds on his bound wrists. He found Jim Quail in the middle of a ponderous lecture — more out loud contemplation, really — about the state of the world. Sarah sat in her cell looking up at the ceiling, still as a statue.

"And that's why I – oh, hello Stuart. How was the night air? Have a nice dinner with Mr.Flemm?" asked Jim.

"Just splendid," replied Stu.

"I was just explaining to my enraptured audience here why I believe Phoenix has less than a month left before the sand finally swallows it completely. A week before the water runs out. Did you ask him about the ground water?"

"I did."

"And?"

"He was nervous. He lied. The water's drying up."

"I knew it!" Jim Quail punched the air in a little moment of victory, then realized what exactly he was celebrating, coughed, and got back to being serious. "And of course, rather than prepare, he pretends it's not happening." Jim let out a big sigh. "Well, I suppose we won't be around when it happens anyway."

"I'm scheduled for Tuesday... and I'm to see you two off before I get my turn."

At this, Jim turned more pale than usual and looked into the floor. He was a good man. Smart. Studious. Polite. Still afraid to die. All qualities that made him remarkably unsuited to the present circumstances.

Sarah broke her gaze away from the ceiling and faced Stu. She said nothing, but Stu thought he could see real defiance in those shocking blue eyes. He didn't know Sarah as well as he knew Jim – didn't know her *at all actually*. She seemed to have a strange way of communicating things without words, and it made him feel like he knew her. But then Stu'd remind himself he only knew her name because he'd been told. She peered into him now, and Stu returned her gaze with emptiness.

"I thought I'd die a long time ago. but honestly, I'm still not looking forward to it. You'd think I'd of come around by now," said Jim. "You – did he say... how, he was…"

"I think his words were, 'a good show, for my good citizens,'" said Stu.

Jim gulped.

Chapter Three

Fred Windsley

THE dunes had reformed outside of Dallas. He was close now, though. He could feel it. The wind had piled the sand a hundred feet high, and Fred had no choice but to summit each hill and hope it was the last. The new sand was so slippery and liquid, it often took him the better part of thirty minutes just to get up one side. The trick was to go slow. *And at night*, if at all possible. *If the stars were out.*

He sat now on the crest of a huge dune. A crescent moon hung lazy in the sky, surrounded by a crowd of twinkling night lights. Fred could see across the sand for miles from here. Illuminated by that soft starlight, the sand was a beautiful blue black ocean. *Marvelous.* Though Fred was too thoroughly chilled to care too terribly much about it.

His body was very near hypothermia, he suspected. Not that he could do anything about it. He couldn't decide which he hated more in this new world: the night, or the day. The day brought that all powerful lamp that burned and beat and clawed at Fred's skin unendingly, like an blinding bobcat. The night started with a promising kiss of cool — a light breeze or a little pocket of cool air — but then the cool would turn mean. *Cold.* Until Fred shivered violently and prayed for some of the warmth that seemed so brutal in the daytime.

It'd been five days since he'd crashed the Triumph. He supposed the responsible thing would've been to turn back and shelter in the gas station, if he could find it again, that is. *If it was even still there to find.* But he'd known even then that it wasn't right. There was a purpose to his current suffering, and the unseen road eastward called out to him. Jerry, the little black cat with the green eyes, had confirmed Freddy's intuition the next day, by speaking with the voice of God. Or something like it.

It had scared Fred terribly. A voice that came from everywhere, and filled his body from his toes to his inner ear, that seemed to flow into him so freely, that he wasn't sure it was real. Yet, it was. *Oh, it was.*

Fred had stopped and kneeled in the sand. Two days after his wreck, he had no water, no food, and every direction looked the same, yellow and brutal, yet Jerry had stayed with him. *My little companion for the end.* As the sun beat down, he had become convinced of his imminent death, could feel the life melting out of him. Then he'd heard *that voice,* and felt for the first time that stomach churning fear and awe that now accosted him every time he looked at Jerry.

"FRED WINDSLEY," the voice had said. "STAND."

Out of respect — *no, **fear*** — for the booming authority of the voice. Fred had obeyed. Then he'd felt the soft flick of a tail on his shredded pant leg. Jerry sauntered out in front of Fred like some pitch shadow in the white sunshine. The house cat seemed not to require water, nor food, nor rest. Nor did the sun seem to rip at him the same way it wailed on poor Freddy. Jerry would disappear suddenly at times, only to reappear on the crest of the next sand dune, waiting patiently, licking his paw.

"I CAN'T ALLOW YOU TO DIE YET. THERE IS A SPIRIT IN THE EAST WHICH REQUIRES I KEEP YOU ALIVE. YOU SHALL HAVE DEATH. BUT ONLY WHEN I GRANT IT. NOT YET. **WALK**," said the voice.

It boomed through the dessert silence like thunder, like Mufasa speaking to Simba. Jerry sat and looked deeply into Fred's eyes then. Fred had begun walking.

Three days on from this first *revelatory* experience with *the voice of God,* they had spoken many times. He had become thoroughly Jerry's, and the collection of memories that had once made up Fred Windsley were becoming fuzzy and twisted, mixing with visions of the desert and of the cat he now called lord. The cat, he suspected, was just a fragment of some... *thing. Something much larger.*

He would die for Jerry, he knew. *Must die for him. MY LIFE FOR HIM.* He had said as much, days ago. *But not here. Not like this. I'm so close. I have work to do.*

Sitting on his high dune, Fred felt that he could no longer go on. His body was broken. Four days without food, and three without water had left him a husk, a marionette, barely capable of walking. But as he sat looking out over the indigo ocean of night, and shivering like a chihuahua, he saw Jerry on the next hill, framed in pale moonlight. A black shape with a liquid tail flicking in the wind like fire. And beyond Jerry, in the not too far distance... *spires. Yes, skyscrapers*, jutting out of the sand like salted razor clams. It looked like some alien civilization.

Fort Worth.

Chapter Four

Sarah Bracken

HER back was starting to ache again. The poured concrete of Sarah Bracken's Phoenix jail cell was hot. Just hot enough to make her sweat wherever her body touched it, which was mostly her ass and shoulders.

They'd taken away her cot yesterday because she'd bitten off the ear of a guard who'd attempted to rape her. Hardly a fair trade, but hey, that's the dust-pocalyse for ya. It hadn't been the first time a guard had tried it, and she expected it might not be the last, even with her execution later that afternoon. Despite her feelings of pure revulsion towards The Penguin, Hugh Flemm, she had to allow for a bit of gratitude towards him. Though he could've, if he'd really wanted to, had Sarah tied down, *beaten, broken, etc.*, forced to become a sex slave, he hadn't. He was just going to kill her. Not because she'd 'stolen' some aspirin, but because he wanted her, and couldn't have her. So now, nobody could. *What a child.*

There are worse things than death. She put being The Penguin's toy about on par with hanging, though neither options were really appealing. Relatively speaking, of course.

She liked her cellmates though. Jim Quail could talk for about ten hours without stopping, but at least it wasn't empty talk. He was a smart guy, and well-rounded in lots of different subjects. A bit ponderous perhaps, but she liked to listen to him, and sometimes his voice reminded her of her father – took her back to a very different time. Stu Black was a good man, too. Nearly as quiet as Sarah, which was okay when Jim was there to fill the silence. He gave her confidence for some reason, a feeling like things might just be okay somehow, despite their dire circumstances. He radiated a kind of calm goodness. The antithesis to Hugh Flemm.

Sarah wasn't afraid to die. She was, however, afraid for her baby. ***My*** *god damned baby.* She hadn't wanted a child. Ever. Even before the world went all shitty — which was a question with widely varying answers depending on who you asked. She hadn't wanted to believe it. Even now, she hoped it was all in her mind, just the placebo effect or something. But it wasn't. The period for doubt was closed. She was pregnant. Three months pregnant, and starting to show. Just a little.

Despite the indifference Sarah wanted to force on herself, the attitude of *not caring,* that she had so often protected herself with, she couldn't bear the thought of her body swaying in the wind at the end of that rough rope, and her baby dying inside her. Her baby hadn't done anything. Hadn't tried to steal aspirin, or asked to be conceived. Sarah hadn't wanted a baby. But she wanted this one. Her child. Wanted it to have a chance, at least. *We all deserve that much.*

Willpower alone wouldn't save her child however. The Penguin had removed any hope for mercy. Stu said they were to be public examples. The latest in a long and illustrious line of human sacrifices he'd slaughtered for *"the benefit of law and order in the good Capital of Phoenix." That's the way it is. Convince people – scared people – that what they're doing is for the good of something bigger than themselves, and you've got 'em. Suddenly genocide is actually just a social welfare program.* Sarah had been there for the last execution. When she was captured on the edge of town, having just come out of the desert, they'd brought her straight to The Penguin. Who happened, at that moment, to be warming up a crowd at the newly christened Chase Field Gallows.

"By the power vested in me by the good people of the capital city of Phoenix, within the independent nation of Arizona, for the crime of public water theft, I, Hugh, The Gambler, first, and chief officer of this blessed capital, hereby sentence this man, Pete Brovnivinsk, to hang by the neck until dead." *A pompous show, but effective.* A muttering hush from the crowd. The gallows were built simply and crudely. Just sturdy enough of a structure to hang one person at a time from a center beam. Nothing as sophisticated as a trap door, or a lever. The hangee had to climb up three terraced milk crates to meet their maker.

Pete Brovnivinsk was crying when he died. He'd committed the crime of stealing water from a public well, the most grievous of offenses in the eyes of the new Arizona government, if it deserved to be called that. His tears had soon dried on swollen cheeks, and the crowd had watched in silence. The Penguin mirrored the tone of the mob with silence and a stern face. Oslo was the one who'd kicked the crates out from under poor Pete.

Sarah closed her eyes at the memory and leaned back against the warm concrete. A short moment later, a voice came from outside her cell bars.

"Hello, love."

Her eyes sprung open to find Hugh Flemm standing squat outside her cell in his strange, ill-fitting tuxedo, hands gripped around the bars, face smiling down at her. She thought he looked nervous.

"I have a couple things ta ask ya, hun. Just before we say our final goodbyes," he said.

Chapter Five

On the End of the World

THE midwest states, including the entirety of North Dakota, South Dakota, Nebraska, Kansas, Iowa, Minnesota, Missouri, Illinois, Indiana, Michigan, Ohio, Wisconsin, and pieces of all the surrounding states, were turned into an uninhabitable desert wasteland in the span of about five years. A combination of countless factors led to this desertification, including but not limited to, massive mono-culture agricultural operations, radical global temperature changes, a weakening of the atmosphere and a variety of other environmentally destructive human activities. The reader can fill in the blanks.

The change was gradual at first. People dealt with the sand until they realized they were being slowly buried, and then they'd moved somewhere else. People tried to stop the change. Many technological solutions were implemented, and all failed to halt the slow, *mighty* advance of the sand. The government tried quarantine, building blockades and re-locating cities and towns. It was a case of too little, too late.

As the sand rolled over the fields and forests, it became a self-perpetuating machine, grinding and consuming, multiplying exponentially. Then there was nothing to do but run. And run they did. People fled the region in the millions, flooding cities like New York and southern capitals like Nashville. Any kind of organized efforts to reverse the desertification were hopeless in the face of such an overwhelming humanitarian crisis. Some left the country then. They found themselves facing similar situations the globe over. In the vast tundra of Asia, and the rapidly expanding Sahara. Australia was already mostly desert anyway.

Even through all this, most of the United States remained liveable. And those who could find work and support themselves did alright. The news called it the second dust bowl. The second Great Depression. A terrible, but temporary cataclysm, that would surely be solved by the next candidate in office. This honeymoon with fantasy was cut short by two successive blows to the guts of the human race. First came a year of storms. Terrible, godly, storms that ripped houses from their foundations and tossed forests into the air like a child throwing confetti. When at last the storms began to ease, many cities were collapsed or collapsing. And without the means to make repairs, their populations dwindled. The natural human instinct to flee drove people to the far corners of the country. They found only more of the same. And all the while, the desert kept coming, urged on by a terrible wind at its back.

The next blow was the solar flare. The biggest in history. And it came down like a steel-toed boot upon a planet already on its knees. In a terrible cosmic joke, the sun added its wrath to Mother Earth's own. The power went out all at once around the globe. Fires caused by electrical grid damage brought down cities and *seaboards*. Communicating with people on the other side of the world, which had once been as easy as reaching into a pocket, became, once again, a dream of science fiction. The satellites which rained down into the atmosphere for the better part of a week, made beautiful patterns in the sky. Patterns that said, *welcome to the end.*

All this, and yet people are adaptable creatures. The story of humanity did not end. No, not really. Things actually got a lot more interesting.

Chapter Six

Keith Lonnagan

KEITH Lonnagan sat criss-cross-applesauce atop the Edge observatory building in New York City, overlooking the lower half of what used to be the island of Manhattan. He supposed it was still an island, though the sea had changed color. Where once the murky waters of the Hudson had frothed against the concrete foundations of New York city, now lay only sand. *Sand. Sand. Sand.*

Keith wasn't sure why the ocean was gone. He hadn't thought the shrinkage would be so dramatic. He wondered where all that water could've gone. *All that water…* The Solar flare had been unexpected, but explainable. And it wasn't as though global warming had been some surprise. No, they'd all known it was coming, and it hadn't made a difference. The Apocalypse had been long in coming, and incredibly… unexciting. Predictable, really. At least Keith thought so. But there was something fishy going on now (no ocean pun intended), something *beyond explanation*. And that was scary.

Sitting a thousand feet up in the air, gazing across the slowly shifting sea of sand, Keith felt quite peaceful. He'd been practicing here often lately, and the words of his old guru, Kathy, rang in his brain. *"Yoga is not about touching your toes. It's what you learn on the way down."*

He wondered why that had come to his mind, and he fought against the other voice in his head that raged at the rancid cheesiness of the quote. Keith stuck his legs out and reached to grab his feet. Something popped in his groin and he rolled backwards in pain. After a moment in the fetal position, he let out a low groan.

It was hard to say how many people were still living in New York, but to Keith, it felt like an absolute ghost town. The panic had really set in when the rolling sand dunes had started trampling over New Jersey. The first sand storm, *the first real storm*, had caused three million to flee the island. Of course the roadways had become impassable almost immediately from the traffic, and the wind, and the sand… so most of those fleeing were forced to continue on foot. By the time the sand had started to accumulate significantly on Manhattan and the ocean was beginning to recede, Keith could've walked down Broadway and not seen a soul – maybe the odd wanderer in wind-ripped clothes, trudging along through the buried streets with dead eyes and no real direction. Winds passing through some of the valleys created by the skyscrapers could reach nearly eighty miles per hour. Keith tried to warn anyone heading for such streets, but often as not, they would ignore him, or even run at the sound of his voice. He had seen several such travelers bashed against the side of buildings by the wind, or tossed down the road like plastic bags.

Keith had absolutely no idea where everyone had thought they were going. Surely most were buried under the sand by now. Perhaps they had thought it was just here. That maybe if they left, that if they were anywhere but here, they could find a good hole to hide in until it was all over. He knew that they hadn't. And they wouldn't. Everywhere was like here. And here was like everywhere, except some of the buildings were still upright. *And I'm a New Yorker, God dammit. I like my skyscrapers standing.* Keith himself had survived this exodus and ensuing wasteland almost by pure luck. During the first storm, he'd passed out drunk with a friend in an underground bar called *Sheemie's*. That next day's hangover had been a particularly brutal wakeup call.

Keith unfurled himself from the fetal position and lay on his back, facing up into the heat of the sky. Under him was a purple yoga mat with a word cloud printed in yellow on its front, most prominently featuring the words *spirit, love, think* and *mindful*. Eyes closed, Keith reached over to his right and grabbed a giant bottle of Gatorade Zero, orange flavor. It was hot and tasted like vitamin C vomit. It was the only bottled liquid left on all the shelves in all the corner stores and grocers south of 51st street that he'd checked. *Sand-pocalypse problems.*

Keith wore a simple white toga fashioned from a Hyatt hotel bedsheet, his latest residence, and he let the heat of the sun wash over his rapidly tanning body.

He didn't really like thinking about the apocalypse, though sometimes it was hard to avoid. The end of familiar civilization had offered him an escape from his life that he'd been in desperate need of for nearly two decades. At thirty-eight, Keith had been working in the financial sector at the same company for twenty years. When the sands came — the storms, the solar flare, *the end* — he'd finally decided to follow his dreams:

He would become a yogi. A yoga teacher. He would become one with the rhythms of this new life and abandon his worldly possessions. He would be flexible, and make kick ass playlists for all the hot yoga babes that he anticipated teaching in the future. *Well,* if he was lucky…

He had begun this process of change, of soul cleaning, by leaving his Brooklyn apartment of twelve years — rent stabilized, that had been tough, with only what he could carry in a small rucksack. Since then, he had gone from building to building with his alms bowl in hand, which really just meant looting the place, and began honing his craft.

This new pursuit of enlightenment and physical harmony turned out to be much more difficult than expected. Kathy had made it all seem so much easier. *I guess that's why the YMCA paid her so well.* And perhaps he had ought to of stretched a bit more before the end of the world.

Chapter Seven
Hugh Flemm

HUGH Flemm. Hugh Flemm. **Flemm.** *Like that shit at the back of your throat that you cough up when you're sick, or after drinking a big lemonade. You know the stuff. Who the fuck thought that would be a good family name? Probably German.* It wasn't.

This is what was going through The Penguin's head as he sat behind his big oak desk at the Best Western hotel. He'd had Oslo move his desk and chair out into the lobby, as to commander the whole first floor his personal office. He felt a little more naked out here than he'd anticipated. A bit exposed. A lone desk island in a sea of laminate. Presently, a man with no shoes or shirt was begging for his life and bleeding on the patterned red carpet in front of Hugh's desk. He'd dropped to his knees crying, so that Hugh couldn't see him. Not that he wanted to look at him. *My dear subject.* The sight of the man made Hugh a little sick. For a number of reasons.

Lately there had been fewer and fewer stragglers coming out of the desert. That was good. Just the way Hugh wanted it. But there were other problems that made him very scared. Namely that the ground water was drying up. And worse, that Stu Black *knew. How could he know? Probably professor bug eyes.* He should have them killed quickly and quietly. But that presented other problems. His control over Phoenix was tenuous at best. And completely based on fear. He had no illusions about that fact. His power resided in people's perception of him. In the early days of his claim to Arizona, he had killed many. Some for 'treason', and some for nothing at all. It was the idea that *anyone could be next* that kept people in line, he knew. He needed a fresh public execution, and Stu was perfect, but if he opened his big mouth before they could execute him... there might be *complications*. And complications made Hugh's head hurt. *No bueno*. All this on top of the fact that he wasn't sure his men would actually do it. Oslo enjoyed killing, but his other employees might have qualms about hanging Stu, and especially about killing the pregnant woman.

A strange thing had happened with Stu Black. His arrival in Phoenix hadn't been any different than the other stragglers, but he'd had an impact on the... *the what? The mood? The vibe?* They'd found him trying to start up a motorcycle on the edge of town — a good enough pretense for an *arrest* — but it was the idea that he didn't *want* to stay here that had surprised people. *He was going east. Why? Where?* The idea that Phoenix wasn't the only option left to people was dangerous. And hopeful. Hugh hated it.

"Please... I'm beggin ya sir... I – I – didn't know it belonged to you…" the man on the floor said.

"Everyone says that shit!" Hugh snapped. "I'm tired of that excuse. Phoenix belongs to me – and everything in it. Oslo." Hugh gestured harshly at the milky shadow from out of the corner of the lobby. He knew nothing of the Swedish man other than that he was terrifying, and that he either couldn't, or wouldn't speak – though he understood English well enough. But that was all to the better. Hugh didn't like talkers. He pretended he wasn't intimidated by the Swede, but it was sometimes a bit hard to contain his fear.

From the beginning of Hugh's rise to influence here, he'd felt like everything was some kind of political game – a show. He was terrified that someone might catch on that there was really nothing behind the performance – just empty, hot air. A frightened child. Cruelty seemed to be the most effective route in maintaining this illusion. In the short term, at least. But Stu Black's prison guards were getting pretty chummy with him, despite putting them on a rotation. The man just had a way with people. They were starting to think there might be some other way to run a city. Even out in the streets, people were becoming restless. Change was in the air.

"What did you steal, again?" asked Hugh.

"A – a gatorade sir, just a gatorade. Orange... flavor, I think it was," the man on the floor responded.

"That's the worst flavor, my man. Hmm. Not as bad as stealing water, I suppose. But a *sacred*, *precious* liquid nonetheless. Are you right or left handed?"

"Si – sir?"

"Do you use your right or left hand?"

"I – I'm ambidextrous."

"...Wow. That is a new one. Actually, that's the first time I've had that answer... I don't really know what to do with that. Cutting off both hands seems a little excessive. But taking just the one you use the least isn't quite enough. What do you think, Oslo? Take em' both? A foot instead, maybe?" Hugh asked. Oslo just looked at the man with old blue eyes, and with his hand on the large bowie knife that sat quiet on his hip.

"Oh no... please. It won't ever happen again sir. I – I promise. I promise, I promise... oh god..."

Hugh let out a big sigh and stood, hands on the desk. "I know it won't." After a moment's pause, he said, "You can go. But make sure you tell others about what happened here. That The Gambler is merciful, as well as strong."

"Oh, thank God – thank you! I will sir. I will," said the man.

"Go on."

The man scrambled to his feet and ran out of the lobby, leaving a trail of blood from his bare and torn feet. Oslo looked at Hugh with something like distain. Hugh met his gaze and feigned boredom. He hoped he wasn't sweating as badly as he felt like he was.

"Let's go hang Stu Black."

Chapter Eight

Billy Thompson

"YOU really believe that?" asked the guard with the crinkled blonde hair – who really wasn't a guard at all, but a nineteen-year-old former poetry major from Connecticut. Yes, Billy Thompson from Connecticut, who now stood armed guard over Stu Black, Jim Quail, and Sarah Bracken in a mostly abandoned jail cell in Phoenix, Arizona at the order of a strange and overweight psychopath, who went by 'The Gambler'. Though everybody called him 'The Penguin'. He'd been writing recently about how strange it all was, and how he regretted attending his friend's bachelor party in Vegas – the party that had left him stranded out here in this strange American West when the storms and the flare had come. *Definitely my luck.* Billy was now talking with Stu Black through iron bars about what might be in store for the future of the human race.

"Funny enough, I do. Like I said, I'm not a religious man, but I do know one thing for sure – that fuckin' desert shoulda killed me... and it didn't. Something was – not *guiding* me exactly, but – you could say it put the wind at my back. I sound crazy, I know," said Stu, leaning against the warm concrete of his cell and smiling bashfully up at the tall boy.

"No, no – I believe ya, Stu. I do. I been out there myself. We had..." Billy's voice caught in his throat, and suddenly he looked like someone had twisted his stomach all up in a knot.

"…The desert closed in on Vegas… and we had no choice but to move on. We were being buried alive there. No one knew where to go… Basically just pickin' a direction to die in. I left with around three hundred people. Fifteen of us made it to Phoenix."

A heavy silence fell as Stu absorbed Billy's story. Across the hallway, and in the adjacent cell, Jim Quail and Sarah Bracken listened quietly to the conversation. Jim was failing at meditation, so was happy to have something to occupy his brain. Sarah was doing what she usually did these days, stare at the ceiling and hold her stomach.

"I'm sorry you had to go through that, son," said Stu. "Nobody should have to bear that, 'specially a kid."

"…You're right about that." Billy was still looking at the floor. "Ya know, Stu. I didn't feel any kind of guiding 'light' out there, and I suspect God is looking the other way right now, otherwise we wouldn't be in this mess in the first place – but I – I believe you. I do. Maybe Jesus did show up inside a bluebird. All the same, I won't be walkin' out into that desert unless I'm walking behind you."

Stu laughed. "Well, might be you're waiting a good long while for that. I'll be dead here in, well… who knows when. Maybe a few hours. And that son of a bitch is gonna hang my two friends here before then."

At this Billy suddenly seemed to remember he was supposed to be *guarding* Stu, not talking to him like a surrogate father. Billy straightened himself, adjusted the Winchester .22 caliber rifle that hung over his left shoulder, and looked back into Stu's gray eyes. They looked at each other for a moment in silence and Stu nodded. A simple thing, but Billy understood what it meant. *It's okay. I understand.* It made Billy feel like throwing up. He turned and began to walk out of the cell block. His shift was nearly over anyhow – but as he reached for the door, he stopped and turned around.

"What is it exactly you think is out there? East, I mean?" Billy asked.

Stu pondered for a moment. "I don't know. But I know that staying here means death."

Billy took this in, then asked, "You think The Penguin has someone – or something – watching over him?"

"I'm sure I don't know, Bill," Stu replied.

At this, Billy turned to leave, but before he could grasp the knob, the door to the cell block came flying open. The door opened with such force that it bent Billy's pointer finger back to a right angle and sent the kid sprawling to the floor. He yelped and grasped at his hand. In the opened doorway stood Oslo. His pale blonde, almost white, hair was up in windblown tufts. He could've passed for some kind of eccentric European couch designer if he'd been wearing a turtleneck and some round rimmed glasses that didn't actually do anything. But the illusion of his playful, childlike appearance was shattered as soon as you looked into his eyes. There was hate there, voiceless and directionless. Billy thought his eyes were more doglike than human.

The big man pushed into the room, completely ignoring Billy. Behind Oslo was Hugh Flemm. The three prisoners watched as their captor strolled lightly into the room.

"Finally feel like paying your taxes, Flemm?" chided Jim Quail. "I've got the paperwork all drawn up."

The Penguin sighed and smiled. "Oh, Jimminy Crickets. That mathematic brain of yours really is something. I appreciate all the work you put in at my… request."

"Truly, it was my pleasure," said Jim, placing his hand on his heart. "All I'd like in the way of compensation is my freedom, and the liberation of my two innocent friends here."

"Innocent, are they? Well. That may be, but unfortunately the courts are a little backed up right now. No time for an appeal I'm afraid. And sadly I must deny your request for liberation – though in return for your loyal service to the new empire of Arizona, we have decided to kill you first."

Chapter Nine

Stu Black

STU was on his knees in front of the crudely constructed gallows in the middle of Chase Field stadium. The goal of restoring electrical power to Phoenix had slowly been pushed to the bottom of the list of priorities, and now in the fading light of the 7th of August, Stu felt the darkness. All around him, as on Van Buren street, trash can fires lit up the field like flickering orange pillars in some sick pinball game.

"Gooood Peooooople!" The Penguin bellowed from his spot on the raised wooden platform. He looked absurd and violent in his strange tuxedo, bulging out around his wide, round stomach. "We have quite a piece of entertainment for you tonight, three pieces actually..." Some laughter bubbled up from the crowd, but not as much as Stu had expected.

Jim Quail and Sarah Bracken stood on the raised stage, each balancing atop two stacked milk crates, and each wearing ropes around their necks. The milk crates were all bright colors, so if you squinted it looked like they might be standing on some oversized stack of legos. Like a couple of little action figures getting ready to bite it.

The Penguin's voice carried over the open field cleanly and with bravado. The Stadium seemed to amplify him, make him bigger. A few hundred people milled around in the stadium stands, and a crowd of about two hundred stood around the crude gallows in a silent mob. They listened to The Penguin with dark eyes and hands hidden away in pockets. Stu was among them, forced to his knees by Oslo and looking up at the flightless man on the stage. Tears hadn't come yet, but he knew it wouldn't be much longer. He felt a hand on his shoulder. Turning, he saw it was Billy Thompson, with a serious and sympathetic look on his face. It scared Stu, but before he could say anything, Oslo was there. The Swedish monstrosity planted his right fist into Billy's stomach – hard. It made the sound of a pillow being hit with a baseball bat. Billy crumpled to the ground.

"And so tonight, oh goodness. I'll say again. Please do refrain from touching Mr. Black. We don't want anyone interfering with his viewing experience," The Penguin said, acknowledging the scuffle. "And maybe... you could all – scoot back a couple of paces. Just – back up a little."

The crowd looked up silently at The Penguin. He began to sweat. A few people shuffled around, but the mob remained tight around the platform. "Ah, well. Let us – continue." The Penguin's voice faltered in the increasingly unsettling vibe radiating from the crowd. The people milling in the stands had turned to look at the sound of The Penguin's command. Some were hopping the fence and walking across the field towards the crowd.

Struggling to regain his composure, The Penguin continued. "For the crime of theft, the theft of sacred liquids, I, Hugh, The Gambler, wielding the power vested in me by the citizens of the new empire of Arizona, hereby sentence Jim Quail, Sarah Bracken... and Stu Black to death by hanging." At this proclamation, Jim Quail's legs began to shake horribly. He muttered under his breath some kind of prayer to the numerous gods of math and social studies, but he didn't cry. Sarah just gazed far away into the blackening night sky. It looked to Stu like she might as well have been on Mars for all the attention she was paying the whole affair.

Suddenly, someone in the crowd shouted, "Stu didn't steal no water!"

Silence fell. "Who… who said that?" asked The Penguin, with just a dash of panic, and more than a little anger. "Who *said* that?" he asked again, with increasing bile in his voice. No hands were volunteered. "He tried to steal gasoline. And with things the way they are, it's just as important. Now, please, no more interruptions."

At this, Stu found he had more courage than he would've guessed. They'd already beat him to shreds on the walk over from the jail, so he figured one more outburst couldn't really do too much more damage. "Why don't you tell em' about the ground water there, Flemm –" Before Stu could finish his sentence, Oslo's iron fist slimmed into his jaw and sent him spiraling to the turf. Stu felt a tooth fall from his mouth, and the warm, metallic taste of blood flooded his mouth.

"What *about* the ground water?" another voice in the crowd shouted out. Then another chimed in, "We're gonna kill somebody over gasoline?" and another, "This ain't what I signed up for."

In that moment, the tide turned. Stu could feel it. Suddenly, the crowd was pushing and shoving their way towards the stage. Oslo tried to hold the wave of people, but was forced backwards and fell under the feet of the rushing mob. Stu was stepped on and kicked. A boot came crashing down on his head. He heard a crunching sound and terrible pain shot through his already ringing head, then a hand grabbed him by the shirt and yanked him up like a hooked fish. Billy Thompson brushed the dirt off Stu's face, and held him firmly by the shoulders.

"We wouldn't let ya go that easy, Stu. You alright?" Billy asked.

Stu was too dazed to answer, and he looked confusedly at the hundreds of people rushing around him like a river of meat and dirty clothes. They had swarmed the stage and were closing in on The Penguin. The big man was sweating bullets, and shouting at them to stay back. They weren't listening. Oslo was gone, flattened by the rush of people.

Suddenly, The Penguin stood still and seemed to take a deep, considered breath. In an act of unexpected athleticism, the rotund man ran and dove head-first off the stage, vaulting over a mob at least ten people deep. Just before he hit the ground, he tucked and rolled, so that by the time people realized what had just happened, he was up and sprinting for an exit door on the side of the field. In his tuxedo, he looked like Humpty Dumpty running a high kneed hundred meter dash. *I guess Penguins can fly.*

About half the crowd tore off after Hugh, trying to beat him to the exit door. Stu turned from the chase and met the eyes of Jim Quail. He was crying now, but also smiling, as several people helped untie his noose. A darkening stain was spreading out over his khaki cargo pants. Stu tried his best to return a smile, but his mouth seemed to not be working quite right. He turned and saw the noose come off of Sarah Bracken's neck. She was looking at Stu hard, with grateful, but strangely sad eyes.

Chapter Ten

Keith Lonnagan

HE'D found the water. Oh, yes.

Keith Lonnagan's view from his new residence on the 86th floor of the Empire State Building was splendid. It was the kind of view Keith had dreamed about as child, the New York skyline, surrounded by the shimmering waters of the Hudson and the upper bay. Except the Hudson was no more, nor was the bay. Both had been replaced by ever growing golden dunes. *Over the dune, down in the dune lives the former talk show host, everybody knows his name…*

As beautiful as it still was, it felt somehow hollow and strange to him here. Empty. There was no one to congratulate him on the enormous success he must've achieved to afford a spot in the Empire State Building. *The freakin' Empire State Building.* No one was around to pop a bottle of champagne. It was depressing.

These feelings knocked at Keith's brain like unwanted salesmen. He took a deep breath and remembered the solemn vows of Yogi-ism he'd sworn. He tried to let go of his worldly disappointment and bring himself into the present, as Kathy had taught him so many times during their Thursday grounding sessions. It was difficult now, because as much as he knew it was true, Keith was having trouble accepting the reality of what he was seeing. A *storm* was coming.

The sky stretching across the southern horizon of the Manhattan desert was black and green. It glittered with evil, pulsing light, and like a terrible black mold, it was slowly absorbing the sky. Moving closer. Under the path of the black clouds Keith could see jade lightning flashing like sulfuric gunfire, and even from a distance of thirty miles, the ground seemed to rumble with anticipation. *It's gonna be one of **those** storms.* Keith wasn't sure if he ought to stay on one of the higher floors, or shelter in the basement. Both seemed like really, *really* bad options. He supposed he'd rather be thrown from a toppled building than drown in a basement, so he settled on the edge of an abandoned office desk and watched as the monster crept forward.

There was something hypnotic in the way the storm was moving and swirling. Thirty minutes passed. Giant naked gods seemed to be leaping and dancing wickedly in black folds of rain and wind. In the dead silence of the Empire State building, Keith almost forgot it was real. Gazing out his little window, the storm was like some fantastic living art piece, nicely framed. Benign. *Just kidding.* But then it was there, and one of the dancing gods of the storm reached down, smashed Keith's window into a bijillion bits, and tried to drag him out into the open air.

Keith flipped in space. It was as if the window had been an air lock on a spaceship. The pressure dropped and Keith realized he couldn't hear. Everything was a dull knocking in his brain, but in his spinning fall, his body instinctively reached out to grab the jagged glass ledge of the window. As if in a dream, his right hand caught. A sharp pain shot up through his arm, but his fingers held. Keith's body slammed on the outside of the 86th floor of the Empire State Building and flapped in the wind like a worn out flag.

The rain was thick. It felt like he was under some great faucet. Far below, Keith could see only water. The storm had turned New York into Venice in the space of just a few minutes. Waves were crashing over 33rd street, surging into buildings through the shattered windows and carrying away anything left on the street. In his nauseating glimpse downward, he saw a wave of muddy brown water, at least a hundred feet high, flip a semi-truck into a neighboring building. Even in his mortal peril, Keith was glad he hadn't gone to the basement.

The world came rushing back into Keith's awareness like a swarm of angry bees. The wind suddenly became a scream in his ears, and the beating rain was making his hand slip. Keith let out a heavy gasp as he reached up for the ledge with his other hand. He realized he wasn't breathing, his impact with the wall had knocked all the air from him. His lungs fought to suck in, yet still his fingers gripped with frantic strength to the window ledge. He managed to get a hold with his left hand, and felt the pain as a shard of glass on the window ledge punched through his palm and out the back of his hand. *Ow, ow, ow, owowow…* He grimaced and tried to pull himself up, but just as he lifted his eyes over the ledge, he saw a large metal work desk skittering over the office floor, coming right at him, propelled by a strong gust from the other side of the building. Keith lowered himself back down, but just as the desk tipped out into free fall over his head, it caught on the window ledge. Keith yelped as his pinky and ring fingers on his left hand were smashed between the heavy desk and the metal ledge. *Hard.* When the thing finally finished its arc over Keith's head and into the ocean below, two of his fingers went with it. *Uh, oh.*

There was no pain. In a huge burst of shocked adrenaline, Keith managed to pull his chest up and over the ledge, back into the relative safety of the building. The wind seemed to grab and pull at his legs as he hauled himself up, like some clawing toddler from hell. The shard of glass made a terrible unsheathing sound against his flesh as Keith pulled his hand free.

He looked at his maimed hands and the copious amount of blood now streaming from his wounds. He breathed deeply, leaned back against the wall, and fainted.

Chapter Eleven

Fred Windsley

HE looked like some hobbled brown hermit crab crawling out of the desert. Some poor sea creature that had suddenly had the terrible desert sun thrust upon him and long since dried out, yet refused to die. And sauntering at his side, *his God*, in the shape of a cat.

Fred was grinning madly as he made his way into downtown Fort Worth. His lips were split in deep white seams, crusted over many times with sun-dried blood. He hadn't had water in almost three days. His throat was a dry wound. It had seemed so close when first he'd glimpsed Fort Worth, but it had taken him days to finally reach the buildings poking up through the sand. He had thought he might not make it, and the elation of finally reaching something real had plastered an oversized smile on his face. The downtown Skyscrapers jutted out of massive golden dunes like strange alien obelisks in an ocean of dust.

Fred was hallucinating quite badly. A little gnome with a pointy red hat had been following him for the last day or so, he was convinced. Every time he turned around to catch him, the gnome would dart behind a dune or a rock, giving Fred only the quickest flash of red. It was incredibly frustrating. The large rotating cast of cartoon characters dancing in his periphery at all hours of the day, however, had come to be really quite valuable entertainment. Despite the hallucinations and his utter exhaustion, Fred felt good. God had been talking to him often, *making promises*, and as they'd approached Fort Worth, he had told Fred what to expect. And what was expected of him.

"THERE ARE PEOPLE IN THIS CITY WHO DO NOT YET KNOW OF MY COMING. YOU MUST SHOW THEM. TEACH THEM. EVERYTHING RETURNS TO THE DESERT," God had said, his green eyes twinkling behind heat lines rising from the desert sand.

"Everything returns to the desert, yes, lord. Not America no mo. *Not no mo*. Everything returns to the desert… everything, everything…" Fred had replied in what had become a ritual chant for him. *Guess I was wrong about being alone in the whole southwest.*

Two years before meeting his God on the dunes outside of Fort Worth, Fred Windsley had been a cashier at Piggly Wiggly in Hartsville, South Carolina. Things had been very simple then; show up, work, go home, go to the bar. A simple life that Fred had enjoyed immensely, though maybe hadn't appreciated as much as he should've. Everything had changed when the storms and the sand came. The prevailing idea in Hartsville had been that California was the place to be to escape the rapidly expanding desert. So, Fred had followed the advice of his neighbors and packed up the car for California, only to find, upon arrival, that California was indeed, *not the place to be*. He'd watched many of his friends and neighbors die in swirling masses of refugees and sand.

It was somewhere in there where Fred had begun to lose his mind. The world had changed in some way beyond the physical reality of desertification. Old things wandered this new American desert in search of followers. Their footsteps were getting louder. Fred was one of the first, he knew. He was important. *I'm… important. God said so.* And as the importance of his role in this new world overwhelmed his mind with visions of fire and glory, Fred had forgotten himself. He was a blank canvas — untrodden sand — to be repainted.

Fred's arm was still terribly mangled. He knew that, but the pain had become a far away thing in comparison to this new purpose. His hand hung limply backward at his side, and the large gashes on his legs were unwashed dinner plates of blood and bruised skin. Yet still, he smiled. He smiled and limped, until Wiley Coyote wandered out of his peripheral vision and smacked him with frying pan. Fred passed out face down in the sand. *Thud.*

He lay there for two hours before they came out to get him. Slowly, hesitantly, strangely shaped figures began to emerge from the surrounding buildings. One wore hundreds of pieces of note paper fashioned into a great cloak of shingled manila yellow. Another wore a backpack with a big multi-colored beach umbrella sprouting from the main compartment. Others wore ragged clothes and odds bits of cloth tied together to form desert style garb. Picture modern day Texas meets Bedouin.

The twenty or so who had come out to get a look at Fred formed a ring around his lifeless body. Looking down at Fred, they were the image of some lost tribe of rogue businessmen. A few wore crude masks made of various office supplies. One of the Fort Worthers reached out with a closed umbrella and poked Fred's thigh. Fred let out a low groan. Some of the group backed away at this, but it was such a pitiful sound that most of the office tribe didn't budge. The man with the great cloak of note paper whispered something in a low voice and two young men grabbed Fred by his arms and legs. One of the boys let out a choked gasp when he grabbed for Fred's hand and saw how hopelessly broken it was. He grabbed again, at the elbow this time, and they hoisted Fred into the air like a pig on a spit.

As the group made their way down into one of the nearby buildings, the man in the paper cloak stopped to gaze back out over the sand. He could swear he'd seen a cat.

Chapter Twelve

Hugh Flemm

THE desert was eating him. Every piece of exposed skin burned with the fury of a thousand fire ants. His tuxedo sticking against the raw red flesh of his chest made him look like some kind of bastardized Emperor Penguin. He sat like a human beach ball on the back of a Harley Davidson chopper. The steering rails had been extended a whole foot, and the bike looked like some ghost rider parade-float parody. It might've been intimidating if not for the comical roundness of the man riding the thing.

Flemm was entering his 25th hour of continuous riding, and his eyes were closing at the wheel. He'd managed to flee Phoenix with his life, but just barely. *Just barely.* And he didn't intend to give anyone in Phoenix the chance to drag him back. He would rather not face the judgement of the new council he was sure would be forming around Stu Black. *Just classic empire stuff, isn't it? They think they want "the good guy," until shit gets real. Then they come crawling back. They will.*

It was pure luck, or some divine gift, that he'd found the Harley, and even better luck that it had had a few bottles of water stashed in its side bags. A *Bluebird, eh, Stu? Try a hundred horses.* It had been hidden in the dark behind a mostly sanded over Taco Bell on the edge of town. Hugh had been in full panic then, panting and exhausted after his narrow escape from his 'loyal subjects'.

He'd surprised himself with the sprint from Chase stadium. A deeply buried, long forgotten athleticism had seemingly taken hold of his bones and propelled him with unnatural speed. He felt the repercussions of his Phoenix 5k now though, as he trundled along the dunes of middle Texas… at least he thought it was Texas. His body ached, and every rumble of the motor beneath him sent terrible shivers up through the fat of his soft frame. He was freezing and melting at the same time, and he thought much more of it might kill him.

The roads were gone. All gone. The great American blacktop serpents which had once ranged from Californ-I-A to New York, New York were buried and dead. Maybe someday, someone, somewhere would dig them out. But it wouldn't be Hugh Flemm. With the roads gone, feeling Phoenix had been as easy as picking a cardinal direction. Stu was going east, Hugh knew. And before he could even think about what might be waiting for him out in the desert, he had struck out East as well. *Maybe I'll beat him to it. Whatever **it** is. Wouldn't that be swell.* It seemed like the right way to go. And something down in the darkness of Hugh's brainstem, some little voice, seemed to be shouting, "GET THERE FIRST."

Get where? Hugh didn't know. But the first stop would be Dallas. It was the only place relatively close to Phoenix that might still have eyes above the sand. He'd just hope that whoever was there — and there surely would be people — wouldn't ask him too many questions about why he'd fled the West.

The desert around Phoenix had been reasonably flat, but was piled high at the city's edges. From the Taco Bell, Hugh had summited a fifty-foot dune just to get out into open desert. He'd seen Phoenix's true peril then. It was some kind of meteorological fluke, some rogue weather pattern that had saved the city. It wouldn't last. The whole of what remained uncovered in Phoenix lay at the bottom of a massive basin. Walls of sand stood fifty to a hundred feet high on all sides, like the waves of some slow-moving golden tsunami. They were easier to ignore from the city center, but having to climb out had rearranged Hugh's perspective on the matter. The people down there would be buried alive if they didn't move. Hugh had laughed then. A wet, crackling laugh, his lungs still recovering from his run. He wasn't being driven out: he had a head start.

He'd made good progress at first, but the sand had turned loose somewhere around what he guessed was El Paso. A terrible smell had come bubbling up from the sand there. Something reeking of death and decay. Whatever had happened in that place, even the sand was having a hard time covering up. Hugh sped right on by.

After the change in the sand, the going had become much tougher. His life became up and down, up and down, up and down... Dune after dune, he summited and descended, until the motion became like the rocking of a boat at sea. And it *was* a sea. Endless and golden and terrible. It was becoming clear to Hugh that it might even have a mind of its own, as it seemed to work against him at certain times, and carry him along at others. *Guide him.*

Hugh awoke from some kind of trance, like snapping out of a restless power nap, and he found himself perched on the crest of a massive dune. His Harley was no longer rumbling, and he knew somehow that it was out of gas. How he'd made it up this monster of a sand dune, he couldn't have said. Out in front of him lay a wide plain of sand, shifting in a gentle southern breeze. He didn't remember the sun going down, but the moon was already high in the night sky, casting its subtle white glow on the open expanse, as it once had on the great wide oceans.

In the distance, Hugh could make out black needles against the starry horizon. *Fort Worth. Dallas.* He gazed for a few moments at this and smiled. He would make it his. *Yes. And the people too.* In his silent reverie, Hugh felt something brush up against his leg. Soft, like the light touch of an inviting hand. He looked down to see a black shape sauntering by his ruined dress shoe. The shape had a tail that waved and flicked like some possessed black fire. *Too long, much too long*, he thought. Then two green eyes turned on Hugh like laughing headlights.

Chapter Thirteen

Wilma Nettlebee

GOD, my fuckin' feet, Wilma Nettlebee thought as she propped up her wrinkled pink doggs up on a brightly colored beach recliner. The plastic straps barely budged under her weight. Eighty-five pounds. Age had robbed her of so much; sight, hearing, motor skills. And like a hungry monster, hiding away in some unseen place — always lurking, always nearby — time had melted the meat off her bones until only a thinly wrapped skeleton remained. A thinly wrapped skeleton that frowned most of the time. And smoked cigarettes like some tacky halloween animatronic.

She supposed it could be worse. She could be a three-hundred-pound old lady, and able to move even less than she already did. Most of the time though, she didn't really think about her age, just the ache in her *fuckin' feet.* It was particularly bad today, which was unfortunate. Though it did provide a wonderful excuse to spend her time lounging under her new multi-colored sun-brella. Harold had dug it out of a Walmart in Sevierville on their way here, along with a few cases of diet Dr. Pepper. *Here,* being the summit of Clingmans dome in Sevier County, Tennessee.

Wilma sat on her lounge chair at the top of the swirly concrete ramp that afforded her a spectacular view of the surrounding mountains. To be honest, she'd seen better. *Lotta trees. Few little streams.* It was okay. *Now, Yellow Springs, back in the 70s… that* had really been something. Though she guessed, with the country in the shape it was now, this pretty much passed for paradise on Earth. Even in the middle of what remained a lush, forested mountain side, she could see signs of the vast desert that surrounded her on every face. When the wind blew up through the trees, it carried a fine brown dust with it. And the smell of dryness. Of bone, and ash, and sandy oblivion. She shuddered.

Wilma reached over the side of her chair and groped for her warm, flat Dr. Pepper. There was no better reminder that the world had ended than a warm, flat soda. *Depressing. Absolutely depressing.* She got a grip and brought the can to her thinly stretched lips. Before she could get any of that sticky brown gold down her gullet, a huge black fly shot out of the can. It flew straight down her throat, and even made an audible buzzing sound as it went.

Wilma shot up in her chair in a fit of coughing. It felt like somebody had shoved their fist down her windpipe. It was burning, and she… She could feel the fly moving in her esophagus like some horrible alien parasite. Through choked gasps, she mustered the biggest breath she could get and loosed one, giant, wracking cough. The fly came out in a spray of spittle and landed on the concrete. Wilma looked at the fly in strange horror. It got up, seemed to shake itself off like a wet dog, and once again took to the air. It hovered in front of Wilma's face for a moment, and she was certain it was laughing at her.

Breaking the spell of paralysis that had gripped her, Wilma shot her hand out to swat the fly. It dodged lazily, and did a few little loop de loops as it flew away, seeming to enjoy the frustration it'd caused. *Too slow, ya old hag!* It seemed to say.

Wilma watched the fly disappear into the breeze, and the lines of her face slowly pulled back into that scowl that she wore so often. *That... bastard*, she thought. And she was certain it was, *that bastard*. She didn't know what to call *him*. Just that she knew it was a *him*, and that *he* didn't like Wilma very much. Or anybody really, that she could tell. Except himself maybe. The wild animals that survived in this new world seemed to have aligned themselves with either *him*, or unexplainably, Wilma herself. She seemed to have gotten most of the birds, though not all of them. Vultures prowled the desert, dark shapes against the blue sky like silent bombers. They were *his*. And the cats. *Christ, the cats*. They were *all* his.

It was small things at first. Back in Fair Garden, on the porch of her little three room cabin in the hills, where she'd been born, raised, and had planned to die, back when the sand was just starting to take hold in the Midwest, a bluebird had come to Wilma. And it had spoken. Not in words exactly, but in essence, and in direction. It had told Wilma where to go and how to get there. And that there would be *things* trying to stop her.

Well, she had listened to the damn bird. Not necessarily out of some secret knowledge of divinity, but because when birds start chatting you up telepathically, it means you're either going crazy, or something important is going on. And Wilma wasn't crazy. At least not really. Not *yet*. And by God, they'd made it to the top of this damned hill. And they'd made it *first*. She knew that was important somehow. And *he* was pissed about it.

The fly had disturbed Wilma, but she knew that if that was the worst he could do, she was winning. *Winning what?* She had no idea. The thought comforted her, but also slipped a little feeling of unease into her otherwise — relatively speaking — relaxed afternoon, because she knew it might not always be so. A winner meant there would be a *loser*, and the race wasn't over. She'd thought that making it to the top of the mountain would be the hard part, but it was occurring to her now, that that was probably not the worst of it. She would need help. And soon. More than Harold's, good kid though he was. Surely there would be others coming. It was hard to miss such a towering beacon of green in this new yellow world. But whose side would they be on? She shuddered to think of the ones who chose the cats over the birds.

Wilma sighed and sat back in her recliner. *God, my fuckin' feet*. The sun seemed to shine a little brighter. And a little hotter.

Chapter Fourteen

Sarah Bracken

SARAH Bracken was sitting in a terribly squeaky folding chair at the back of the Phoenix Symphony Hall stage thinking about, among other things, her last conversation with Hugh Flemm. He had come to her a day before she was supposed to be hung, which of course, hadn't exactly gone according to his plan. Even with a rope around her neck, she'd had to stifle a laugh watching him sprint across the stadium field like a weather balloon on stilts.

On the symphony stage in front of her, speaking to about twenty-five hundred people, many of which were crammed into dense pockets, standing any place they could find room, was Stu Black. He was speaking into an oversized, battery powered megaphone that made him sound like a carnival hawker.

"If we stay here, we die. It's plain and simple, folks. You have eyes just like me, the walls are closing in."

"Quite literally," chimed in Jim Quail from his position on Stu's back right.

"Listen, I can't tell you what to do, hell, I don't even know what I'm doing up here, but you asked me to talk, so I'm talkin'. I'm going East. Tomorrow." The crowd let out a skeptical sounding murmur. "Yes, tomorrow morning. Mr. Quail here reckons Phoenix's only got about a week left before it's swallowed by that God damned sand, and I don't plan on staying here to find out if he's right about that, though I gotta tell you, I'm pretty sure he is."

"I am," said Jim, leaning in to get his voice into the megaphone mic.

Stu gestured to Jim with a, *'you see what I mean'* kind of shrug. "I mean shit, the sand is already a hundred feet high on every side of this place. We're at the bottom of the cereal bowl folks, I'm worried we won't even be able to get out *now*."

At this, the crowd began to murmur anxiously. They didn't want to go back out there, Sarah knew. Back into the desert. To the Sand and the sun. Sarah herself was rather ready to return to the wasteland, as others called it. She'd stayed here out of a sense of responsibility to Stu and Jim, whom she liked quite a lot, though she was reluctant to admit it. Funny how the apocalypse does that.

Before she'd arrived in Phoenix, after the fiery death of her old life, she'd felt free. Really. Free. For the first time. The desert was just *right*, like an old, worn pair of shoes or a chewed-up piece of gum stuck behind the ear. Even now, she felt it calling to her. Just quietly, subtly, beckoning… like a spring breeze whispering, *"come play."*

And that attraction was just what Hugh Flemm had wanted to know about.

"I'm going to ask you… one last time. Okay? And I'd like an answer. Where did you come from, and who told you about Phoenix?" he'd asked.

Nowhere important, and nobody. That's what she would've said, anyway, had she felt compelled to respond. She hadn't. When it had become clear that she'd had no intention of answering his questions, Hugh had let out a big sigh and leaned back in his shitty, faux leather office chair in the Best Western lobby.

"You…" He had looked at her long and hard then, and she'd seen inside him, past the show he put on to maintain his position as dictator of Phoenix, and into the child's eyes at the bottom of the well that was his soul. He was just a person. She knew that. And he had fallen for her. It wasn't the first time it'd happened. But power had corrupted his heart, and the expression of his desire had come in the form of brutality and force. It revolted her. But that child deep down was still just that, a child. Children could be sweet. And cruel. In this instant she had seen this child drowning behind Hugh Flemm's deer shit brown eyes, and she had felt sorry for him.

"You compel me," he'd said. "It's obvious you have no interest in remaining here, but I can't let you go free, lest you spread the good word about Phoenix." *That statement hadn't aged well*, she thought. *He would be the one protecting a sinking ship.* "But, keeping you in a jail cell is like caging some exotic animal, some wild thing meant to be roaming the earth. It's breaking my heart. I really hate to boil it down to something so asinine, but it's come to… if I can't have you, nobody can."

At least he'd put it simply. He'd talked for another hour or so then. Cried, yelled, calmed, apologized, then reiterated his death sentence and dismissed her. Oslo had escorted her back to her sweaty jail cell. She shuddered at the thought of that milky, towering monstrosity. She'd said nothing over the course of the whole two-hour ordeal. But it wasn't necessarily out of character for her to keep quiet. She found that people often talked their way through things easily enough without help.

Suddenly Stu Black was looking down into her face and shaking her gently by the shoulder.

"Hey – you alright? Thought we lost you to the ceiling fan there for a second, you were staring so hard. I wish your eyes could fix the son a bitch. It's hot as… well, I won't say."

When Sarah pulled herself back from that black ocean of deep thought, she saw Stu reach back and scratch his head in a kind of Charlie Brown, 'well shucks' motion. *I like this one.* The assembly was disbanding. People were shuffling out of the Symphony house in slow hunched lines under dead exit signs. Sarah realized she'd missed the last half of whatever had been said. She'd live. Though she wasn't sure about everyone else. In the few moments since Stu had shaken Sarah out of her meditation, Jim Quail had silently tiptoed over to the duo and poked his head over Stu's shoulder.

"What're we talkin' about friends?" Jim said, rather loudly.

Stu jumped like a cat pawing a cucumber. "Fuckin' Christ, man. Didn't I tell you about creeping over my shoulder like that?"

"Sorry Stu – didn't mean to scare you. Just a – a bad habit. My Dad did the same thing."

"Well, cut it out – por favor."

Sarah felt a smile creep to her lips. Stu saw it and raised an eyebrow in a questioning arch. Sarah opened her mouth to speak and found her voice hoarse with disuse. She coughed and leaned forward. Stu and Jim both rushed forward to support her, but before they could touch her, she was up again, steel in her eyes.

"We need to leave tonight. I can show you how."

Chapter Fifteen

Keith Lonnagan

THE Primal Shabda: "Auuuuummmmmm...*suuu*... Auuuuuummmmm...*ssuu…*"

Keith Lonnagan inhaled a fly. It flew down his windpipe, did a twirl, then exited, riding the extra velocity of his wracking cough into the blue air. Keith looked up at the fly with disinterest. He was glad he hadn't killed it, that would've been against his pacifist ideals. Even so, he sensed some bad vibes in that fly. As it drifted lazily away, Keith's eyes returned to the problem in front of him. The desert. Always the desert.

His brush with death at the top of the Empire State building was the final straw in a long series of events that seemed to be telling Keith it was time to leave New York. He had been procrastinating, waiting for some contradicting sign, and had gotten none. The storm was as good a message as any. *Time to go.* His life in New York was over. He'd thought he'd made that distinction even before the sand had come. *Apparently not.* And even now, sitting criss-cross on the lower cliff of the island of Manhattan, he was having a hard time convincing himself to leave. He'd been born here. Raised here. Spiritually died, and been reborn here. Travelled, sure. but always with the expectation of returning to that big slab of American concrete, NEW YORK, NEW YORK, that shouted, "Here! Here! Here is where anything is possible!"

It was dead. The people were dead. Drowned or dying of thirst. The city was just a carcass now. Keith let out a big sigh. His hands were wrapped in big rolls of brown-red bandages, like some buddhist boxer. He'd been lucky enough to find a first aid kit on one of the lower levels of the Empire State Building, but he was no doctor. Not for the body at least. The most he'd been able to bring himself to do was wrap up his shredded hands with some Neosporin, shaking tremendously the whole time. The sight of his two missing fingers, snipped cleanly off at the first knuckle by a desk — how exciting — made him blindingly nauseous. He wondered if his contemplation of the desert before him would really matter all that much: if he would die of fever and infection first, or thirst would be the one to take him. He sighed.

The city had not weathered the storm well. And what a storm it had been. It was as if the ocean had been dropped from the sky. The water had come up at least eighty feet by the end, and many buildings had started to crumble and collapse under the pressure of the gale force winds. Behind Keith, the city looked like some clumsy giant's childish attempt to build a stick teepee. The skyscrapers leaned against one another like dominoes in a sandbox.

Keith was still wearing a bedsheet as a robe, and had added a small white sling bag, which rested over one shoulder. There wasn't much in it. Two bottles of orange Gatorade Zero, a moldy loaf of bread, some grape Hi-chews and a bottle of Banana Boat SPF 15 sunscreen. His purple, and considerably more dirtied, yoga mat sat in a roll next to him, a shoulder strap binding it tight.

When finally Keith had ventured back out onto the street after the storm had subsided, he found the dunes had turned to mud, ten feet deep in some places. In fact, his first step outside had almost sucked him down to a gritty, suffocating death. A rogue street lamp, knocked loose by the storm, had been just close enough to provide a lifeline to pull himself free. His white robe was now mostly brown from the ordeal, making him look something like a human roll of (soiled) toilet paper.

The storm had brought one small pleasure with it at least. *Water*. Fresh, potable water. And it had even been cool. Keith had gone from one puddle to another, gorging himself on that sweet, sweet liquid. It hadn't lasted long, though. The sun had returned with a vengeance and turned the city into a terrible moist sauna. Keith had watched in awe as the water returned to the sky from whence it had come in huge rising columns of steam, some so thick, they turned the world into a white sheet. It had only occurred to him afterwards that he should've found a way to save some of it for later. He'd been too excited to think ahead. And maybe a little shell-shocked too. *Too late*. And now, looking out into the sand, it was like it hadn't even rained at all.

From behind Keith came the sound of fluttering air, and suddenly he felt a small weight land on his head. He didn't move, but shifted his eyes upwards. A little hop, and the twisting, curious head of a Bluebird looked down over the expanse of his forehead. In a smooth, almost casual motion, the Bluebird wiped its beak on Keith's forehead, tweeted, then launched back into the air. *South*. Keith watched until it had blended into the blue sky over what had once been the eastern coast of the United States. He wondered how it was surviving out there. If it had taken shelter during the storm, what it was eating, drinking. Then he smiled, and he knew it was time to go. Time to follow.

Keith stood, hoisted his bag to a comfortable position over his chest, grabbed his mat, and began to walk.

Chapter Sixteen

Fred Windsley

THE desert had changed the citizens of Fort Worth, Texas.

Fred awoke to the sights and smells of office-themed tribal ritual. Far below the shifting sands of the new American Desert, in one of the towering glass skyscrapers, Fred Windsley awoke from his exhaustion induced sleep, strapped to a first aid gurney by several bands of leopard print duct tape.

He was in some kind of lobby, wide, with tall ceilings and a large, diverging staircase. All the furnishings had been shredded and strewn across the lobby in the fashion of some kind of bizarre cave animal. Strange huts made of lobby couches and other office supplies littered the dark corners of the main floor and first landing of the staircase.

The electricity was long gone, and as a result the room was drenched in darkness. The tall glass windows of the lobby allowed no light. Sand, fifty feet deep, covered the windows in blackness. A single, massive fire raged in the center of the room like an angry orange tongue. From Fred's vantage point, towards what had once been the main entrance, it looked like some kind of Office Max hell. Figures in hodgepodge costumes danced wildly around the fire. They seemed to be fighting invisible demons, punching and kicking wildly as they raced around the blaze. He was reminded briefly of some National Geographic film he'd seen in what seemed like a previous lifetime, of a group of native people in some far away land performing a rite for the dead, a play for the fire. Stranger still was the fact that there was no sound. Fred had thought for a moment he might be going deaf, until he finally clued in on the crackling of the fire, the wet thumping of feet on tile and… *what?* A strange chorus of clicks and a deep, metallic rumbling sound.

It was hard to make out in the orange tinted darkness, but Fred finally found the source of the noise. In the corner of the room, perched on a set of stairs in almost total darkness was a three-man band. One was playing the stapler, one the desk, and another, a rusty paper cutter. The man on the desk was setting the beat for the others by hitting the back of the steel desk with his forehead in a slow, "THUmppppwwaaa… THUmppppwwaaa… THUmppppwwaaa…"

The man on the stapler was reminiscent of an Appalachian spoon player. He flicked the heavy metal bars between his upraised knee and left hand in a fury of clicks and ker-clacks.

The last man, wearing no clothes — save a long, scraggly beard — was operating a paper cutter. The thing had seen better days as far as its usefulness in actually cutting anything, but the rusted metal blade and squeaky hinge were making for an excellent, gritty accent to the bass of the desk. The man was drawing the blade up and down in sporadic, practiced motions, almost like a washboard player.

The result of this mixture was some kind of music (?) unlike any Fred had ever heard. Yet they kept good time and reacted to the rhythm of the dancers like trained musicians. Fred liked it. He smiled. Then remembered he was alive. And his throat cried out like a dying and neglected houseplant. His mouth was so dry he thought he might choke on nothing. He tried to call out to the dancers, but found he could make only a wheezy, rasping noise. Air on cracked leather.

Suddenly, a hand was on his cheek, and his vision was being pulled away from the entrancing orange vision of the fire and the pulsing shadows. A woman was kneeling above him. She wore a sort of mask about her head, fashioned from yellow construction paper and secured using safety pins, so that only a small slit of her face remained exposed. Dark brown hair sprung from the folds of her paper mask in haphazard braids and curls, making her look like the child of a Spongbob piñata and the flying spaghetti monster.

In the small gap of her mask, Fred saw two bright green eyes. The right eye stared down at Fred with an intense curiously, the other pointed distractedly at the hearth fire, far to the left. Fred opened and closed his mouth soundlessly. With an audible snap, the left eye flicked into line with the right to gaze down at Fred, then, just as quickly, turned back to the fire. It was like watching some terribly malfunctioning doll trying to rewire itself, though Fred was far too thirsty to care.

The woman reached for something down to her right in the darkness, and then lifted it to Fred's lips. Cool life flowed down into the cracked earth that was Fred's mouth and throat. *Water, water, water*. He gulped like a guppy gasping for air. After a few swallows, the woman pulled the bottle away from Fred's lips. He tried to chase the water, but was restrained by the tape. His head thumped back down against the hard plastic gurney. Gradually, Fred began to remember where he'd come from… though, that only meant the desert. His life before meeting God was all… *fuzzy*. He looked down at his arm and saw that it had been set straight, though it still felt useless. Several rulers were holding the arm in a line, acting as a splint, held in place by more leopard print duct tape. Something told him that rulers wouldn't be enough.

Despite the strangeness of everything, Fred felt at home. He smiled up at the woman in the yellow mask and said, "Have you... Have you met God yet?"

He promptly slipped back into a black, sweaty sleep.

*   *   *

THE second time Fred Windsley woke, he was alone. He was still in the lobby, but the fire had burned down to little more than embers, and the duct tape that had been restraining him was gone. Slowly, Fred sat up and checked the state of his body. The hair on his arms where the duct tape had restrained him was gone, and he felt like some strange, hairy, striped caterpillar. The orange coals left by the fire cast only the slightest glow over to his corner of the room, but he could just make out the rulers binding his arm.

He was sweating profusely. The gurney he'd been resting on was slightly cradled, and a small pond of Fred juice had puddled there. The room was stifling, and a thin layer of gray ash rested over everything like a choking blanket. His thirst wasn't as dire as the first time he'd woken, but it still hurt to swallow. The water the woman had nursed him with was still there and he sucked it down greedily, throwing the cap and the bottle down once he'd finished. Slowly, easily, he got to his feet. His knees shook like bendy straws, and he wondered how long he'd been out.

Across the room, the fire flickered, and for a second Fred thought he'd seen the silhouette of a long black tail against the orange glow of embers. *No, Lord. I haven't forgotten.*

Fred made his way towards the fire. He hobbled like some broken old man, shuffling. Wet footprints trailed in his wake as the sweat poured over his back and down his legs. Arriving at the fire, he saw it rested on a massive pile of ashes. It seemed they'd been burning whatever they could find; couch cushions, paper, plastic — *fuck the fumes* — anything that would catch. A burn pile rested next to the embers and, despite the oppressive heat, Fred tossed a pillow on the embers and sat down. The cotton caught quickly and sent orange light racing across the room. As he looked through the flames, Fred realized that the woman in yellow was sitting across from him. Her green eyes shone like God's. Fred let a little pee out.

He tried to speak, and once again found he had no voice. A wheezing cough sprang from his chest, then a big black gob of snotty mucus followed. He swallowed hard and tried to speak again.

"Wh – who are you?" said Fred. His voice was different than he remembered. But then, what did he remember? *Only God. Only the desert.* He sounded strong. Confident. And suddenly, he felt it too. He was filled with purpose and gasoline. The Yellow Woman's eyes shimmered. She had noticed the shift. Her eyes twinkled between the yellow sheets of construction paper that covered her face. Fred asked again, "Who are you?"

The woman didn't answer, only stared in silence. Fred raised his hand and beckoned her gently over to his side of the fire. He felt a grin creep across his face, unprompted. Something felt good here. Felt right. And it made him smile. The Yellow Woman stared for a moment longer, then clumsily, childlike, got to her feet and plodded over to Fred. She sat down criss-cross and leaned in. Fred met her face to face, his smile reaching for his ears. The woman reached up slowly, and then touched Fred's hair curiously. He followed her hand with his eyes, letting her examine him for a moment, then reached up slowly for her mask. The woman jerked back, but remained sitting.

"It's alright." Fred's voice seemed to fill the lobby, reverberating and harmonizing with the close acoustics of the room. "Let me see."

The woman seemed to respond to the increasing fluidity of Fred's voice, and eased into his advance. He gently lifted the yellow paper mask away from her face. Underneath, he found startlingly normal features. She was older, maybe in her early thirties. But the strange, jungle-like braids made her seem much younger, and her body language was that of a child. She reached up, wiped her nose and mouth with the back of her hand and gazed at Fred.

He soaked in the sight of her, and suddenly he felt like he had been here before. God had shown him things out in the desert, and he recognized this woman. Suddenly he knew. These people had been changed. Irrevocably. The desert had wiped them clean. *God wiped them clean.* They were his blank canvas. *My blank canvas.* And Fred knew he was the brush. The paint was coming… He had been changed too, and yet some parts remained. These people, this woman, were *his.*

The woman's left eye darted from Fred towards the dimming flames. It startled him to see her left eye move so independently of the other, but he followed her half-gaze and realized that shadows had begun to gather around the fire. The dancers from before stood naked, or half-clothed in paper cloaks. They were looking at Fred. He smiled up at them. His teeth glowed yellow in the dimness. He knew then that they had been waiting. Waiting for someone to show them something. To take them to… *to the mountains. Yes. The mountains.* And Fred felt that glorious, decadent… *violent,* sense of purpose well up in him like a chocolate fountain. And he laughed.

Chapter Seventeen

Stu Black

HE didn't know it yet, But Stu Black was in last place. Along with his ragtag flock of former penguins. Though they hadn't really been following Hugh Flemm. They just happened to be living in 'his' city. They were just scared. Stu was too.

Only a few months ago, there had been thousands of people in Phoenix. Some had weathered the slow end of the world there, long time residents, like Jim Quail. Some lucky bastards had been stranded there by chance, like Billy Thompson. And still others, who had wandered out of the new American Desert by luck, or inside information. It didn't matter. Whoever they had all been, they were gone now. Phoenix had been slowly jettisoning its population, and when the sand started to tighten its grip — *really tighten* — they had run. In all directions and toward nothing.

Stu felt completely unqualified for the responsibility that had been thrust upon him as makeshift leader of this new world, nomadic tribe, but Jim kept telling him that's why he was perfect for the job. In truth, Stu knew they would've started losing people to the desert days ago if not for Sarah Bracken. Every day they spent out in this wasteland seemed to provide more evidence that she was some kind of silent desert angel. It was like she had been born to this kind of life, and the desert seemed only to make her more beautiful, where it turned others, like himself, into bent-over, walking scabs.

About three hundred people had decided to follow Stu. A relatively small group, considering how many remained in Phoenix, but a whole hell of a lot more people than Stu thought he'd ever be responsible for. Others had opted to go west, some south. And still more had chosen to go east, just not with Stu. In the absence of Hugh Flemm, a few had seen the opportunity to seize power, what little remained anyway. One woman in particular had been especially persuasive in her argument to stay in Phoenix. Like moths to the flame, she had drawn them in with promises of water and safety. At least a thousand had decided to stay with her, and Stu was fairly certain they were buried under two hundred feet of sand. Or would be soon. Jim Quail seemed pretty sure anyway. He kept imagining the last citizens of Phoenix, Arizona hiding in hotels and gas stations and office buildings as the sky collapsed in on them — an airless blanket of grit — as the sand came to fill in the whole.

They were somewhere vaguely northeast of Phoenix now, surrounded by nothingness. Two weeks had passed since that little town hall meeting they'd hosted in the Phoenix Symphony building. They'd left that night, and though Stu had been a little hesitant to leave in such a hurry, he was glad they had. The cliffs of sand around Phoenix had been moving before his eyes, shifting and tumbling in on themselves like great writhing, blue-black beasts. Sand being blown over the top of the rise had started to coat everything in the city – a beautiful sparkle in the air that quickly turned everything shit brown once it settled. The walls had steepened even as they had discussed their plans earlier that night, and it had been a *struggle* to make it over the rise. Certainly no vehicles could make the climb. Sarah was the first up. She had this strange way of sidestepping back and forth up the slope to avoid backsliding. Many of the three hundred wouldn't have made it without her help. Once a few people had made it over the top, they lowered a rope, which eased the ascent considerably.

Summiting the sand revealed just how bad things really were. The city was doomed. And everyone in it. This is what the Penguin must have seen when he'd somehow managed to haul his fat ass up the wall. Stu had almost laughed at the sight. Almost.

When the last member of their newly formed group finally flopped themselves onto the plateau of sand above Phoenix, the journey had begun in earnest. Stu had forgotten what it was like. A couple of weeks in a nice comfy cement jail cell had made him forget the desert. He was reminded quickly enough.

The weather was getting more extreme. It brought back memories of the year of storms that had been the right hook to the left jab of global warming. Terrible, violent things that had routed cities, and seemed to claw at the very surface of the earth. Though when Stu had finally been forced from his home in Colorado, the first time he had braved the desert, it had been relatively still out there. The nights were cold, and the days were hot. But this new rapid change, this devouring monster of sand coming from all sides was different. Above Phoenix, the wind had been blowing like a motherfucker, and the cold stung like knives. Every night since had been some variation on the same, yet it beat walking in the skillet that was daytime out here.

Stu, in his infinite wisdom, had wanted to pack light; bedsheets for sun protection and warmth at night, shorts, a few long sleeve shirts, etc. It was Sarah who'd known really what to expect. She had some kind of other worldly gift for reading the sand, even though from the bottom of the Phoenix bowl, you could hardly tell how brutal the weather would be at the top. She was a woman of few words, and she didn't argue. Stu's protestations that they didn't want to overburden themselves for the long, hard march that surely awaited them was met with silence. In the end, he had talked himself into a compromise and brought along several more layers of clothing than he had originally planned. But less than Sarah had recommended. He'd regretted that the first night. Then again, he felt like they'd done pretty well for themselves with the time they'd had. *Best we could.*

Water had been the biggest issue. The Penguin had stockpiled all the most valuable items in his domain, including potable, bottled water, in various buildings throughout town. When he'd escaped into the desert, his already flimsy organization of goons had imploded, and the stockpiles had been raided almost immediately. Some had even been forgotten and lost to the desert, a nice little treasure for some far future subterranean civilization. Or a thirsty mole.

They'd scrounged all they could then, from the bones of possibly the last American city to know real fresh air and sky; non-perishable foods, clothes, backpacks, and as much water they could find. It hadn't been nearly enough. That said, they'd been lucky. Despite the wind, the desert had been kind enough.

Two days out, Sarah had seen a dip in the sand a half mile south, and sure enough, a lone Texaco had poked its ugly head out of the sand like some endangered species trying to take one last breath of air before the big sleep. Stu supposed it sort of was. There had been some water there, and a few items of unspoiled food. The following weeks had been dotted with similar oases, though now the remnants of the old world seemed to be thinning out, and the true desert beginning.

Stu sat shivering next to Jim Quail. They were looking out over their future in silence. It was empty. Sarah sat down the dune from them, criss-cross and straight-backed like the desert monk Stu was beginning to suspect she was. Her mismatched clothing fluttered in the screaming wind, making her look unfairly dramatic, especially against the blue-black sandwich of sand and sky in front of her. Stu felt like an old man in a pity blanket compared. Jim Quail felt the same.

"Here."

Jim nudged Stu with a gloved hand. He was palming a mickey of Jack. Stu raised his eyebrows and nearly gasped.

"You've been holdin' out on me?" said Stu, his voice muffled by the high collar of his jacket and scarf.

"Well… I don't think Furiosa over there would be very approving of any *intentional dehydration*. Thought I'd keep it to myself for a bit. You just looked so miserable, I couldn't help it."

"Glad to see I can still inspire a little pity, if not confidence, in my loyal subjects. Thank ya kindly." Stu took the whiskey gingerly, undid the cap and took a hearty swig. He let the fire sit in his mouth before swallowing. He'd never been much of a whiskey lover, but the warmth it brought, like a little furnace in his tummy, was glorious.

"Are you still confident about going East?" asked Jim.

"I don't think I ever was, to be honest. But if you're askin' if I feel like turning back… not really. Something *is* out there. Behind us is nothing. That I know of, at least. You saw that bird yesterday, same as me. A fuckin' Blue jay. Out *here*. In the middle of nowhere. Where did it come from? What's it eating… I just can't help but feel like it was here for us."

Stu took another small sip of the whiskey, capped it and gave it back to Jim. He nestled back into the sand. They sat in silence for a moment and watched the wind blow south over fields of nothing, dragging lines across the world like huge invisible fingernails.

"We moving soon?" asked Jim.

"Yeah, probably oughtta get a move on. Wind seems to be comin' down a bit. Better make the best of the good moonlight."

As if on cue, Sarah stood and began to zag her way up the hill towards the pair.

"Hey, maybe we're getting better at this desert navigation thing. Ms. Atreides agrees with our assessment."

"Is that a Dune reference?"

"Oh, he reads. That's good."

Up the rise, in a hollow of sand, only partially shielded from the wind, lay the sleeping bodies of three hundred desert nomads. They pimpled the desert surface like cellulite on a sandy stomach. Sarah, Jim and Stu began to wake the sleeping travelers gently, rousing one at a time and urging them to get ready to move. It hurt to wake them. Some seemed to be sleeping so peacefully, even in the cold. But it was kinder than making them walk in the sun. The *All powerful* sun. Billy Thompson was one of the first up, and began to help wake the rest of the travelers.

They'd stopped to rest because the wind had been blowing too hard for some of the frailer members of the group, and because frankly, everyone was exhausted. But they couldn't stop forever, couldn't stay. Not yet anyway. *Not yet.*

Finally the troupe was up and bundled. They looked a sad thing, like a group of hunched old ladies in trench coats. But they were strong. Stu could feel their strength behind him when he said, "Let's do it."

And off they went, like a line of shriveled raisins on god's cruel, peanut butter lined celery stick. Stu just hoped there was something waiting for them. *Something good. Or anything…*

Chapter Eighteen
The Black Cat

"MMMMmmmmm... Aaah..."

The sound of low rumbling earth, twisting like an upset stomach. And then a sound like a gasp after a deep swallow of Coca-cola. *Refreshing. Blood has been given to the desert. That's good.* He'd like more of that. *I'll have more of that.*

A black cat with green eyes and a writhing whip for a tail, or was it some kind of a man? In the shape of a demon? A terrible black shadow that made one want to look away for fear of drowning in it. Only in quick glances, out of the corner of the eye, did *He* let his true shape show. But now, on the crest of a gentle dune, sitting on his back legs and slowly flicking his tail, he was a cat. Or rather, he appeared as a cat, to those who couldn't yet comprehend God. Above, in the electric blue sky, dark wings circled ever wider like B-52 bombers on standby. His birds. His vultures. *That pruny bitch on the mountain can keep her bluebirds and her rabbits.*

He was one with the desert. And the desert was him. They had been born from one another, you see, equal parts in an unravel-able whole. Snake and tail. Yin and Yang. Sky and sand. There was something dimmer, in his memory of birth. It was the vague, almost metallic, sensations of uncurbed greed and fury. Upon his birth into this beautiful world, the only mothering he'd had was this feeling. He knew somehow then, that this is what had begotten the glorious desert, his birthright, and thus himself. *Human Greed*. And it was this at the core of him.

The desert wanted more. Always more. And he would *always* lust to bring more into the fold. And when this world was one, golden, shimmering — *perfect* — hushpuppy, he would go on to the next. And the Next. And the next.

For all this confidence, there was… some small, doubt. A few, tiny, *itsy-bitsy, teensy-weensy*, frail little things, that made his tail flick back and forth in agitation. Made him itch, ever so slightly. As if they were ants walking across the plain of his mind, the Black Cat — *God* — could feel the steps of those players in his great opera, as they traversed the desert. And there were a good few. To the west, a man named… *Black*. And with him, a woman with no real name, though some called her *Bracken*. She frightened the Black Cat, for she too had been born of some greater, primal, force. One that he could neither see, nor discern. *It makes no difference. She isn't the only one.*

A student from the North comes as well. A little bit of a silly one, but strong. He may be a problem. And then there was Wilma. Wilma Nettlebee. She was not of the same brand as him. She was no God of sand or sky. Simply an old woman from Tennessee with a timeshare in Florida. Still, The Black Cat couldn't fathom why such a mysterious power had been given to her. Long nights he had prowled at the base of her mountain, waiting like a predator who knows his prey is trapped. Yet he could not touch her. And the desert seemed to flow around her mountain like a river around a boulder. It had been a mistake to let her take that place. Now she sat like a queen on her throne of greenness. *Hideous green*. And in *His* desert. *IN MY GODDAMN DESERT.*

All the same. He would prevail. The sand *was* rising. He felt it even now, the weakening of the woman's resolve. Soon, the battle would be one of physicalities. And in this, he would surely dominate. Even now his legions grew, and soon they would march to bring everything and everyone into the desert. And when their job was done, and there was nothing left to conquer, they too would come to dust, though he hadn't yet felt the need to share that vision with his generals, his *Penguin*, and his *Chief*. A curious pair, and so... *eager*. So empty. Like the desert.

There were others out there. Many others. Less every day, every hour, but there *were* others. He didn't think they mattered much. Not yet anyway. Not here. Still, he felt them all the same. *First, comes the old woman and her little island of green. Her lifeboat.* Like the last pull on a champagne cork. *She must come first, and the rest will follow.*

Thunder under the Black Cat's paws. A great gasping, and a crash. His pitch black fur shimmered with soft, deep vibration and pleasure. What was once the city of Nashville was trembling beneath the weight of his sand, his desert. A skyscraper imploded, shaking the earth and giving motion to the sand which rushed enthusiastically to fill in the new void. *Godly work. Glorious sound. I'll have more of that.* There had been a few people in that one, he knew. Ones too terrified to join his ranks, and too cowardly to seek out the old lady.

Damn her. His thoughts always came back to that flip flop wearing, beer drinking hag. The thought snaked into his brain, and his orgasmic pleasure at the fall of life and creation, the greedy feast of sand upon the carcass of human civilization, was soured.

"Meow."

Chapter Nineteen

Fred Windsley

FRED was feeling good. *Yes, yes*. Much better than he'd felt…
well, *ever*. And God had praised him. *Praised **me**.*

It had been a few days since Fred had awoken that first
time, strapped to a gurney in the bowels of — as he had come to
find out, after reading the words plastered above the no longer
functioning entrance to that underground lobby — the D Horton
Tower building. A bank. A bank that had become a cave/shelter
from the sun, and stocked with a ready supply of burnable items.
And some water. But one thing *had* worried Fred… the seventy
feet of sand piled against the tall glass windows. It was a miracle
that they hadn't shattered inward from the weight of the stuff
long ago, and a few visible cracks in some of the panes was
enough to tell Fred that they might not hold out a whole lot
longer. *Soon it'll be time to breath the fresh air again, folks.* He would
give a sermon today, to get these cave dwellers accustomed to
the idea of it.

That feeling of purpose which had so gripped Fred
Windsley down in the depths of that orange black pit had
seemingly extended itself to these strange Fort Worthers, *the
blanks, the office workers.* Fred wasn't really sure what to call them,
and so he had resorted to *"my people."* It seemed right, though
they weren't truly *his* people, but God's. Regardless, they had
become infatuated with him, or rather, with the green eyes that
loomed behind him and lent him their power.

This kind of *king of the poor lost natives* type situation didn't strike Fred as out of place at all. He'd almost forgotten he was in Texas. Though, was this still really *Texas* anymore? Fred thought not. The desert was coming alive. He could feel it. And funny things were beginning to happen. It was as if the land itself was waking from some long, deep slumber, and tossing about in its bed. Fred pictured a giant boy under the sand stretching out and rubbing his eyes. *Getting ready for Saturday morning cartoons.* These people, who had been wiped clean, *mind and soul*, were just another ingredient in this big stew. Fred had a feeling the same thing was happening to him. He was getting crazier, and he didn't much care.

The effects of this restlessness of the earth were beginning to make themselves clear. For one, the sand was moving. *Shifting.* Fred had only realized after the fact, though even his memories of even the last year were beginning to turn fuzzy, that his journey from California should have taken much longer than it did. He had been helped along by the desert. And by God, he was sure. And speaking of God…

"GOOD PEOPLE," said Fred, his voice echoing through the sandy lanes between the decapitated heads of Fort Worth's remaining skyscrapers. The words sounded as if he had spoken them softly, but another voice, crouching just behind his own, *God's voice*, lent them a frightening bass. "I THANK YOU FOR YOUR HOSPITALITY. I WAS LOST AND DYING, AND YOU… YOU GOOD PEOPLE – *MY PEOPLE*, TOOK ME IN. TOOK ME IN AND GAVE ME WATER. SWEET WATER… IN RETURN, I WOULD LIKE TO GIVE *YOU* SOMETHING…"

Fred stood in the center lane of what used to be Main Street, on a small stage of milk crates, plywood and other scavenged materials. He wore a cloak of multi-colored construction paper, and in the afternoon sun, he gleamed like a beachball. Around three hundred office workers stood in the lane before him. Some had looked bored, or been wandering aimlessly from building to building, but Fred's voice, backed by that alarming bass, had transfixed them. *All* of them. In the front, closest to Fred, stood the woman with the yellow mask. He winked at her.

"PURPOSE!" shouted Fred, and the echo of his voice seemed to expand until the sand itself was shivering with awe. He raised his arms above his head, the right one crooking into an unsettling claw shape. He had forgotten the pain. "IN THE EAST LIES GREEN. EDEN. THE GARDEN WHICH MUST BE RETAKEN, FOR OUR LORD HAS TOLD ME SO! AND YOU… *YOU* ARE THE CHILDREN HE HAS CHOSEN TO DO IT. FOLLOW ME, AND I WILL GIVE YOU THE FUTURE."

The words tumbled out of Fred easily, like practiced poetry, and he was aware of the shadow of the Black Cat — Jerry, *God* — looming behind him like a dark cloak. It felt like warm sand. *I am a prophet. A conduit for his words.* Never had puppetry felt so good. He knew he was being used. Being used like a baby rattle to hide a pair of green fangs. But that was alright. *They don't need to know everything. I don't need to know everything. He's enough.* And it was enough. Enough for the several hundred pairs of watchful eyes in front of him, who began to bow and cheer.

Fred could feel the inky blackness behind him, and the deep, velvety black confidence that flowed from it. He felt a cat move between his legs like a soft snake.

Then the voice of God whispered in his ear, "NOW COMES OUR GENERAL."

In the distance, stumbling out of the afternoon desert, seemingly propelled by the sand, came a chubby man in what looked like a ragged tuxedo. Fred lowered his arm, and shaded his eyes with his crooked right hand.

"Is that a penguin?"

Chapter Twenty

Hugh Flemm

THE king was waiting for Hugh in his sweat-box of a lair, his *den,* deep in the bowels — in reality, the first floor lobby — of a green glass building on the corner of West 5th and Throckmorton. It might've been cooler down there, away from the sun, if they hadn't been continuously feeding a central bonfire with couch cushions and whatever other shit they could find. Hugh could smell the heavy chemical fumes resting on the walls and hanging in the air. His throat and mouth were dry. *So dry.* And this place was making him sweat the last of his bodily fluids out faster than the desert sun, which he was, despite the stuffiness, glad to be out of.

When he'd first arrived, he'd seen the apparent king/prophet giving some kind of speech on a stage… and the Lord's shadow looming behind him. *I'm in the right place,* he'd thought then. *My conversations with God weren't just hallucinations.* But when he'd stumbled towards the conglomeration, he'd been quickly restrained by some funny looking fellows in scant outfits, and ushered into a small office room in a green skyscraper. An hour or so later, when the king was ready for him, he'd been brought down into the pit. And so, here he was.

There were people milling about the room that might've once been a lobby, but was now some kind of strange Neo native American office worker base camp. Most were naked, but some wore improvised clothes, like the man in the huge construction paper cloak. Over by the fire, a group sat in a semicircle, like some elder council. One was smoking out of a tin-can pipe, and failing to blow smoke rings. In the middle of the half circle sat a woman wearing a yellow paper mask, and… and a man with twisted arm and a black smile.

"Hello, general," said the man with the terrible grin.

"Hello… King," said Hugh hesitantly, his dry throat catching on the words.

Freddy laughed loudly. Like rocks in a tumbler. "So, God *has* spoken to you. Where is he?"

"He left me on the outskirts of the city. He said he had other places to be."

"Ah, yeah. I'm sure he does. He's in lots'a places at once, I think. Though he is often… *more,* in one place than another."

"I wish he were more here than *there,*" said Hugh. "He could have at least introduced me."

"… It sounds almost like you're questioning God's will… *Penguin.*"

At this, the room stopped. All eyes moved to Hugh Flemm, and the only movement was the flickering of the flames and the orange reflections they cast on the faces around them. Hugh swallowed. Or more aptly, went through the motion of swallowing. He had no spit to down. He was suddenly aware of the currents of violence running through these people, of the tenseness of their attentions and the possibility of *blood.* He really did *hate* when people called him *Penguin,* though. Almost as much as *Flemm.*

In this moment, Hugh almost wished he'd stayed out in the desert. *These people are nuts,* he thought. *But I guess I'm not that far off. I did spend all yesterday talking to a cat…* but even the thought of that was enough to make Hugh shiver. *That weren't no goddamn cat. That was God.* And he knew it was true. Despite it all, he hadn't been hurt here, and God had promised him refuge in Fort Worth… if only he would do his bidding. He'd agreed readily enough then.

"…I only meant, I feel, what is it, *vulnerable*, with him gone. And I fear for what those on the green island might attempt against him. That's all. *Freddy*, baby."

Fred ignored the mention of his name and eased his tone. "We are all *vulnerable*, comrade. All except the Lord himself, right? And those green islanders are gonna find out real soon just how true that is. And by your hand, ironically."

"By, my… hand?"

"Oh, he didn't tell you? I guess I still have to do *some* things. As you can see, I'm recovering from a little spill I took a while back… As much as there is to recover anyway." Fred lifted his mangled arm, splinted with rulers and bound with leopard print duct tape. "But soon, we'll be as mobile as a jackrabbit. And you'll be leading my army. And be the first to strike."

"I guess… this is your army, right?" asked Hugh.

"Oh yeah, Jack. And ain't it somethin'?" replied Fred.

Hugh looked around at the blank orange faces surrounding him and asked hesitantly, "And, uh, how'd you swing that, if I might ask?"

"The power of God, my *sphe021sciformine* friend!" Fred roared the words and suddenly the fire seemed to shrink, and the black shadows on the edge of the room began to curl in towards the fire like smoke. *Suffocating.* The office workers began to cry out and bow and scream. Fred laughed, and seemed to let the shadows retreat to their corners. "I gave them a little demonstration of… the power our God has bestowed upon me.

Earlier today actually, just as you stumbled into town. They'll obey his will, just like you and me."

Hugh took this all in without peeing his pants, though it was a close call. He played it off well. Not even a voice crack. "I… see." *Gulp*. "And why the, uh… why are they so…?"

"Stupid?" asked Fred. "Yeah. I don't really know, to be honest. They were like that when I got here. The desert does funny things to people. Certainly did to me, eh?" Fred chuckled. "Though she's different." Fred gestured to the woman in the yellow mask sitting next to him. "I think she's smarter than all of us combined, tell ya the truth. She can't talk though. Least not that I've heard."

"That so?"

"Yeppers."

Silence hung between the Penguin and the lunatic king for a few seconds.

"So… what now?" asked Hugh.

"Well… first we've gotta get you some iron."

Chapter Twenty-One

Keith Lonnagan

THE bluebirds abandoned him after three days in the desert. Even they didn't like going this deep into nothingness it seemed. Except, that wasn't quite right. It wasn't *nothing,* it was just different. But Keith somehow got the feeling that it wanted to be everything, that the desert wanted to consume. *To eat.*

Keith Lonnagan felt as if he had been staggering over sand dunes his entire life. There seemed to have been nothing before the desert, and nothing except the desert. The sand was fine as powdered sugar in some places. Golden sugar.

Sometimes, when the sun hung low in the sky, and the horizon transformed it into a giant heavenly tomato, Keith forgot he was on Earth. It felt like he'd stumbled onto some alien planet by mistake, or unknowingly passed into the land of the dead. Purgatory. And his thirst induced delirium almost made him believe it. Still, he practiced his meditation every morning. Though on the beginning of his 7th day walking south, the raw burning of his skin and throat had been hard to overcome. He was pretty sure this would be his last hurrah. His last day conscious. The last trot before reincarnation, if that was still a possibility in this barren world.

It was midday. The sun overhead was an all-consuming spotlight. It seemed to reach down and press on Keith like he was a panini in a frying pan. His rucksack was empty, and he'd repurposed it into a sad looking head drape. He wore his bedsheet like a robe, trying to cover as much of his fried red skin as possible. From afar he looked like some bleached hermit crab, meandering his way zig-zaggedly across an endless beach. But no matter how he arranged his garments, it felt like the sun always found a way to reach inside and sear him, burn him with its long hot fingers.

His last sip of gatorade had been three days ago, and it felt like it. Keith had never known such thirst and hunger, like there was some kind of Tasmanian Devil eating him from the inside out. He was sure there were worse ways to go, but at the moment, he couldn't think of any. *Fitting for an aspiring yogi, really. A good, long, harsh march to the end,* to that clearing at the end of the path.

It was the rise of another cursed sand dune that finally crumpled his legs. Keith could almost hear his knees sigh, '*O fuck*' with relief as they plunged into the boiling sand. He sat there, at the bottom of a desert valley, and looked up at the sky. The sun slapped his face hard, and Keith closed his eyes. *About ready to call it.* But just when the heat seemed unbearable, just when he felt his mind slipping away into that final abyss… fingers snapped, and the heat of the sun was replaced with a blessedly cool night breeze. It felt like someone had dumped a bucket of refrigerated 3% milk on him. *Orgasmic.* He opened his eyes to the sight of a million billion stars, blinking in the black sky like a river of silver and polished pewter.

"SIMBA!" cried Jeff Bridges.

"Huh…" said Keith.

Jeff chuckled. "Just kidding. Never seen the Lion King? Brutal, man."

"I, uh, I had a pretty sheltered childhood. And adulthood, really," said Keith.

"Yeah, I can tell. But hey, you're doing great now! You look so cool, really, I mean it. You're like this wandering ascetic dude, all emaciated and tan… dressed in white. Kind of. Really showing your commitment to the bit."

"No bit, man. I'm in it for real. I want to be the real deal."

"Well… That's good. That's good, man," said Jeff Bridges, with both skepticism and hope in his voice.

Sitting in front of Keith was some part of the old world. A piece of energy that'd been evicted from its old home and now wandered the desert, somewhat lost, like Keith. To some it may have looked like nothing at all, to others, the very face of God. To Keith, it looked like a frog. And then a spot of starlight. Then both at the same time, and finally, Jeff Bridges. *Or all three?*

"You looked like you were about to give up there for a minute. I happened to be in the neighborhood, so I thought I'd drop in… introduce myself, ya know, give you a little bit of a helping hand, one yogi to another," said Jeff Bridges.

"I'm cooked, God – I really…" said Keith.

"Woooah, there. Woah. Woah. Man. Not God." The frog pressed its flippers to its chest in a, *'you got me all wrong'* kind of gesture.

"Well… I just thought…"

"Jumping to conclusions is a bad habit, dude. Really should work on that. But hey, I didn't mean to interrupt."

"I was just saying that, I'm cooked. Toast. Goosed… wait no, that's not right. Does goosed mean like, juiced? 'Cause that's not what I mean, unless it's like literally juiced, in which case…"

"I think the expression you're looking for is 'my goose is cooked,'" said the puddle of starlight.

"That's the one. My water is all gone, I feel like I'm about to… wait…"

And suddenly, Keith didn't feel like he was about to die. His skin felt smooth and hard, but not burnt. He licked his lips. *Moist.* That burning sandpaper in his throat was gone. He felt... *good.*

"Hey now... I feel good?" said Keith.

"I had some spare fairy dust, so I hit ya with a little sprinkle." Jeff Bridges winked at Keith, then ribbited.

"Swell..." said Keith.

The pair looked at each other in silence for a little while. And it was comfortable, like two friends okay with sitting next to each other in a silent car. Keith was the first to speak.

"So... One yogi to another, I've been wondering if I really have what it takes to... to be this teacher I always felt like I could be. *Should be.* I don't really know much about Hinduism and all that. I just learned from Kathy at the Y. But I have to say, it always felt like she really got to the *core* of things. No messing about with Samsara, and Atman and Brahman, and the paths and vehicles, and blah-bah-blah-bah-blah..."

"Hey, I know Kathy," said the lily pad of silver light. "Hell of an instructor. I took her class a couple times. 151st street, right?"

"Hey, yeah! That's the one."

"Ya know, I really wouldn't be too concerned with all that stuff about reincarnation and Nirvana and whatnot. Kathy had it figured. Just follow your instincts, and you'll be fine." Jeff Bridges leaned in then, and said in a hushed voice, "The truth is that nobody really knows shit about the afterlife. Well... except Ozzy Osborn. But, that's, err, a *special case.* What matters is what we do with the time that is given to us, *here,* eh? That's a Lord of the Rings reference. In case you didn't catch it."

"...I suppose you're right."

At this, the apparition leaned back and nodded. "Right on, man. Right on. Keep on keepin' on dude. You got some fans on the bench cheering for ya. I unfortunately do have to go now. An acupuncture thing I signed up for, we'll see if they're still in business, despite the weather." Jeff Bridges waggled his finger in the air, as if the desert were just a passing drizzle. "Hey, one last thing, though. We're, uh, not exactly alone out here. There is... another... *A black one.* Just keep an eye out, mmm?"

And with that, the frog sunk into the sand like a fishing bobber being pulled under the surface of the water by a fish, and was gone. The night air remained, but felt a little bit cooler. *Cold.* Keith found he had somehow migrated to the top of the dune he'd previously been looking up at. He was still seated, but now with his legs crossed above the knees and with his back straight.

Far out over the black ocean of sand, he thought he saw something moving. A black shadow with a long wriggling tail, and green headlights.

Chapter Twenty-Two

Hugh Flemm

HUGH Flemm. Hugh. Flemm. Flemm. Flemm, Flemm, Flemm…

Hugh Flemm let out a big, wet cough. A greenish yellow ball of spit was propelled from the back of his throat and swallowed up eagerly by the midday desert sand. The loogie stayed whole for a few moments, rolling on the ground and collecting a gritty coat sand on its exterior like a dead grasshopper attracting ants. Hugh looked at it disdainfully. *My namesake. Thanks pops.*

Hugh raised his eyes to the scenes of strange barbarism and Neo-medieval extravagance that had become common in the wasteland of Dallas. The sky was a searing blue, almost itself sizzling. The sun hung right up top, like some terrible, terrible, heavenly heat lamp, and below it, the Fort Worthers toiled under the whip of their self-made master.

Hugh did not like Fred Windsley, but he had to admit there was something intriguing about him, though he knew a lot of this charm came from his contract with God. His mangled, hooked arm, weathered skin, badly healed wounds and crazy eyes made for a compelling package. *He was chosen by God. Like me.* And now, dressed in his new office king finery, Hugh thought he looked like some inbred peacock, Office-Max freak. A cloak of multi-colored construction paper hung about his shoulders, while his body remained mostly naked, save for a bedsheet diaper, and on his head rested an ornate crown fashioned out of leopard print tape, construction paper, an array of colored markers and what looked like a brass doorknob.

Fred's pavilion consisted of several massive red and gold rugs thrown over the sand, and a series of white bedsheets, strung between metal signposts into a flowing canopy. It had taken the office workers days to find the right materials in the labyrinth of sewage passageways and uncollapsed buildings under Fort Worth. But they had.

Hugh shuddered at the thought of the darkness and the stench they must've braved to haul those huge carpets out, to wrestle them free from the desert, like a rope toy from a determined dog. One party had blown themselves to smithereens trying to light a torch in one of the sewer tunnels. Methane trapped in the tunnel went up like a bomb at a spark from a BIC lighter. It sounded like little more than a mole fart from the surface. Another group went down into the sewers and never came back. *Just got swallowed.* It was a few days after this that king Fred had commanded the tribe move to Dallas. And then... *And then East. East to Tennessee. Yes. On this, we agree.*

Fred sat in a burgundy Lazyboy recliner, his feet tucked up in the seat and his chin on his palm like a bored child. The woman in the yellow mask sat beside him. Two half-naked office workers stood on either side of the pair, gently fanning the air with big sheets of green poster paper cut into the shape of palm fronds. They were watching the good Lord's work being done. *Excavation.* It was more of an undertaking than anyone would have imagined. Hundreds of office workers were roasting out in the sun like little pale salamanders, digging with anything they could find. A few were lucky enough to have actual shovels. Most sat and pawed at the sand like dogs, flinging it behind them through spread legs, only for it to slowly roll back down into the pit.

Despite the lack of equipment, Hugh was surprised at their speed and progress. *They're determined, these psychos.* They'd made what looked like a giant ant-lion hole, or the Sarlacc pit from Star Wars. A cone in the sand that narrowed to a point. *Just enough to scratch bottom…*

One of the parties sent down into the depths of the Dallas sewer system had come back with a map. On it showed a number of stores specializing in weaponry. *Guns. Explosives.* Whatever automobiles remained above ground, above the golden sea, were the last. There was little hope of ever being able to dig a car out from under seventy feet of sand. And even if you got it out, even if it ran, there would be no more gasoline. Maybe someone, somewhere would figure it out, but for now, the golden age of the car, of the American highway, was gone. It made Hugh a bit sad. But if you could just reach the roof of a building, one that had coped with the weight of the sand above it, you could tap whatever resources lay inside, like a buried egg. And guns were better than gold. They were power.

The progress was slow. And hard to watch. Hugh was content most of the time to just sit inside, stare at the wall and drink water. His brush with death out in that *shit* between Phoenix and here had given him a new appreciation for such simple pleasures. A few of the office workers had fainted from heat stroke already, and one had died. Fred had then said, "We didn't want any weak links in our legions, anyway. Not no mo." *Not no mo.* It was like a ritual response to the office workers, and they shouted it back at Fred like Nazi fanatics screaming "Heil!" Hugh had wondered on several occasions already if they were even *capable* of saying anything else.

Hugh's journey across the desert hadn't changed him too much, though he'd lost about twenty pounds, and the sunburn had darkened his skin considerably. What *had* changed was his *purpose*.

God had come to him outside Fort Worth and named him a general in his new army. *Third in command*. Fred was the profit, and king among *blanks*. Hugh Flemm would be master of war. God had need of such a person, and Hugh fit the bill. Who's more cruel than a child? Deep inside, that's what Hugh was. A bitter child. And ever since God had come to him, he felt that child's anger rippling through his soul, laughing and raging to be set loose.

Hugh made his way towards Fred's pavilion and stepped under the bedsheet canopy.

"Freddy baby, how goes it," Hugh said, as less of a question and more a string of syllables.

"Hello, Flemm," said Fred.

Hugh hated when people called him that. And it didn't help with his already growing distain for the Black Cat's choice of prophet.

"Making progress?" asked Hugh, trying to keep the annoyance out of his voice.

"Well... they dig alright, but the sand keeps falling in as fast as they can shove it out."

"That does seem to be the way of it. Phoenix got swallowed up by that shit like it was water. No way you could dig it out... no way. I still think you're a little crazy for trying here."

King Fred looked up at Hugh with glinting hazel green eyes and smiled wildly. "Only a little? Don't insult me, Milly-bo-billy."

The two chosen men watched in silence for a few moments, squinting against the bright golden light of the sand in the midday sun.

"When are you sending me out?" asked Hugh. They hadn't discussed this topic much, but Hugh knew he *would* be sent out. God's promises of life and pleasure had all come at a price. A price Hugh had been more than willing to pay. *And first comes the old hag…*

"Well…" Fred reached up with his splinted, but still twisted, arm and scratched his stubbled chin. "I guess as soon as we can get you some firepower. A master of war outtgha…"

And just then, a cry came hurdling out from the dig site. It was an animalistic shout. A sound like an ape might make after a bloody and brutal battle for tribal dominance. *The first kill.* It was dry and horse. A shout of triumph. Of Victory. Fred looked at Hugh, and winked.

They'd struck roof.

Chapter Twenty-Three

Sarah Bracken

SHE felt herself melting again. And not from the heat.

Her name was Sarah. *Sarah Bracken. Yes.* She remembered that name. It was the name of a girl from... *somewhere. Montana? Colorado? No, not Colorado.* That was where Stu was from. She remembered a big back yard with a tire swing and green grass. And no neighbors. There were other things about that place too. The faces of sisters. The face of a mother. The terrible smell of a father.

It had been easier to remember herself in Phoenix. Easier to *focus,* even in that warm concrete box. She'd wandered out of the desert like an unsuspecting woodland sprite. She couldn't even recall why she'd chosen to go to that rotten place. *Ah, the baby.* It was still possible to forget she was pregnant. But harder every day. Even the desert couldn't seem to wipe that fact from her mind.

Sarah's days now consisted mostly of helping the poor people who'd chosen to follow her and Stu Black into the desert. Like a shepherd herding sad, tired goats. She had told them to come, told them she knew the way. And she did, but she didn't know if she could get *everyone* across the finish line. *No,* she was sure she couldn't. They were slow, and the sun and sand didn't seem to be the antidote to them that it was for her. *The desert.* It cradled her like a soft crib. Like she had been born to it. She hadn't been.

There was the time before the desert, that was the tire swing and the sisters and the green. Then the sands and storms had come, not just for her and her family, but for everyone. Something had happened then. She couldn't remember what became of her family, and for some reason she didn't much care. They were probably dead. Like most people. But she wasn't. The desert had chosen her. *Her*. And every day she spent out here, leading this flock, she became more and more sure she was losing her humanity, that it was being replaced with dry nature. The life inside her seemed to be excited by the thought.

"Hey, Sarah… You alright there?" asked Stu Black. Sarah looked at him blankly for a moment, then shook herself with conscious effort.

"…Yeah. Just thinking, for a second," she responded.

"These dunes are a bitch, pardon me sayin' so, but I'm not sure how much more we can take… Jim's knees are in real bad shape. Not that they were ever tip-top… But you seem to scamper up these hills like it's child's play," said Stu.

It is.

"Just had more practice, is all," said Sarah mildly. Behind Stu and Sarah, a long train of desperate journeyers trudged up golden curves of sand, almost seeming to move backwards with each step. The Dali painting with the melting clock came to mind. And the sun was frying them all, like little donut holes in a vat of golden oil.

"Most of us'll be out of water by the end of the day. It's gonna start getting a little dicey. Don't suppose you can pull another one of those magical Texacos out of your hat?"

"I told you to conserve what we had." Sarah's voice came out harsher than she'd intended, and Stu moved back an inch, hurt.

"I did what I could, Sarah. We're no group of desert commandos. I mean Billy's from fuckin' Connecticut. I'll be alright, but we have a responsi –"

"I didn't ask for that," interrupted Sarah. Stu opened his eyes in wide incredulous circles.

"You didn't ask for that?" said Stu. "The fuck you didn't. If I recall correctly, I believe it was something like, 'we have to leave tonight. I can show you how.'"

Sarah turned away from him, facing up the dune. Her bleached hair fluttered in the breeze, then, after a breath, she turned back around to gaze at the trail of slow moving people below her.

"We're two days from… something. I can smell it. It's scraps, but it'll have to do," Sarah said into the wind. And it was true. She could sense something ahead of them. It was leavings from that *other*. *The Black other*.

She could feel him in the icy nights, circling and sauntering across the desert, like the dark angel from *American Progress*. A massive black panther with soft, dangerous paws and terrible green spotlights for eyes. He'd unearthed something, and the stench of the old world was thick on the air. There was a race on, and they were in last place, she knew. She didn't want to participate in this race, but something told her she had no choice. Things were converging on the back of a great green turtle somewhere in the East. How she knew this, she didn't know, nor did she question this knowledge, granted to her by an unseen hand. And she wondered how much Stu could sense. *Not enough*.

Stu turned and studied Sarah for a moment, then sighed. "Well, I suppose that's what it is, then. I'll let the people know."

Stu turned to pass the message along, but before he could

go, Sarah grabbed his arm and pressed her water sack into his chest. It was almost full.

"… *Jesus Christ* – this was from three days ago! Are you human? What about the baby?" Stu held the sack, stunned. Sarah just shrugged.

"I wasn't thirsty."

A hand grasped at the top edge of the crest on which Sarah and Stu stood. A moment later, an exhausted and sunburned Jim Quail flopped over the edge.

"Oh, fuuuck," Jim moaned, breathing heavily. Stu reached down and gave him a hand up. Jim could see the uneasiness in his eyes. "Everything alright?" he asked.

"...Yeah. Sarah says it'll be two days before the next pit stop, though."

"Two days! Oh Jesus – I don't know if –"

"You can," said Stu, reassuringly. "We got no choice. We knew it'd be hard, right? This is us. We keep going."

Jim looked like he might protest, then shut his mouth and nodded.

"Help me spread the word," said Stu, giving Sarah's turned back one last searching look.

Sarah peered out over the rolling dunes ahead, letting the hot air blow through her. *That smell again,* of a rotting city. It made her sick. She was coming to understand that she loved the desert. She loved the desert, and she hated what had come before. She knew then that she wasn't *so* different from that black other. He loved the desert, in his own way. Though he wanted more. Always more.

And maybe... she did too.

Chapter Twenty-Four

Wilma Nettlebee

WILMA Nettlebee sat under her multi-colored beach umbrella, a warm, flat Dr. Pepper and a pack of Hillsborough Cigarettes on the ground by her side. A number of song birds had landed around her and were chirping excitedly, almost like they were having a conversation. Wilma lay back, completely still on her beach recliner, her eyes fixed on where the electric sky met the edge of her sun-brella. A bluebird did a little hop-glide and landed on Wilma's boney chest. It turned its head to point a beady black eye down at Wilma. She stared back, only moving her eyes.

It started as a low groan, then quickly exploded into a full blown shout. "GET THE FUUUCK OFF MEEE!" Wilma cried. She sprang up off the back of her chair and waved her arms around, like a someone whose been assaulted by fruit flies past the point of rational behavior.

"I can't stand this shit anymore!" she screamed as loudly as her smoker's throat would allow. "Like I'm fuckin' Snow White over here. God *Damn*." As the birds scattered, Wilma slumped back into her recliner and reached lazily for a cigarette. Finding the little red and white box on the ground, and the pink mini BIC lighter on top, her practiced hands sloshed one of the cigs free and brought it to her lips. Wilma tossed the box back to the ground and brought the lighter up to her face, but just as she struck the flint wheel, a bluebird swooped under her umbrella and landed on the arm of her recliner.

"Tweet."

Wilma didn't move, but her eyes snapped to the intruder. The flame flickered silently in the stillness. The bluebird twisted its head and chirped again. It sounded like, *"Bitch?"*

Wilma slowly brought the flame up to the fuzzy end of her cigarette and inhaled, pulling that wonderful chemical smoke bomb deep into her bosom. She wiggled her wrinkled toes in the opening of her fluffy pink house slippers with satisfaction. She kept her eyes on the bird. At that moment –

"Nana! Nana! I finally got one!" said Harold, hauling his two hundred and fifty pound ass up the Clingmans Dome ramp one labored step at a time. He was holding a small fish of some kind by the gills. It was still flopping around in his iron grip, and its eyes looked like a human's might when on the operating table of an alien spacecraft: Wide and fishy.

Wilma turned back to face her only grandson, breathed in some fresh ciggy, and with smoke blasting out through her yellow teeth, said, "That's great baby. Lemme get a look."

Harold hobbled up the slope to Wilma's perch, abductee in one hand, and Walmart fishing pole in the other. He wore a massive white Hanes t-shirt that had turned mostly a brownish-green from river love, AND1 basketball shorts, and a huge smile. He only vaguely looked like his grandmother. Perhaps if you'd removed the excess hundred pounds from his body, you could've guessed they were related.

"Wowy, a big one too," said Wilma. Her voice was soft and careful, very different from her 'bird-shooing' voice. Speaking of, a few birds had returned to the shade of her umbrella and had resumed their chirping. The sight of Harold had apparently not been enough to discourage them.

"Think we can cook it up later?" asked Harold. The fish had about a gulp of meat on it. And half of that would be bones.

"Sure, honey. I'll leave that up to you. Just be careful with the fire. Keep it in the pit, and make sure you cook it all the way before you take a bite, akay?"

"Sure, Nana."

"You finish all the rest of your chores?"

"Yeah... 'cept measuring the sand." At this Harold looked down at the ground, the excitement instantly vanishing from his face.

"Oh baby... I know you don't like it. I don't like it, either. I'd do it myself, but I don't think I could make it back up this... fuckin' hill if I did. If I had a scooter or somethin' maybe. It's gotta be done, honey bun. We have to get an idea of how much time we have." Wilma delivered this information gently, but firmly. "Now before you go cooking that poor fish..." The poor fish flopped in terror at the mention of his demise. "I want you to go check by the stream. You don't have to get too close, in fact, *don't* get too close, just have a looksie and see if it's starting to rise up to the tree line, akay?"

"Okay..." Harold nodded, but did not look resolved. "You think... you think he'll be there again? Like last time?"

Wilma's face turned grave. A bluebird jumped up onto her lap and pooped on her blue shorts quietly. "Might be, baby. Might be. But you just don't worry about him. He can't touch you here. *Not here.*"

"He's... his eyes..."

"I said *don't* you worry about him. You don't listen to a word he says. You hear me? Not a word. Don't even look at him. Just keep your eyes on the ground, then I want you to come right back here, akay? Then we'll cook us up a nice fish dinner." The fish's eyes seemed to somehow get even wider.

Harold brightened at this thought and said, "Okay. You watch him and make sure he doesn't go anywhere. I'll go and come right back." Harold dropped the pole, and gingerly laid the fish on the searing concrete. If fish could scream, he woulda. Harold then began his long waddle back down to the edge of the forest to see how quickly the desert was eating their island oasis. And maybe to face that black other. *The black cat.*

Wilma watched him go. Her cigarette had burned down to the filter. It was hot on her lips. She tossed it aside and accidentally hit the fish with the butt. The fish had already made peace with its maker. The cigarette was but a dim thump on the way out the door.

Wilma turned back to her view of Clingmans dome. It was spectacular, though Wilma still thought it was just alright. It was also shrinking. The ocean of sand was rising, as once the polar ice caps had melted and caused the seas to rise. The desert flowed like water and was slowly eroding the island on which they had taken refuge. She could see the sand now. Could see the trees falling one by one into yellow death.

Wilma didn't sleep much. It seemed the older you got, the less your body craved that dark relief, and the more it wanted to just sit down, smoke, and *watch shit.* She'd taken to star gazing and looking out over the mountains and into the desert. She saw him then. Every night. *Every night.* A giant black cat with a writhing tail, circling, and pointing his virulent green eyes right at her. *Right at her.* The longer she looked at him, the more she was convinced he wasn't a cat at all, but something much worse. Some kind of a half-formed demon, his body composed of a million wriggling worms and serrated claws. But always with those toxic green, spotlight eyes.

Wilma did not shudder at these thoughts. She just lay back and let the bluebirds crowd around her like she was a loaf of bread. Their chirping seemed more urgent now, and she felt like she could almost understand them. Almost. It was still far too annoying to pay attention to.

Chapter Twenty-Five

Fred Windsley

"OH Captain, my captain!" Fred Windsley shouted whilst giving a somehow simultaneously patriotic and mocking salute to his number one general. *Gambler. Penguin. Flemm. Numero Dos. Mi teniente primero.*

Three bikes were humming in the sand, each loaded with a sled full of supplies and four riders. Hugh Flemm sat at the front of the formation, looking up at Fred's half constructed palanquin. He gave a nod and rolled his eyes. *Ungrateful son of a bitch,* thought Fred, though his smile only grew larger.

"Good luck! And make sure to leave some fun for the rest of us, eh?"

The crowd of office workers gathered in the sandy lane between two Dallas skyscrapers, or what remained of them, cheered at the jest of their prophet king. Fred knew that it didn't much matter what he said. Their ears were all hearing the same thing: *Come! Come! Follow me to Mecca! To the Kaaba! To **salvation!** Or don't, and burn in eternal damnation.*

Hugh Flemm would be the first ambassador for their beautiful movement. The first missionary to bring the good news to the heretics living on that green island in the East. *How dare they…* The idea made Fred so angry that he nearly lost his smile. *How dare they put such a blemish on God's fine desert? Blasphemy.*

He didn't like Flemm's attitude, but he saw why the lord had chosen him. *He's cruel and vicious. A cruel and vicious boy, for a cruel and vicious job. He's perfect. Though it's important I don't hurt his pride. Gotta feel cool and in charge… cool and in charge.*

With a final swing of his hand, the riders were off, flinging sand up from their back wheels in flowing golden rooster tails. *Only three bikes in the whole goddamn south, don't wreck em', Penguin.* He knew they should have enough gas to get to Tennessee, if they drove straight, at least. *God will help with that.*

Fred Windsley didn't know exactly what to expect in the east, as far as resistance, but the Black Cat had made it seem like it oughtta be a piece of cake. *The guns will help.* The roof they'd managed to break into from the desert's surface was an armory, though not the kind Hugh had been expecting.

Fred Windsley, though a good orator, was not always the brightest crayon in the bunch. He'd thought it would add a touch of *style* if his subjects were wielding muskets instead of AR-15's. And so, on the map of gun shops they'd found, he had picked a historically-themed armory, specializing in seventeenth century firearms. He'd been right in that it certainly added some style to things, though it had thoroughly enraged Flemm, who was more of an Uzi guy — shocker.

Nonetheless, his first emissaries from the Black Cat would climb that green hill armed. And that was good. *Now…* Now it was time to turn his eye to the runners in last place. *Stu Black and that other one… Sarah Bracken.*

Fred watched Hugh Flemm and his riders speed off into the afternoon sun until he could only see their dust trails, then he turned back to his people. He cleared his throat. *Outside voice.*

"GOOD PEOPLE!" he shouted. He had their attention easily. "It's time to leave this place and put destiny in our pocket. These skyscrapers, these affronts to God's new order, are from an old world, a *dead* world. They have no place in the desert... Others will come here after us and try to take nourishment from their remains. We must guide them towards a better path, mustn't allow them to ruin their standing with God by sinning." Fred took a deep breath and called on that bass which the Black Cat had given to him. "BURN! BURN EVERYTHING! LEAVE THEM NOTHING BUT ASH AND BLOOD!"

And so it was done.

Chapter Twenty-Six

Harold Nettlebee

HE was there. *He was waiting*. And no matter how much Harold wanted to look away, he couldn't.

"Oh, Harold. There's really no need for all that fuss. Just look at me. *Look into my eyes*," said the black cat, though his mouth never moved.

"...N no. Nana said not to listen to you – n-no matter what," said Harold, struggling to keep his eyes on the ground.

Out of his peripheral vision, Harold could see a small black shadow sitting primly on the edge of a great golden sea, the sky buzzing blue above him like an electric fence. The Black Cat put a paw up to its mouth and licked it, tail flicking and waving like black fire. Two green saucers shone out of the blackness of his fur like nuclear reactors in squid ink.

"Do you always listen to your... *Nana*?" The voice spat the word out like poison. "She seems a tad *bossy* to me. Does she tell you when you can take a shit as well, Harold?"

"You shut up! Why don't you just leave us alone?"

The cat laughed, or rather, the voice laughed. It sounded as if it came from everywhere at once, and it thundered through Harold's brain like the deep rumble of an avalanche.

"That wouldn't be any fun at all. You know what I want, don't you? The desert demands it."

"W-what?" asked Harold.

The black cat sprung from his sitting position and began to pace back and forth at the edge of his great litter box. The moist brown dirt and greenness of the forest seemed to repel him, like some invisible barrier. His tail flicked and jittered with irritation.

"This island of green is an affront to the new world, Harold. Your grandmother, that *bitch*, up there, is exercising power over a domain to which she has no right or claim. This place is *mine*. This is *all. Mine*."

"...Then why don't you walk over here?"

The voice was silent then, and the black shadow stopped moving. Out of the corner of his eye, Harold could see the green headlights boring into him like drills, vibrating with fury.

"Well, maybe you aren't such a moron after all, Harold. Since you're so observant, you should be able to understand what I'm about to tell you. Ready? When my army arrives here, and they are *coming*, they'll walk right over your little island like ants over a dead cricket. And there won't be a thing you can do but watch as they disembowel your grandmother –"

""Stop!"

"–And mount her frail, *weak* body on a spike like –"

"I said stop!"

"–the swine she is. And you'll be dessert, Harold. Yes... You've got quite a bit of meat on you, eh? That's good – that's *good*. You can make up for the piece of gristle I'm sure your grandmother is. I'll make you last a week. At least."

"I said *stop!*"

Harold's voice rang out into silent air. In the fright of the conversation, Harold had shut his eyes tight. When at last he opened them, the cat was gone. He could see out of the corner of his eye that the pitch shadow had vanished, and been replaced with the emptiness of desert and sky. Slowly, Harold raised his eyes to look out into the desert. Nothing but the breeze stirred.

In that blankness, there was nothing, not even a paw print remained from where the cat had been walking. Though the more he thought about it, the less sure he was that it had actually been a cat at all, and not… *something* else. The memory of their conversation too, was fading quickly. Harold shook his head, blinked, bit the inside of his cheek. The urge to turn around and sprint, as much as Harold was capable of sprinting, back up the hill to safety was intense. But he had to see how quickly the desert was moving, how much it was rising. *Nana needs to know.* And it *was* rising.

All along the edge of the forest where the trees met the desert, fallen pines jutted out like needles from an earthly pincushion. As the sand rose to overtake the black soil shore, the trees fell one by one into that yellow void and were swallowed whole. Harold could see the sand moving before his eyes, almost like liquid water, and it seemed that with every tree, every foot of new land that was absorbed by the desert, it gained more momentum. More *urgency*.

Harold had tied a piece of cloth to a small Oak just yesterday, at least twenty feet from the edge of the desert. Yet today, he couldn't find it. It was in his searching along the shore that he'd encountered the Black Cat. Still, he didn't want to believe the sand could be moving that quickly. He especially didn't want to have to tell Nana that.

Harold walked downhill ten feet or so, to the very edge of the desert, and tried to recover his nerves from the confrontation with the cat. *Nana wouldn't want me this close to the sand,* he thought. But he also wanted badly to find his piece of cloth, his marker, something that could assure him that they had more time than he was beginning to think they had.

He looked left and right, down the shore of their earthly green lifeboat at the slowly falling pines and maples and oaks. And then he spotted it: about thirty feet down to the right, he saw his piece of cloth. It was just where he'd tied it, about six feet up a small little Oak sapling, except the tree that had been twenty feet clear away from the sand just yesterday, was teetering on the edge of death, almost touching the sand, and already leaning out over the edge due to the crumbling earth beneath its roots.

Harold leaned out over the desert to get a better look and confirm his sighting when he felt something grating on his shoes. He looked down to see the sand vibrating and pulsating, moving like some giant sub-woofer lay underneath it, pumping out deep, violent bass. It was puddling around his sneakers, rising like bathwater.

The smell hit him first. The stench of a thousand deaths. Rotting carcasses, fields of slaughtered animals, vulture picked roadkill. It came from out of a black hole of deep purple gums and dripping, motor oil saliva. Harold's eyes were a split second behind, but they turned just in time to see unhinged jaw bones begin to click and snap beneath wet, glistening skin, stretched tight. He felt the teeth against the back of his neck before he even realized what was happening. *It's a mouth. It's a huge, stinking mouth. And my head is… in it.*

Then something was racing past Harold's right arm and launching itself into the terrible maw. Something pushed him backwards hard, a hoof, and he fell to the ground with a heavy thud.

It was a deer. A big buck. A deer had raced out of the woods and leaped into the terrible jaws that were now closing around its body. Perhaps it had thought it could fight the horrible mouth, use its antlers to gore the thing. It couldn't. And the buck screamed, only for half a second, as the toothy black pit closed shut and turned the deer into *two halves* of a deer.

Suddenly, the black cat was back, and sitting casually on the shifting sand. Next to him lay the back legs of the deer in a steaming pile of deep, red, organ ravioli. Already the desert was swallowing the color eagerly.

He was laughing. The sound filled everything. His green saucer eyes peered down at Harold, terrible humor and violence in the black slits that were his pupils. Harold didn't remember turning and running, only the last words of the Black Cat as he fled back up the mountain,

"–Haha – Golly I hate venison, Harold! I much prefer Tennessee hick, with a side of old hag! Haha –"

Part Two: The End

Chapter Twenty-Seven

Stu Black

THE sight of Fort Worth sent the ragged band of ex-Phoenicians into an uproar. As much of an uproar as they could manage, anyway. Which amounted to a few dry squeaks and raised, triumphant arms. Stu contained his excitement, though inside he had to admit he was a little proud. *Not one loss*, he thought. *Not one person dead, and a thousand miles done*. But it was all wrong.

A thousand miles… That can't be… But it was. *Even if we'd done twenty miles a day, it should have taken us months to get here… And we were **not** doing twenty miles a day*. Then suddenly, Stu realized he *couldn't remember* how long they'd been walking. Time had become a yellow blur in his mind, where seconds and weeks were a tangled mess of slippery, yet sticky spaghetti noodles. Jim Quail wore a similar expression of consternation that told Stu he was thinking the same thing. As if reading Stu's mind, the sand seemed to move beneath his feet and *hiss*.

But when something inexplicable — the good kind of inexplicable — happens, there's really no point in complaining. *Roll with the freakin' punches*, as they say. Especially if the punches seem kinda nice, and come carrying water bottles.

They couldn't have known then, but their expedited journey across the desert had *not* been a gift freely given. The desert giveth and taketh, and the powers set loose in the new American sandbox do what they want.

*   *   *

FROM far away, Fort Worth looked like a field of salted razor clams, plunging up into the fresh air at almost, but not quite, straight angles. It was only as they got closer that Stu realized a lot of what they were seeing was smoke. *Black* smoke. Someone had burned the city nearly to the ground.

As they made their way over the buried suburbs and into the outskirts of town, where the first buildings began to peek above the sand, it was clear that Stu's traveling desert carnival would find little of value. Most of the buildings were blackened hollow sticks of concrete and rebar. Everything that remained inside was well and truly cooked. Still, they clung to the hope of finding water and maybe some food. *Anything* really. *We **have** to find **something**.* And they surely did. Though afterwards, Stu would wish they hadn't.

The sand dipped into shallow, canoe-shaped lanes between the remains of bank buildings and long abandoned office skyscrapers. Stu and his herd shuffled along in the dryness and the quiet. Overhead, black winged silhouettes glided silently against a blue canvas. Stu looked up to catch one turning in a wide circle above him. *We're not dead yet,* he thought. But it wasn't as comforting a thought as he'd wished.

Stu wasn't in the front of the disorganized column, but close enough to be one of the first to see the ragged man approaching. He was wore only a tan T-shirt that was more stitching than fabric, and one white sock. His hair and beard were long, untamed, and singed at the ends. One side of his head was completely bald, and squiggly pink with burns.

As he limped down the sandy lane, he made no attempt to divert course. He didn't see Stu, or anyone else for that matter. The silence remained unbroken as Stu's mob of nomads slowly opened up to let the man pass through them. As the man shambled along, Stu considered grabbing him, *helping him,* but the look in the man's eyes said it all: *I am already dead.*

They let him limp by, no one uttering a word.

*   *   *

PRESSING on, Stu's nomads spread out and searched the charred buildings one by one, looking for *moisture. Anything at all.* And one by one they were blown to pieces by the ghosts of some sadistic, recently departed tribe of savages.

The first trap went off when an old man stepped through a broken window of one of the shorter skyscrapers. It wasn't very tall, and seemed to be in relatively good shape. *No burn marks.* Stu had been thinking of checking it himself, but moved on when he saw others already going that way. He regretted that bitterly.

The old man took one step into the dark interior of the building and, after hearing a soft clinking sound, looked down. Stu was gazing forward to see if the distant towers of Dallas were also burning, but he turned at the faint clinking sound. It seemed to happen in slow motion: Stu saw the man lift his foot up and began to yell, "*No–*" but it was too late.

The old man vaporized. He'd stepped on a pressure mine. Stu, and an unlucky few others close enough to the explosion, felt, *for the first time in years,* rain on their skin. They wished they hadn't. The blood was hot and sticky, and the dust in the air stuck to it like Fun Dip.

Stu held a ceremony there and then for the old man, still smeared and peppered with his blood. He hadn't even known the old timer's name, a thing for which he felt incredibly ashamed, though Jim Quill assured him that three hundred names was a lot for anyone to memorize.

It was George, for the record. His name was George. A few others said some words, but since there was nothing to bury, and time seemed to be running faster every second, thirst was responsible for that, they moved on.

*   *   *

STU'S Phoenicians weren't the only ones that had been burned by these traps. As they journeyed deeper into the heart of Fort Worth, those dark shadows overhead began to grow more numerous, *thicker*, like the black undersides of the Luftwaffe. Stu almost expected to hear the scream of dive bombers, but the only sound was the soft hush of desert breeze.

Bodies littered Main Street. A terrible feast laid out for the Black Cat's detritivores. Some were fresh, their blood still soaking into the sand. Others were buried under layers of windblown dust. More than once, someone in the grim column tripped over a sand-covered body and got a face full of dust. Stu watched as Billy Thompson accidentally put his foot through a hidden ribcage. The sound made Stu want to vomit. Billy did. But still, they had no choice but to keep searching the ruins for salvation.

Stu was the first to enter one of the larger skyscrapers. A hole had been smashed through the wall of a towering green glass building, providing a cave-like entrance. From inside came the dark smell of sweat and fire. Of *humans*. He'd only taken two steps into the mouth of the cave, when someone shoved him backwards hard, sending him sprawling into the sand. There was a small '*click*' sound, and in the next instant, an explosion that left Stu's left ears ringing and bleeding.

A trip wire. An invisible cord rigged to — Jim Quail reckoned after the fact — about six full tanks of propane. Stu didn't know how the man had seen the wire, or how he'd had time to react, but his quick reaction had saved Stu's life. And again, Stu felt that hot rain on his skin.

Shaking his head hard from the shock of the blast, Stu found his feet, and stumbled back to the entrance of the building, hoping to find his rescuer still alive. He found red stains on concrete. There he fell to his knees.

"What the FUCK!" His voice was hollow and hoarse. He unconsciously wiped at his eyes with a dirty sleeve, streaking blood across his face.

Jim Quail came up from behind Stu and sheepishly put a hand on his shoulder. Stu turned, quick as lighting, and grabbed his collar.

"What the fuck is *happening*?"

Jim tried to back away, frightened, but Stu held him close. "Jim. What the fuck is happening." This time, it wasn't a question. Stu could see the look of fear in his friend's eyes and was only filled with anger. He shoved him away hard, putting his ass into the sand.

Behind Jim stood a silent crowd of strangers who had decided to follow him into the desert, into this *shit*. He could see the fear and sorrow in their faces.

"Keep moving. Be careful." And with that, he turned and resumed his walk down death lane. Jim and the other's watched him go silently. After a moment, they followed.

No one cried, and this time, Stu didn't learn the name of the person who'd saved him.

*   *   *

THEY came across a few more walking dead as they soldiered on through Fort Worth, poor, ragged things with eyes much like the first one they'd seen, each searching for a place to die. And in all the buildings they searched, they found pitiful little water. Enough to keep them moving. But barely.

After the fifth explosion, *the fifth death,* Stu made the decision to press on to Dallas. *There's nothing here worth more lives. Perhaps the trap-laying bastards got lazy in Dallas*, he thought. They hadn't. And in fact, it seemed they'd even had a burst of creativity.

It took them another day and night of walking to get there, and Stu was unsurprised to learn that Dallas would be offering much the same as Fort Worth, charred and smoking buildings, propane traps, and precious little in the way of sustenance.

The worst had come on the western edge of town.

A great funnel of sand had been dug down to a squat building of some kind, like a human-sized Antlion trap. In hindsight, that's exactly what it had turned out to be. *Someone was digging here*, thought Stu. *But what? Why?* He was still dazed from his brush with death in Fort Worth, though he wouldn't admit it, to himself, or anyone else. *I'm the leader. I'm responsible…*

The sight of a building without the marks of fire had quickly drawn in a mob of Stu's people, all dying of thirst. They'd rushed down the steep sandy slopes like kids running down the stairs on Christmas day. Thirst has a way of making people forget about booby traps. By the time Stu saw what was happening, it had been too late.

The first one to make it to the roof of the building plunged through almost immediately. A muffled 'BOOM' rumbled through the soft ground, and the funnel began to implode, sinking in on itself.

The sand moved like whitewater, sloshing and swallowing and frothing. The ones who had plunged giddily into the depression were buried alive, *screaming. Though only for a few seconds.* The part Stu would never forget was the way their cries were cut off, like a severed cassette tape, silenced by sand. Even an unlucky few on the edge of the wide sinkhole hole were dragged in, kicking and screaming.

The only reason Stu himself had escaped suffocation was Sarah Bracken. As soon as the explosion had gone off, she'd grabbed his shirt and hauled him backwards. He'd fought her, but she'd had a frighteningly tight grip and the leg strength to back it up. In the moment, even whilst watching the devastation unfold in front him, he wondered where she was getting such power, what she was, *really.* He was dragged backwards like a baby, unable to look away as the people he was responsible for, were murdered by the desert.

When finally the ground stopped moving, and the earth was quiet again, Stu got shakily to his feet. He stared blankly, and let his mouth fall open. Where the at least hundred foot wide pit had been, lay only flat, empty desert. It was as if there had been nothing there at all.

*   *   *

THREE days after the sinkhole, Stu was trying and failing to forget about Fort Worth and Dallas. They'd been lucky enough to find a small string of gas stations of the eastern edge of the city with un-looted supplies of water and other drinks. It wouldn't get them to the Atlantic, that was for sure, but it was enough to keep them going. *For now.*

The significantly reduced line of travelers was once again trudging through open waters. Far behind them, the skyscrapers of Dallas were little more than blips on the horizon, specks of gray against a massive, beet-red setting sun.

Stu was failing to suppress his anger. It wasn't a feeling he was used to. But then again, watching people die wasn't something he was used to either. Or *wanted* to get used to. But he was angry all the same. And as he marched along, just as tired and brutalized as the rest of his people, more and more of his anger was shifting onto Sarah Bracken. *Who is she? I mean, who, **the fuck**, is she?*

Stu had also been dwelling on the bluebird he had taken for a divine sign. *You idiot. You killed yourself because you saw a bluebird? Just decided, 'It's a sign!' Like some God happy ding-dong. Just walked into the desert without so much as a map? And you had to bring all these people along for the one way ride into Hell. You're a murderer. No if's and's or but's. A murderer.*

The natural way of dealing with self-loathing usually comes down to shifting the blame. Stu decided it was time to do just that.

"Sarah," Stu called out to the front of their sad column of marchers. Sarah stopped and turned. Her eyes were hard rings of blue. Her clothes flicked about her in swirls of white fabric. Stu hadn't spoken to her since Dallas. *She was supposed to be our guardian angel, God damnit. Our lantern in the black night.* Yet, she had led them into a trap, and Stu was now convinced that she'd known it.

Stu approached her calmly and gestured for them to step out of line. A few of the hunched and scabbed marchers watched them as they trudged past, but made no move to stop or listen in.

"Where are we going?" asked Stu.

"I thought you were the one leading," replied Sarah.

"Cut the *shit*, Cleopatra. You know more than you're saying."

Sarah looked at Stu long and hard. The only sound was the shuffle of sand as the last citizens of Phoenix wandered by in a desert-blown daze. They looked like little brown mice. *Dying*, little brown mice.

"East is the only way left to go, Stu," said Sarah. Her voice had softened a bit.

"Well, you're fuckin' right about that. I mean what are we *heading* for? What's waiting for us out there?" Stu paused, and tried to look into Sarah's brain. He didn't want to believe she had known about the traps. "Did you know what a… *mess*, Dallas was going to be?" Stu asked.

Sarah held Stu's gaze. "No," she said.

"I think you did."

Sarah turned away from Stu and looked out over the shimmering, empty golden sea before them. "I didn't know," she said. "But I could've guessed. It wasn't as if it were some big secret. You could've done the same."

Stu suddenly reached out and grabbed Sarah hard by the shoulders. He turned her and shoved his peeling sun-burned mug into her's, a face somehow smooth, tan and unblemished.

"And you didn't say *shit*! Didn't try to stop us. Not a… God damned word. When it's time to leave, it's time to leave, eh? '*We go tonight*,' she said. '*I'll show you the ways of the desert*' she said. Ain't that just fucking swell. Didn't feel like sharing when lives were on the line though."

Sarah was quiet for a moment. "We needed to move faster. And they wouldn't have made it anyway."

This admission was like a fist to the stomach. Stu let go of Sarah and stumbled back a step.

"What… what are you?" he asked.

Sarah stepped towards Stu, suddenly looking very solid in the breeze. Very, *real.* "I don't know. But the farther we get from the cities, the less human I feel… the more confident I grow that I am, *myself,* part of the desert. Just as *He* is. The last thing keeping me anchored is this." Sarah placed a hand on her stomach, which was growing day by day, and suddenly scared the living bejeezus out of Stu.

"You mean…"

"You know who I mean. The Black Cat. The other. I know you've seen him walking. Prowling."

"But that was just… an illusion. A mirage, *surely…*"

"You know it wasn't."

Stu slackened his body, and looked frankly into Sarah's icy blue eyes.

"So, what? I'm just a person, not some desert goddess, or cat demon. Are you going to help us?"

Again, Sarah turned to face out over the desert. "Something's happening out there. You want to find out what it is? Or not?"

Stu supposed that his options were rather limited.

Chapter Twenty-Eight

Fred Windsley

Well, here I sit high, getting' ideas
Ain't nothing but a fool would live like this
Out all night and runnin' wild
Woman sittin' home with a month-old child
#
Well, dang me, dang me
They oughta take a rope and hang me
High from the highest treeeee
Woman, would you weep for me?

"A-bebebeb-bop-a-didididideee!"

Fred Windsley road high above the sand in a plasterboard Cadillac. One that had swapped its wheels for sixteen human legs. It tipped and swayed through the sand like a beetle floating on ocean waves. He was humming and mumbling his way through a song that only he could recognize. The office workers laboring underneath him weren't appreciative of his lack of rhythm, though they were careful to keep that opinion to themselves.

Fred stumbled his way through the next verse like a child stumbling through briers. In his mind, he could hear the words clear as sunshine.

Just sittin' around drinkin' with the rest of the guys
Six rounds bought, and I bought five
And I spent the groceries and half the rent
Like 14 dollars and 27 cents
#
Well dang me, dang me
They oughta take a rope and hang me
High from the highest treeeee

He managed to get the last line out, almost in one piece this time, as he turned and screamed it into the ear of the Yellow Woman sitting beside him.

"Woman would ya weep for me? AA-bebebeb-bop-a-dididididideee!"

The Yellow Woman looked straight ahead, through the slit of her mask of construction paper. Her eyes glittered like cold emeralds in the back of a dark cave. Fred finished his verse and quieted, still looking at her.

"Man… you're no fun."

Fred rolled his head lazily over to his left shoulder to gaze down at the man sweating furiously under what passed as the driver's side door. The multi-colored umbrella perched in the center of the mock Cadillac cast dark rainbow shadows and changed Fred's face from red, to green, to yellow, to match his passenger. The poor saps laboring underneath the car-shaped palanquin of plywood and cubicle plasterboard were afforded no such shady luxury. Their exposed shoulders were red as lobster shells. Fred reached down with his left arm and flicked the top of one of the laborer's heads. The man flinched, but kept struggling forward. Fred, bored again, lolled back to an upright position and sighed.

Behind the Cadillac litter trailed several hundred men and women, as well as about twenty children. They might've once called themselves citizens of a city called Fort Worth, Texas. Might have once owned houses with green backyards and tire swings, and owned white Ford F-150s. No more. *Not no mo.* Now they were followers of God and his prophet. Like Fred himself, their minds were being claimed by the desert. Wiped clean. In most cases they were already gone. Whatever vestiges personality that were left manifested in only the most unconscious of ways; how they scratched their ass, how they walked, how they talked. *Or grunted.* They were the Office Workers, and as though he were Simon, they did as Fred said.

The queen of this strange tribe, the Yellow Woman, was different, in so much as she said nothing. Fred had often tried to provoke her to speech, but whether she *could not*, or *would not*, she made no sound, formed no words. Only her actions spoke of intelligence. Since she had resurrected Fred in the dark stomach of that Fort Worth skyscraper, she had been leading — really leading — from behind the terrible twisted arm of Fred.

When finally he'd recovered from his near-death journey across the western desert, awoken to the yellow woman drip-dropping him sweet water, Fred had become something new. Of whatever kind of person he'd been before, only the cruel bits remained. That, and a black, furious drive to push east. *East. Ever east.*

Fred had demonstrated his communion with God on the second day of his awakening, out in the sand above main street in Fort Worth. The Black Cat, the *other, Him, God,* was there. In his terrible shadow, Fred had raised his twisted arm in exaltation of his new people, and their images had converged and coalesced into the form of a wormed demon. One that blotted out the blue of the sky, the orange of the desert, and replaced them with a great, hot darkness. A blackness whose breath had been the smell of death, buried under great dunes. From that moment, these people had been his, though he'd had to kill a few dissenters for good measure.

Fred sighed and gazed off into the desert-sky sandwich. Suddenly, a silver glint caught his eye, something flashing blue and metallic on the horizon. Fred stood violently, causing the office workers underneath him to lose their balance and drift to the right.

"There," said Fred. And the Yellow Woman stood as well, peering through her mask. "Forward! Faster!" Fred shouted. His legged Cadillac tried its best, and about forty minutes later, they found the source of the glint.

Fred jumped from the Cadillac into the hot sand, a five and half foot drop at least. Fred's thin body gave the impression of frailness, but his legs caught his fall easily, and the sand seemed almost to part for his very footsteps. *Like Moses, baby.* The men carrying his litter collapsed into heaps of sandy, sweaty limbs, and panted like overworked oxen.

Fred slid his way through the fine sand over to the corner of blue metal poking up through the desert's surface. He fell to his knees and started digging (as effectively as he could with his twisted right arm). The Yellow Woman stepped out from the litter, walked over to Fred and began to help him. As more of the road sign revealed itself, they dug faster, frantically, until at last they had enough free to haul it out of the ground.

By the time they got the whole thing out, a crowd had gathered around the royal pair. With a sweaty brow, Fred stood and turned towards his people.

With raised arms, he exclaimed, "We'll soon be reunited with our warrior brethren, and our noble general, who showed such courage in leading the advance party. We are nearly there!"

At this, a weak cry of mingled joy and fear came from the gathered crowd, though many could hardly speak through the sandpaper dryness of their throats and the blur of their heat stroked minds. Fred took no notice of this, but kept his arms raised and smiled. *Yes, lord. We come.* And his mind began to sing again:

> *Roses are red and violets are purple*
> *Sugar is sweet and so is maple surple*
> *Well, I'm the seventh out of seven sons*
> *My pappy's a pistol, I'm a son-of-a-gun*
> #
> *Well, dang me, dang me*
> *They oughta take a rope and hang me*
> *High from the highest tree*
> *Woman, would you weep for me?*
> #
> *"A-bebebeb-bop-a-didididideee!"*

Behind Fred, the unearthed green road sign screamed, "Tennessee welcomes you!"

Chapter Twenty-Nine

Hugh Flemm

THE smooth rosewood of the blunderbuss stock felt good in his palm. Heavy, but good.

He'd taken up smoking, despite the imminent extinction of Tobacco and a childhood history of Asthma. It made him feel cool. And God knew, he needed to feel cool.

He sat on the hot black leather seat of the Harley that had carried him across the Arizona-Texas desert, recovered from the dunes outside Fort Worth, and one of only three operating bikes belonging to Fred Windsley, king of the Office Workers.

Hugh's two most trusted captains rode on either side of him, one on a similarly decked out Harley with five-foot chrome handle bars, and another on a much smaller, much shriller sounding, de-badged dirt bike.

Though they'd had the chance to reclothe themselves in Dallas, the desert had a way of making it seem as if the fabric had never been clean in the first place. They were, all three, coated in varying shades of brown dust. Desert brown. All wore goggles.

Squished between the cloudless blue iris of the sky, and the ocean of shifting orange below them, they looked like Mad Max's three horseman of the apocalypse, riding through the zip drive of holocausted space and time to finish off whatever remained of America.

Each of the three bikes pulled a sled made of dumpster lids, desk drawers and florescent light fixture casings. On each sled sat four office workers, all in differing states of clad-ness. One wore nothing except for a pair of Converse with the American flag on them, a diaper and a crown of red construction paper — delicately cut paper feathers arrayed behind his head, like a fourth grader's Thanksgiving school project.

Another was dressed in a tuxedo, his shirt cut at the nipples, letting his thoroughly frayed and browned tie hang to his bare belly. Instead of dress shoes, he wore combat boots, laced to mid-calf. On the back of his cut-off shirt, someone had painted a winking penguin in messy red strokes. All fifteen riders had guns.

Hugh Flemm was steering with one hand, holding his 17th century blunderbuss in the other, and attempting to smoke a cigarette with the help of neither. He did look cool, though he thought he might pass out soon from smoke inhalation. Or vomit all over his seat.

Despite the nicotine induced nausea, he was glad to have the rumble of an engine underneath him again, and it felt even better to be back in charge. He'd grown weary of following that Wack-a-doodle Fred around Dallas, digging for buried treasure. He wasn't a man made to take orders, even though the little boy inside him was so often frightened by the thought of giving them. It was, however, easier to command these… *kaishain* — Hugh had taken Japanese 1 during his first semester at Little River Community College. They were a simple people. And eager enough to please, though Hugh felt the need to maintain a certain image to keep his posse's respect. And subsequently, their obedience. *My fourteen commandos…*

Hugh coughed from the smoke of the Hillsborough cigarette he was gripping between his chapped lips and the butt tumbled from his mouth onto the leather seat. The still red-hot cherry burned quickly through his pants and into his crotch. He screamed like a little girl, and in trying to stop the burning, lost control of his bike. The sudden jerking caused the sled behind him to zag and two of the office workers were thrown to the sand, tumbling in their own personal dust clouds.

Hugh let off the throttle, and the front wheel bit into the sand, throwing him forward, face-first into the unforgiving hard-pack.

*　　　　*　　　　*

HIS ears rang as he took a deep breath and inhaled a mouthful of sand. He rose, choking and spitting. The desert enthusiastically gulped down the bit of spittle he could produce. The first thing he heard was the sound of his captains laughing. It was like hot acid to his ears. *Be quiet.*

He did a mental check… *nothing broken, nothing hurting.* The trigger of the blunderbuss was still under his right pointer finger. He could hardly believe he'd held onto it and not blown his own head off in the process. He lifted it now, attempting to wipe sand from his eyes with a sweaty forearm, and only succeeded in making the problem worse. Finally, he managed to blink his right eye open, a hard, brown diamond peeking through a slit of swollen flesh.

He gave no warning before pulling the trigger. The laughing coming from the captain on the dirt bike ended abruptly with a *BOOM-SPLAT-THUMPtsssss…*

All Hugh saw was the man's left leg fly up and over the seat of his bike as he tumbled backwards. Hugh stumbled to his feet, and back to his bike in blessed silence. Without a word, he began to reload. His commandos only watched and waited, guns shifting in sweaty palms. *My 13 commandos…*

"Fuckin' thing," said Hugh as he struggled with his bag of black powder. "Couldn't have dug up a regular ass gun store. *Nooo, noo,* had to be something with *'style,'* he said… *'pizzazz.'* Fuck you, Fred. And your seventeenth century bullshit."

Hugh had lost a significant amount of weight since leaving Phoenix, and now his skin hung loosely over his frame, folding over long buried muscles. The accident had ripped one of his sleeves off, and his chicken wing arm was breaded in sand, as well as his face. With sweat lines clearing paths down his forehead and cheeks, he was the image of some overworked swamp monster coming home from a black tie event. Hugh finally got the blunderbuss reloaded and lifted his bike free of the sand pit that had thrown him.

"Choo-choo! Get on the fuckin' bike. Seems Seesaw lost his grip," Hugh shouted to the office worker in the diaper. There was a moment of silence, and nobody moved. Hugh turned back over his shoulder and gazed at his men. Choo-choo met Hugh's gaze, and for a second, Hugh thought he wouldn't obey. But just before Hugh was going to offer him a view down the gullet of his blunderbuss, the almost naked man shoved off the sled and went to pick up the dirt bike. He stepped gingerly around the body of Seesaw, who lay bleeding out in the sand.

"I don't like to be laughed at," Hugh said quietly to the air in front of him. And again he wiped at his stinging eyes. *Tears? No. No. Just sweat.* Hugh dug into his pocket for another cigarette, even though the thought of smoking made his stomach turn and his throat scream out in terrible anticipation. He finally found the crumpled red and white package deep in his side pocket, as well as the mini pink BIC lighter. He managed to pry a flattened cigarette free and bring it to his lips, shaking. He got it lit and breathed in the daggers.

Hugh stashed his cigs, hoisted his blunderbuss and took off. The two men who had been thrown from the sled had barely had time to recover and get back on when he spurred the Harley into action.

It was a couple of hours later when they spotted it. A smear of green on the endless orange horizon.

Chapter Thirty

Keith Lonnagan

MICHIGAN seems like a dream to me now...

Except it was New York, and it was more like a nightmare. Keith Lonnagan was beginning to think he might be developing some kind of apocalypse PTSD. The desert was driving him mad. Or maybe he was just going insane, and the desert actually had nothing to do with it.

His run-in with the wandering spirit of *The Dude* — or maybe Jeff Bridges — still haunted him. It had been so normal at the time. Like a neighbor dropping in for a cup of tea and a snack, but the more he thought about it, the more it disturbed him. And what disturbed him even more were the small things he was noticing about this new, silty landscape he had been inhabiting for the past… *how long*?

For one, the sand was *moving*. Undoubtedly. Keith had been a cubicle man for most of his adult life, but he had, in his teenage years on Long Island, dabbled in psychedelics — *and much later, after deciding to walk the path of the yogi, had shared shroom tea with Kathy and a stranger named Phil, though all he really remembered about that experience was their heads inflating like those old airheads commercials.*

When he was seventeen he'd taken a tab of acid at midnight in the attic of his mom's house with three of his friends, possibly the last spontaneous act of Keith's life. What he saw now, staring down into the blinding golden sand below his feet was reminiscent of his experience then. The grains of sand were *crawling* like so many little bugs, each grain seemingly trying to squeeze past the others like tiny pedestrians at a crowded crosswalk. And no matter how many times he rubbed his eyes and went back for another look, he saw the same thing. And he *felt* it too, like some planetary subwoofer banging out the baseline from *Breezeblocks*, somewhere in Hell's basement.

He'd come to notice that during the cold, *freakin' cold,* nights, he would, unfailingly, be ferried along somewhere by the sand. There was really nothing to be done about it. The subtle movement underneath him actually felt kinda nice, and it wasn't as if he had the energy to stay awake anyway. Each morning greeted him with a new, yet painfully similar view. Picture it: SAND. Just desert. And more desert. And an equal portion of blue sky pie.

The other trick of this desert was equally as disconcerting as the inexplicably animated sand. He couldn't seem to remember how long he'd been out in this living waste. *A day? A month? Years?* He knew it couldn't be that long, otherwise dehydration would have exacted a much heavier toll by now. But then again, when a desert angel in the shape of Jeff Bridges drops in and magically wets your whistle, minus the White Russian, anything is possible.

But decidedly more disturbing than all of that was… *Him.* The Black Cat. A shadow the size of a football field that was *always* prowling the desert. He was like the cat bus from that Miyazaki movie turned green-eyed demon. Green eyes cast two terrible beams across the desert like searchlights. And Keith was now pretty sure they *were* searchlights. And it begged the question, *what is he searching for? Because it's starting to feel a lot like it's me.*

He'd first seen the Black Cat the night of Jeff Bridge's little visit. He'd been far off then, a black pit with a long, *much too long,* wriggling tail against a starry night horizon.

He'd since paid Keith much closer visits. *Much closer.* Though he couldn't say exactly how many days it had been since then, his rapidly drying mouth and sandpaper throat told him near on three days, the cat, *no, that thing,* was dialing in.

Last night, Keith had snuggled under the top layer of sand to soak up the last warmth of the sun's heat and had fallen asleep. He was awakened by the feeling of a shadow. A sensation of *cold,* more than just the desert night's chill. And the smell of death, hidden underneath sand. He'd opened his eyes to a massive, furry black underbelly. Green headlights shone out into an empty and cloudless night sky. The Black Cat was standing right over him, huge and silent. The toes of a black paw the size of a Toyota Matrix flexed in the sand not ten feet from where he lay. Keith couldn't help but conjure images of Clifford in his mind, though he was really quite terrified.

Despite the size of the beast, his paws seemed to make no impression upon the sand. It was as if he were weightless. An illusion. And though it was a mildly comforting thought, Keith had had no inclinations to test its validity. He'd lain completely still, only moving his eyes to watch the black underside of the cat and focusing on controlling his rapidly increasing heart-rate. The shadow had stood above him, breathing in the night air, for what seemed an eternity before moving on. Keith remained where he was, long after the cat had gone, though he didn't manage to fall back asleep that night.

As he'd lain in his sandy prison, not daring to move, Keith had watched that grotesque shadow trace wide circles in the sand, pacing like an aggravated house cat. And as the night went on, Keith was *sure* the cat was looking for something. *Looking for a meal. Looking for me.*

His tail writhed and flicked in quick, irritated flutters, like an eel going into toxic shock. At one point, Keith had been able to make out the shadow frantically digging, flinging up huge clouds of dust and sand. And when he failed to find whatever it was he'd been looking for, he'd let loose the most horrible roar Keith had ever heard. A thousand-thousand nails dragging across unseen chalkboards. Metal chairs scraping across concrete floors. A hundred broken smoke detectors. His ears buzzed, like clipping microphones. All of it backed by God's tuba, vibrating in some horrible, halftone minor key.

Keith had let a little pee out then.

*   *   *

MORNING sprang on him like God flipping an almighty light-switch. One of those nights that passed in the blink of an eye. And as usual, he found the dunes around him had changed. Or rather, the sand had deposited him somewhere new. Not that it made much difference in the way of scenery.

The cat was gone, and Keith couldn't recall falling asleep, though he must've, as the rapidly rising sun assured him. *Another day. Another day of walking, floating, and... nothing.* Keith wondered if he'd taken those bluebirds back in New York a little too seriously. But he *had* felt it then, that drive towards... *something*. It had been so easy to walk out into the desert, filled with that lunatic confidence that he would reach whatever destination he was meant to reach. The dawning of this new day though, seemed to whisper of other, *less pleasant*, possibilities.

His throat was red raw. Every swallow felt like smacking two dry cat tongues together. And though he took care to wrap himself in his bedsheets each day, his skin was so sunburnt, it seemed as though it might actually be cooking on his bones. *Nothing to be done for it.* He dragged a gritty tongue over peeling lips and peered out from his sandy sleeping nook. The sun was already beginning to warm the sand. Keith thought of eggs under a heat lamp, then sighed and sat up, shaking sand out of his ears. *This is it. Last day. If I don't find something, I'm done for. Unless Jeff Bridges comes back and gives me another little boost.*

Keith's rucksack was long empty, and he had since converted it into a turban of sorts. The only other item he still carried was his purple yoga mat. Rising slowly from his desert coffin, he shook off what sand he could from his clothes and headgear, then slung the mat over his shoulders.

"Two-pence, four-pence, six-pence-a-dollar, all for the sixth grade, stand up and holler." The words came out like wind over a salt flat. An old, old man's voice. But it did the trick, and Keith's feet started to move. *One in front of the other…* Leff, leff, leff-rie-leff…

It was noon before he found a good spot to do his meditation. Good spot meaning: a sand dune slightly higher than the rest. There was no escape from the sun at this time of day, no matter what he did. The sun shone straight down from the heavens, a terrible white death laser. It burned through the thin fabric of his bedsheet robe and bit at his aching red skin. But meditation was necessary, and it always made him feel better. *All for the best,* he thought, *because this may be my last one.*

Though he didn't fully understand why, Keith knew his mediations had become much more productive since his visit with the desert yogi spirit. *He felt plugged in. Turned on, baby. Fully in the biscuit. Goosed.* And something told him that he may be approaching some level of inner peace, heretofore hidden from him. He thought It was a little bit of a bummer that he may die right on the cusp of such a discovery, but *shit happens*, as they say. *Used to say.*

The hour or so of meditation each day gave him some level of refreshment, a small fraction of the magical rejuvenation Jeff Bridges had performed for him that night, though still more than welcome. It was as if he were pulling moisture and sustenance from the air itself. *Photosynthesis, baby.*

As Keith settled into his position atop the dune, something caught his eye on the horizon. Something… *Green? No. Couldn't be.* But it was. A great desert turtle, its shell sloping up and out of the baking desert heat, luscious and wet. It was a mountain. *No, several mountains.* With green trees sprouting from their surface like moss. Keith rubbed his eyes, and though he still had to squint through shimmering heat lines, the green splotch on the horizon remained. He stood and placed his hand over his eyes to shade his view. *Still there.*

"Well. Would you look at that. Hot Dog."

Then suddenly, Keith was seized by an urge to check the horizon line behind him. The back of his mind screamed of danger. He whipped around and scanned the desert. For a moment, he saw nothing. Then… a black dot, bouncing. An itsy-bitsy smear of black and… *green again*? But not the green of trees, *no*. A toxic green. A nuclear green. Postindustrial-apocalypse goop green. Then, for a split second, through the waving spaghetti of heat lines rising from the desert's surface, he saw it clearly. A cat. A huge. Black. Cat. Galloping towards him like Cerberus. And there was no doubt that the monster was looking right at him. A promise of death across a field of fire.

It took Keith a moment to comprehend what he was seeing, and he stood calmly on his little dune. He slowly turned towards the green mountains off in the distance, then back to the black monster racing towards him. He blinked.

A second later, his body took over and he began to run, knees pumping in the air like Tom Cruise.

And the race was on.

Chapter Thirty-One
The Black Cat

RAGE. Something is wrong. I am the desert. And I am greed, but I am not rage.

The black other stalked across the desert, an agitated tomcat, his size and form changing at his whim. His tail fluttered like a scarf in a shifting breeze, *angry*.

He's here! I feel him! WHERE?

Keith Lonnagan *was* there, buried in a shallow grave of sand, peering up at the black shadow's underbelly and trying not to pee. But *He* did not notice. *Could* not notice. His nostrils were filled with a new sensation. One that frightened, but also excited him.

That fat, hick bastard, and that wrinkled hag still defy the desert. Still oppose ME. And it makes me… Furious. The Black Other felt the presence of that green oasis, Clingmans dome, like a raised wart against a razor blade. His razor. And though the sand was slowly, surely winning, rising as the tide rises to swallow the beach, the end was not assured. What was more, he was beginning to doubt the quality of his generals. *And I almost had that jiggling, worthless sack of butter too. That old woman sent the deer. I know it.*

This mounting anger and frustration was compounding with his inability to find the silly little man from New York. *He was helped by something, someone. I can feel it.*

The map in his mind told him where to go, as intuitively as walking. Yet the picture was still *fuzzy*. He could not, as much as he wished to, assault Stu Black's company in the west. *They're getting quite close now.* Although his powers were many… *that woman scares me. If she is a woman.* He wasn't sure that was a fight he could win. Power resides in the minds of those who follow, and minds can be easily fooled. Something as simple as bending light can do the job. A harmless trick, but when employed with a little *showmanship…*

But that woman… She has something more. More than me. This fact burned inside the Black Cat's mind like a red hot coal, enflaming his rage.

But this silly one, this yogi, a voice whispered in the Black Cat's ear, *Him, I can dispatch myself. And better to do it now.* If he could only *find* him. The desert stretched before the black shadow like an ocean. In the blue night, the shifting sands could almost be mistaken for liquid waves. Forces worked against him as well as for him. He could feel them too. Not just Stu Black and the desert horror, Sarah Bracken, that walked beside him, and not just the rednecks on Clingmans dome, but other, less defined things.

The Black Cat's birth had coincided with the birth of the desert and the torrent of human greed and ignorance that had precipitated it. In the beginning it had been just him. *Only Him.* Like that great, greedy, violent American spirit of old. The one that had pushed settlers ever westward and broke against the native people of this land in a great wave of blood. He had driven the desert ever further, swallowing and drowning everything in his path, and sucked the oceans dry like a child's milk carton. But he had failed to kill everything. And now they stalked the desert as well. *My desert!* The audacity of it infuriated him.

The black one prowled and paced a widening circle under the starry blue sky. An urge to dig seized him, and he sank his mighty paws into the sand, sending great heaps of earth soaring into black air. And still, *nothing*. His instincts had betrayed him, for the first time, and the squirming thing inside him that one might think of as a heart, though it was not, pulsed faster, sending hot tendrils of anxiety and fury coursing through his body. His eyes widened into toxic green pools. The black slits of his pupils narrowed to obsidian arrowheads. He meant to say, *'come out now, little yogi, hiding is futile,'* but instead, from the bowels of his being, unbidden, came a shriek of hatred. It sailed across the desert air and died without a response. But he knew that at least *one* had heard it, and that only made him want to scream again.

He restrained himself from spiraling any further into anger, and continued to search for his prey. He did not find it, however. And slowly the sun rose over the sand, a great friend to the Black Cat, and the great killer to what remained of mankind. The heat blanketed him like a soft comforter, and he found, in the light of day he felt more himself. More *attuned*. The map in his mind, and the ants that walked upon it, became clearer. In that clarity, instinct turned his head across the sand, south. *Of course the disciple would be heading to the old bitch. What was I thinking? If I'd just waited on the edge of the mountain, he would have come to me!*

Then he spotted him. A blip of white and red across the desert, standing upon a high dune and gazing about like an idiot. That feeling of rage gripped him again, and the Black Cat began to run. Run with his eyes wide open and his mind fixed on the kill. He could see, for a moment, the yogi looking at him in confusion. Then he too was running.

On the horizon stood their finish line, the shell of a great green turtle.

Chapter Thirty-Two

Sarah Bracken

THUMP, thump, thump – Him.

Thud-thud-thud-thud – Smaller. Running.

MMMMNNMNNM – An engine.

The desert was speaking to her.

It seemed to be doing that quite a lot now, but this time, the information it conveyed came in the form of footfalls. Two sets, one small and hurried, and one… *hunting*. To the south and west of the two runners, the sound of engines. At least three. It was a strange sound in this new world. An old sound.

Sarah Bracken and the group of starving and desperately dehydrated pilgrims walking behind her were still too far from these sounds to catch them. But they were getting *close*. What remained of the people who had followed her and Stu Black from Phoenix were too tired to take notice of much of anything. Not that they could have heard the desert speaking to them, anyway. They had closed their ears to it. Even Stu. Especially Stu.

Sarah had come to have a confusing love and respect for Stu Black, but since Dallas, he had been a cold and unyielding wall to her. Understandably so. She supposed it had really happened now. Her humanity had slipped away like a blanket off the side of the bed. Stu, she knew, was just a man. No more. Yet he was important. A representative for the moral, loving side of mankind. This new American desert was reducing everything to just that, symbols and essences. A big pot of broth, boiling and condensing things down to their greasy, meaty, cores.

The future was still uncertain, but Sarah knew that the "something" she had promised Stu, were these whispers, these vibrations in the sand. They were all approaching a collision point. More, she recognized one of those sets of pounding feet. It was *Him*. The Black Cat. Something screamed in the back of her mind that it would soon come down to the two of them. She was not afraid, but that whispering voice told her that *He* was. The rhythm in his footfalls. Or perhaps the fact that he was losing the race against his mystery competitor. *He is not used to being scared. Not used to losing.*

And what is it that He represents? She knew the answer. *Greed, and uncompromising singularity.* A green-eye which sweeps everything into one, level, clean slate, like a black hand upon the etch-a-sketch of the universe. *And what do I represent?* She didn't know. Though she felt a sort of kinship with the black shadow, they were not the same. *No.* She had not been born from the same spiritual muck as him. She had been human once. Perhaps he had too, long ago… though she doubted it. The last tie to humanity sat inside her. A new life. Though she suspected even that wouldn't hold forever, and the thought made her sad.

These things floated through Sarah's mind like dandelion fluffs. She lay on top of a dune with her ear pressed to the hot sand. The whispers became fainter, and were replaced with the ever present sound of shifting sand. She rose to rejoin the column of foot-dragging refugees trailing through the yellow expanse. She found herself at the back of the line, just behind Jim Quail.

Jim saw Sarah join the column, but could hardly make the effort to acknowledge her. Walking was enough, though after a few moments, and despite his dry, raw throat, he turned to face Sarah. It took two tries to get the words to come out in a recognizable fashion. He swallowed, and Sarah heard the unsatisfying sound of dry tissue bouncing off itself. She pitied him.

"…So, who are you now?" asked Jim Quail.

"What?" replied Sarah.

"You aren't the woman I met in that Phoenix Jail cell. We call you Sarah, but I think it oughta be something different now, don't you?"

"Sarah's fine."

"…No, I don't think it is. Ms. Bracken, either." Jim tried to laugh, but the chuckle ended up sounding more like a sick kind of wheeze. "Tell me. Are we going to die out here? By we, I mean the rest of us *mere mortals*. I know you'll be fine."

"No, Jim – Of cour –"

"Oh, please, stop. Why are you trying to hold onto the niceties now? When we need them the least."

"I don't know if you'll die. But if you don't do it here, you'll do it somewhere else."

Jim chuckled. "Shit. I should write that down. Ya know, Stu's liable to never speak to you again. He blames you for all the… for Dallas. Which I don't think is entirely justified. But hey, who listens to the college educated. All I know is, we wouldn't have even made it that far without your help. Finding the gas station, *water*, *food*, having someone to follow that knew where the hell they were going, really… I love Stu, honest, but all the directional input he ever gave was 'follow the bluebirds.'"

"You would've gotten there eventually."

"I'm not sure about that. And speaking of, what does *there* mean? What are we moving towards?"

Sarah paused for a moment, then, "Some kind of… final spasm. I think. The last fit of a dying world. And they will determine the shape of the new world. Or if there is one."

"There's going to be fighting, isn't there? I'm really no good at that kind of thing."

At this, Jim tripped abruptly and thudded hard against the sandy earth. Sarah, though the remaining human pieces of her brain shouted to bend down and help him, stood still. Before Jim could begin to haul himself up, two young arms looped down below his chest and pulled him gracefully to his feet. Billy Thompson, from Connecticut.

He looked older than he had in the Phoenix jail. Tan and lean. But that's to be excepted when you haul ass through a thousand miles of desert. He looked at Sarah through cold, but wondering eyes. Like one might look at a lion or tiger, enraptured and wary. He pushed Jim gently forward, wordlessly. Jim turned back to Sarah and asked, "And your child. What shall we call your child?" But before any reply could be made, Billy was shuffling Jim off like a grandmother to tea time.

Sarah was the last one in the column now. She could see the diminished troupe stretching out before her like a drowning worm drawn to concrete by heavy rain. Stu was in the middle, helping those who were struggling, and carrying supplies that others had become too weak to bear. *Good man.*

Then the desert was whispering in her ear again. And this time it was asking the same questions as Jim Quail.

Chapter Thirty-Three
Wilma Nettlebee

WILMA Nettlebee stared up at her sun-brella and let the warm bird shit slide down the side of her neck. A particularly runny one. *I could really go for a 100 grand bar…*

About fifty song birds of varying colors and sizes — mostly bluebirds — sat on and around her. She'd stopped trying to shoo them away. It seemed only to make them more determined to stay perched upon her and her beach recliner. Only her face remained clear from the blanket of birds nested atop her, and that solely because she had a lit cigarette resting between her lips.

They were all quite anxious now, Wilma could tell. Hence the fresh outpourings of Oreo colored shit. Her sun-brella no longer shone through with the sun's light, but was darkened with yet more birds and their leavings. Some dripped down onto her exposed toes and mingled with the pink fuzz of her slippers. Wilma remained motionless and continued to stare up at her sagging sun-brella, a cigarette deteriorating below her nose.

There were other shadows in the sky besides her own little crowd. Wide black wings circled, marking Wilma as food-to-be. *Vultures.* She pictured them stripping her bones of what little meat still clung to her body, and imagined she would taste something like cigarette ash and stale jerky. Wilma hadn't ever held a particular grudge against vultures. *They are a part of nature,* she supposed. And aligning themselves, whether consciously or otherwise, with the black cat was likely to get them more meals than if they had joined the songbird team. Still, they made her uneasy.

The birds were crowding around Wilma because they were anxious, yes, but also because their habitat was shrinking. Harold had risked his life, at her command, to bring back the news she had already known to be true: the desert was eating the forest alive. And every day its appetite grew. The birds had nowhere to fly. The deer had nowhere to run. No tree was high enough to escape this slow death.

The Appalachian mountains, which had once spanned two thousand miles across the Eastern United States, risen nearly seven thousand feet into the sky, and had been home to hundreds of species of flora and fauna, had been reduced to little more than a few square miles of dirt and rock. A blip upon a global, yellow sea. What remained of the mountain was small enough now that she could gaze out in any direction and see the desert. It exploded out to meet the horizon in every direction, all the same. Gold and blue. She was also witness to deer and other animals of the forest as they made their way out into the waste, confused and scared, forced from their home, and made to walk into the arms of heat death. *Well, mostly heat death.*

Every so often, she would watch as the Black Cat chomped down on some poor deer that had wandered in the wrong direction. He was taunting her, and often tossed the decapitated bodies back into the forest like, *See? See what's waiting for you? You and that fat grandson of yours.*

Wilma blinked and wondered why she was still here. She cast her mind back to before all this sand. It hadn't been *that* long ago. *If only we'd listened. If only we had been better. Less… human. Maybe it all could have been avoided.* She longed for her porch and a gentle breeze, the comfort of knowing the trees that shaded her weren't in imminent danger of being eaten. The thought made her sigh.

A rough curl of cigarette smoke fell into some part of Wilma's right lung that didn't quite enjoy it. A painful itch lanced through her chest and she sprang up, coughing and crackling. The twenty or so birds that had been nesting on her upper body fluttered up, then resettled almost at once, some on her shoulders and head. At this moment, mid-cough, Harold Nettlebee came running up the concrete spiral viewing deck breathless and sweating.

"Nana! There are people coming – an – an – and *Him*! He's coming!" he shouted, though his breathlessness made it sound more like a whisper.

"Yeah, I know," said Wilma, slowly rising from her bench in a flurry of feathers and quiet tweets.

"It looks like he's chasing after someone."

"Just one person?"

"That's what it looks like," said Harold. "He's really leggin' it, but th – the Black Cat is all big now, *huge*. I'm not sure if the guy's gonna make it. An-an-and someone is coming from the West too. There's a dust cloud, like maybe a *car* or something would kick up…"

"Didn't think I'd see one of those again. Let's go greet our guests, hmm? I wanna talk ta the pussy cat."

"But nana! He's dangerous, you shouldn't go…"

"I'll be fine, Harold. You said he can't step off the desert right? Like he was allergic?"

"Well, yeah, but…"

"If he coulda come for me, he woulda. And I don't care much either way. Help me find my walkin' sneakers."

Wilma bent over, pushed a chickadee gently off her pack of Hillsboroughs and scooped them up, along with the little pink lighter of course. *Ready.*

*   *   *

IT took Wilma Nettlebee about fifteen minutes to waddle her way down the spiral concrete ramp at the top of Clingmans dome, with the help of Harold's arm, of course. And another ten minutes to make it through what remained of the woods, and finally to the edge of the forest. Harold offered to carry her, several times in fact, but Wilma refused adamantly on the grounds that, "Ain't never been carried before. Not once." *Pause for smoker's heavy breathing.* "Not gonna start now. Though I expect you'll have to carry me sometime soon, Harold." *Breath.* "For that final lay down."

Harold looked like he wanted to argue, but was quiet, knowing it wouldn't do any good. She was set. By the time they made it to the desert's edge, Wilma's pink house slippers were thoroughly ruined: they couldn't find her *walkin' sneakers*. They'd each amassed their own bundles of pine needles and other forest detritus, glued with bluejay shit. Strands of Wilma's thin gray hair hung down in her face, plastered against her weathered skin in white tendrils of sweat. The deep lines of her face seemed to have gotten deeper from the journey down the hill, and Harold looked at her concernedly. Wilma smiled a wicked grin at Harold and grabbed a small maple tree for support.

"I'm dyin', Bubbha. I was dyin' before all this shit started, and I'm dyin' now. Probably all those fuckin' cigarettes. Don't be sad when I go. We'll get you set up real good before then." She smiled at Harold again, and her hand unconsciously reached for her Hillsboroughs.

"…Nana, look." Harold pointed out into the waste.

About two hundred yards out into the bright sand stood a long rolling dune which blocked the view out any further into the desert. At first, Wilma didn't see anything, and then…

A white and red blip scrambled over the top of the dune. After giving her eyes a moment to adjust, she could clearly see the shape of a man. He was running towards them. *Running fast.* His knees were pumping up and down nearly to his chest, and he looked to be wearing some kind of toga. Wilma suddenly had a brief flashback to some long forgotten desert scene in an episode of *The Road Runner and Wiley Coyote.* She was about to laugh when something else came tumbling over the dune.

A black monstrosity with green suns for eyes.

It was huge, easily five times the height of the man running for his life, and doubly as long. It was the size one might imagine Clifford, the Big Red Dog to be, if he were real. But Clifford was not real. *He* was. The great shadow kept his head level, like a tiger might when stalking its prey. His eyes were massive in his skull, like two giant glowing planets. And at each of their centers, a slit of black. Vanta-black. The kind of void a person might just fall into and never find their way out of.

By the time the Black Cat was up and over the dune, the man in the toga had crossed nearly half the distance to the forest. But the cat was faster. *Much faster.* And then they were in line with one another, barreling straight towards Wilma and Harold. The sand seemed to shift and whisper by Wilma's feet, as if it were betting on the outcome. Wilma could see the toga man's face, sunburnt and terrified, and behind him, a writhing black and green pit of rage. The cat's shape seemed to change before her eyes, his fur transforming into a mat of squirming, inky worms. His tail writhed like a huge black snake.

Wilma pulled her pack of Hillsboroughs from her pocket and shuffled one loose. She kept her eyes on the man in the toga and the Black Cat, but went about lighting her cigarette casually.

He'll make it, she thought. *He'll make it*. Harold looked between his grandmother and the horrifying race taking place in front of them unbelievingly.

"…Na – Naana – what are you…"

Wilma replied with a bit more ice in her tone than she'd intended. "What're we gonna do about it? Don't you step out into that sand, Harold. Not one toe."

Harold dropped his jaw, then closed it again and watched the race unfold in silence.

The cat was gaining, but the man had kept up his brutal pace and was now only about forty yards away from the safety of the forest. His feet seemed only to touch the ground on every third or fourth step, and his eyes were squeezed shut in a grimace of effort. Behind him, the shadow was a lumbering ball of paws and black fur. Every stride brought it a meter closer to the man, and now it was almost within striking distance. One big leap, and it would be on him. But something caught the cat's attention. Wilma could see the jitter of distraction in his huge green eyes.

It's the forest. It'd be like running into a fire for him. He has to leave room to stop. She was right. She could sense that the cat had to make a choice, otherwise he would crash into the woods, and subsequently, his end.

The radioactive green dinner tables behind the toga man flashed like gunmetal in the sun, and then the shadow was in the air. *One last leap*. Time seemed to hold its breath, and for just a moment the man was shaded by a great, black, furry cloud, hanging weightlessly, black against the blue sky. The cloud's mouth opened impossibly wide, like the unhinged jaws of a snake. Unseen bones and cartilage strained against stretched purple gums, and razor thin yellow teeth sprouted at strange angles out of bleeding flesh. Wilma took a pull off her cigarette.

The great shadow came gliding down to earth, and for a moment, it looked as if his horrible, gaping mouth would engulf toga man, but just as the mouth was about to close over the top of the man's head, he took a leap of his own. Still fifteen feet out from the forest edge, he sprung forward with such desperate power that the distance seemed trivial.

The mouth came crashing down into the sand behind him, brushing against the bottom of the man's upturned foot. And then toga man was sailing over the desert, riding the hot wind like a wave.

Harold stood watching all this, dumbfounded and trying not to pee his pants. It was too late to react by the time the man came flying into the trees and into Harold's thighs. They fell together onto the forest floor in a heap of ragged breathing and sand and sweat.

The Black Cat tumbled to a full stop in a curiously small cloud of dust. He braced his paws against the sand and skidded to the edge of the desert, his face just a foot from Wilma's. The breeze from his dash came billowing past her, blowing a few strands of her hair backwards, and carrying the sweet smell of death.

Wilma exhaled a lungful of smoke and stared into the pulsing green fires in front of her. The Black Cat started to vibrate, his whole body shaking and trembling. Wilma didn't know how she'd ever mistaken it. The monster's coat, was not fur, but a twisting mat of black worms. *Agitated* black worms. It was as if he were boiling. Then his mouth opened and he raged. It was a howl of ultimate fury and pain. The sound of car crashes and the fatally wounded. The sound of cannonfire and tearing vocal chords. Godzilla up to eleven.

The scream lasted nearly twenty seconds, and by the end, Wilma was thoroughly covered in sticky, yellow cat saliva. *Smells like tuna,* she thought. It didn't.

Her cigarette would have been doused, had she not continued to suck on it like a Capri Sun. The smell was overwhelming. Death and rot and warm, sweaty pennies. Once he'd finished his pouting, the Black Cat shut his mouth and breathed heavily through his nostrils like a bull. His body shifted in agitation behind him, but his head remained perfectly still. Wilma raised her hand and slung it clean of cat spittle. She reached up and brought her cigarette from her mouth quietly. She exhaled, keeping eye contact with the cat, then slowly turned around, bent over, and farted.

It was a wet one, like old hot air being forced through two pieces of wet bologna. And then she laughed.

Chapter Thirty-Four

Keith Lonnagan

HIS ears were ringing, he could barely breath, and he'd somehow managed to hopelessly entangle himself in some large, fleshy mass of limbs, but he was pretty sure he'd heard a fart. A real stinker, too.

Keith Lonnagan was unaware of just how close he'd come to being catnip. He was also unaware that he'd just run a new PR for a 10k, though his lungs were quite aware that *some kind of shit* had gone down. He lay, breathing deeply and rapidly, with his eyes closed in a heap of sweaty flesh. Several feet away, an old woman was bent over and cackling like a lunatic. Two massive green eyes burned like hellfire behind her. Keith would have whimpered if he'd had the air for it.

"Hello, hag." The cat's voice was everywhere. It was deep and powerful and seemed to ring inside Keith's head, even though he wasn't the one being spoken to. Picture James Earl Jones with telepathy. "I'm glad you find all this amusing. Laughter is good."

"Hey, somethin' we can agree on." The old woman had brought her convulsions under control, and was now leaning heavily on a small tree, killing the butt of her spit-covered Hillsborough. She stood not two feet away from the black shadow's giant face. *Are those worms in his fur?*

The giant cat was perfectly still, though the slitted pupils of his eyes followed every minute motion of the old woman's hands and body. His eyelids were peeled back, as if on a stretcher, and it gave his eyes a look of supreme, wide-open rage.

"Oh, I think there are many things on which we might agree, *witch*. For instance, your oasis is shrinking. I'm sure your… *special* little boy over there has been reporting as much. I gave him quite the scare the other day, I'm sorry to admit."

A whisker twitched briefly in what might've been a smile. As much as cats can smile.

"I'm sure we'll have another opportunity to talk later, Harold." The eyes briefly flicked to where Harold lay in a heap on the forest floor. Keith, having recovered his breath a bit, had begun to disentangle himself from Harold, but before he could lift himself free, he felt the hot run of Harold's urine down his lower back. *Ah, man.*

The old lady snapped her fingers in front of the cat's pulsing eye. "Hey, pussy cats oughta mind their manners, or they might get the broom."

The Black Cat's eyes seemed to soften from rage to a special sort of contempt, though they remained wide open.

"And what *broom* would that be, tell me? You have *nothing*." The cat said this last word with emphasis, as if he were trying to convince himself. "Just this little… *blemish* upon *my* desert. Soon I will swallow it. And everything that lives on it. You are just a woman. A *dying*, woman. Submit to the desert. Give up your island, and I promise to make your death swift. Harold, I'll only play with for a little while."

The old woman was leaning on her sapling as if she were talking to a neighbor over her mailbox. Which was, Keith had begun to gather, not entirely different from the current situation, though the invisible fence into the *murder free* zone did change the equation a bit.

"Hmmm… Nah. Think I'll stick around a little while longer. We'll just see if you can make good on that promise."

The old woman coughed up a phlegm ball and spat it into the thin strip of desert between her and the black cat. It sizzled as it hit the sand, as if it had landed on a frying pan.

The Black Cat said nothing more, though his green eyes remained tall and violent. And then he was... *peeling*? No, that wasn't quite right. The green eyes were melting, *blending*, as if they were liquid, into the jet fur around his face. The giant body behind the eyes began to squirm and wriggle like air bubbles floating up through water, and suddenly the giant shadow was gone. In its place, sat a normal black house cat, though it did have a rather long tail. It was licking its paw.

Keith had, by this time, finally righted himself and freed his limbs of the young man he now knew to be Harold. The sight of such an out of place little creature made him giggle. The little cat's green eyes flicked to Keith, and his laugher caught in his throat like a jawbreaker. Those little green marbles were a thousand nuclear explosions. Two green singularities. Keith seemed to be looking into the future in those eyes. And it was a very, *very* bad future. What Keith might call, *a bummer*.

"Aww, ya know, you're kinda cute when you're not yowling like a bitch in heat or frothing at the mouth. You been dewormed? Why don't you just step on over here and I'll give ya a good once over. How bout it?" The old woman looked down at the little cat and smiled. It was genuine. And wicked

The cat looked up at her with those green eyes and held her in them for a moment. Keith could understand what they said, though they made no sound. *You are mine.* Keith shuddered.

The cat rose from its sitting position and turned around to give the trio, now all standing at the edge of the forest, a good look at his pink butthole. He sauntered off to the west, treading like a creature that hadn't a worry in the world. And off in the distance, a small dust cloud was growing nearer.

They watched the cat go until he was just a black smudge on the western horizon. The old woman turned to Keith and offered her hand. Keith grasped it tightly, and shook.

"I'm Wilma. Looks like you soiled your bedsheets there, son."

*   *   *

"MAYBE just a little bit. Is it noticeable?" Keith looked down at his ragged, desert worn, and thoroughly browned, bedsheet toga. He was really starting to look the part of the wandering ascetic. He'd also lost a considerable amount of weight, not that he'd been particularly plump before his desert journey. But now his skin was starting to stick to his bones like shrink-wrap. He guessed he'd lost at least a pound in the all out sprint for his life he'd just done.

"Nah, we keep it pretty casual around here, as you can see. Don't think anyone will mind, hun," said Wilma, gesturing to her blue tank-top, pink sweats and ruined slippers. "What's your name?"

"I'm Keith. Keith Lonnagan."

"Where ya from, Keith?"

"Just came from New York."

"Woah! City boy! What brings ya down this way?"

"Well… I'm a, uh, a… A Yogi." Keith looked at Wilma, as if to give her a chance to laugh. Wilma looked back as if Keith had said nothing at all. "I'm on a journey of self-improvement. And a, um, a bluebird… told me to come this way. Sort of."

"Fuckin' birds. All they do is shit and tweet, the bastards. You walked out into the desert because a bird told you to? You didn't take it as some kind of… sign or something did you? I hope you didn't."

Keith coughed a little and adjusted his robe. "Erh – Ahem – No, no – *me*? No. Definitely didn't take it as divine symbol. Who would do that. Not me, for sure."

Wilma raised an eyebrow. "You did, didn't you?"

"I totally did."

"Well, shit. I hope this isn't too much of a disappointment, but there's nothin' much divine going on here, I'm sorry to say. You see the state of things. As they are now, and I hate to admit that furry black *sonofabitch* is right, but we're just delaying the inevitable. The sand is rising, and we, that's my grandson, by the way, Harold…" Harold lifted his hand up and flashed a sheepish smile. "We've just been sitting here watchin' it. Nothin' much else to do really. You a smoker?"

"Eh… No."

Before Keith could elaborate or apologize for his non-smoking preferences, Harold interrupted.

"Hey, Nana. Mr. uh – Lonnagan?"

"Just Keith's alright."

"Mr. Keith… I think those are people on motorcycles." Harold pointed out over the desert to the approaching dust cloud, and against the line of the horizon, Keith could just make out a few dots of silver, glinting in the sun.

"I think you're right."

It was a strange thing, after traversing so far on foot, to imagine that there were still working engines in this world. Keith thought whoever was riding those things must have been lucky enough to escape any storms like the one he'd seen back in New

York. Otherwise, the motors surely would have been drowned. *And probably the people too.*

"There's something kind of… I don't want to be dramatic and say *evil*, but, there's something really not very friendly about motorcycles in the desert. Just seems a little Mad Max-ish."

"Hey! I've seen that movie," said Harold.

"Which one? Reboot, or the 80s version? Because the old –
"

"Keith. You seem like a nice enough fellow…" Wilma paused to take a drag off her newly lit Hillsborough and looked Keith up and down, propping her cigarette-free hand on her back in an inspectorial pose. "Little… strange, Maybe." She shrugged. "But that's New York… If you wanna join us on our little mountain top, you're welcome to. Haven't had company in a good while, eh, Harold?"

"That sounds lovely, and thank you," replied Keith.

"I'm gonna need one of you big strong boys to carry me up. It was struggle nuff to waddle my old ass down here, no way I'm makin' it up on my own power."

Harold, being the strongest and most well fed one among them, promptly volunteered to carry his grandmother, and they began to walk up the mountain.

"Maybe they're friendly," Keith said, as more of a hopeful question.

"Might be," said Wilma. But they all felt that Keith's earlier assessment was probably more on the money.

After about thirty minutes of hiking, they came to the home base of Wilma and Harold Nettlebee. Though it wasn't Fort Knox, Keith thought, it was pretty good for make-shift living.

They'd converted the observation deck at the top of the spiraling concrete ramp into a little hut of sorts. It was already well covered and solidly built, with a 360 degree view, but they'd gone even further and stacked sandbags at the only entrance to make it more defensible. Unless those approaching motorists had some serious artillery, it would be difficult to force them out. On the roof sat a lounge chair and a multi-colored umbrella. Covered in shit, it looked like to Keith.

On entering the small room, the smell of cigarettes hit Keith like a wall. Inside the observatory, was a veritable wall of cigarette cartons. *Hillsboroughs*. But there was also a good amount of canned food, and some water jugs. They hadn't been idle, it seemed. And the view…

For the first time since his childhood, Keith Lonnagan stood at the center of miles of green, lush forest. After the flat emptiness of the desert, he felt drunk. Drunk on oxygen, and dirt, and the color green. But in his revelry, he saw that Wilma hadn't been lying about the encroaching desert. The mountain was being swallowed. He could see trees jutting out along the edges of the forest like porcupine spikes, falling into orange death. *No bueno.*

In his surveyance of the horizon, Keith saw the motorcycles coming from the west, clearly visible now. *Mean looking.* It looked like they might be hauling sleds of some kind. They were almost to the edge of the forest now.

"Hey, Wilma," Keith said, turning from the view. "Is there somewhere convenient I could set up my mat?"

Chapter Thirty-Five

Hugh Flemm

HE'D forgotten what the color green looked like. It was so thick and luscious, he wanted to reach out and bite it, not the leaves off the trees, but the color itself. Hugh Flemm's traveling companions, the remaining thirteen office workers assigned to his Penguin death squad, felt the same, he could tell. One of the Office Workers reached out, as if to grab the color and verify its reality. They sat at the edge of the green island, gazing up at its rising slope. Their motorcycles idled underneath them like humming tigers.

Hugh reached down and flicked his ignition off. His two captains did the same. The quiet was startling. A gentle breeze washed over Hugh and brushed his thin black hair over his forehead. The sound of leaves rustling in the wind was butter on the ears. Hugh closed his eyes in bliss. He felt like an actor in an Aquafina commercial. *Or maybe Pantene.* And then, the sound of the breeze was fading, being replaced with… *grit*. The sound of boiling, dead earth. The air against his skin turned warm and sharp, as if passing over hot metal. Hugh opened his eyes and was greeted by God.

*   *   *

HE sat primly at the edge of the forest, looking directly at Hugh. His eyes shone like nuclear fallout, and suddenly, the green of the trees seemed less vibrant, almost *gray*, in comparison. Hugh felt a spike of terror hit his nervous system. His mind was instantly gripped with one thought: *I'm in the cage with the tiger. I'm in the cage with the tiger. I'm in the cage with the tiger…*

Fury seemed to be radiating off the cat in black waves. The desert was crawling and squirming underneath him like a trench of maggots. The office workers had dismounted their bikes and sleds and were in the sand, bowing. Hugh got of his bike, and lowered his head.

"Hugh," said God. His voice came from everywhere and nowhere. It was the voice of all fathers, with the base of doom.

"Lord," replied Hugh, his eyes on the ground.

"You are late, *General*. And a man short."

"Yes. We had a… delay. It was my fault."

"I'm sure it was. You are selfish and unreliable. Your name is spit."

"Yes, lord." Hugh kept his head bowed and braced himself for the retribution he was expecting.

"But you are, *regrettably*, the only choice I have. Fred is needed to lead the chosen people, and he is still a distance from here. You are here *now*. And you are armed. Make yourself useful to me, and you shall be rewarded. Bring me the hag, *alive*, and kill the rest. Do this now."

"Yes, lord."

God had risen from his seated position at the desert's edge and walked over to where Hugh stood. He weaved in between Hugh's boots like black Mercury. Two green eyes peered up at Hugh, buzzing like live wires. They were open wide. *So wide.*

"And general… should you get any ideas of your own, *any at al,*- don't. And remember my face… **Look!**" The command was one Hugh couldn't even consider disobeying. He looked down into those wide green pits, and saw the future. It was empty.

"Go."

Hugh Flemm went, first driving his bike and sled up onto the mountain to make sure it wouldn't be swallowed by the sand. His captains did the same. When the bikes were secure, they each dismounted and readied their weapons. Hugh carried two blunderbusses, with spare rounds and powder. His captains and commandos each carried guns of similar fashion, muskets and pistols. When they stood, ready to begin their hike, Hugh couldn't help but crack a smile at the sight of them. They looked like ravers that had gotten lost and stumbled into a civil war reenactment.

"Let's go. Watch for traps. And don't shoot unless I give the order."

Hugh began the trek through the woods towards the concrete ramp where his enemies undoubtedly waited. He glanced back to the desert behind him, and was pierced by two green spotlights. God sat at the edge of the forest, watching him. His tail flicked behind him like a black pool noodle. The eyes seemed to shout, "DO NOT FAIL."

Hugh gulped.

It took about thirty-five minutes to arrive at the bottom of the Clingmans Dome observatory ramp. The woods had regained that magical feeling Hugh had experienced so briefly at the forest's edge, and for a moment, he was lost. His mind went back to before the desert. The memories were fuzzy and indistinct, but he could recall the color green. *Yes, green. And the feel of cool air and water.* Looking around him, he realized he couldn't see the desert, only trees and dirt. It was a strange sight, and his commandos obviously felt the same: *Disoriented.*

Then the face of God flashed in his mind, and Hugh saw a thousand nuclear explosions, the egg of the world cracking. He shook his head and coughed. He turned to his captains.

"Wait here. If anyone comes up the mountain, shoot them. I'm going to go talk to our friends in the hut up there. We might not have to waste any bullets."

Hugh started up the ramp. He was about halfway up when he saw the rainbow colored umbrella on top of the observatory. And… *someone doing yoga?*

*   *   *

"THAT'S plenty close enough there, friend."

Two shrewd blue eyes peeked out at Hugh Flemm from behind stacked sandbags at the entrance to the makeshift hut that was once the Clingmans Dome observatory. They flicked between his face and the two blunderbusses he carried by his side. He stood about twenty feet from the entrance.

"You look kinda like a penguin."

The voice was that of the old woman hiding behind her wall of sand. It wasn't mean, just matter of fact. Still, the old jibe cut into Hugh's already thinning patience like an ice pick.

"Hmm… never heard that one before. Shoulda seen me in a suit… Listen, I'm gonna make this really easy, uh –"

"Wilma."

"…Wilma, I'm gonna make this *reeeal easy* to understand. You're coming out of that little hole you've built for yourself, *one way or the other*, and your friends, too. There's someone who wants to see you."

"Let me guess, small, furry, green-eyed and smells like shit?"

"You've met God."

The old woman cawed like a raven, and a few lances of spittle came catapulting out from her viewing slit, actually getting about halfway to where Hugh stood. He looked down where the spittle had landed on the hot concrete and grimaced.

After recovering from her bout of laughter with a wet, wracking cough, Wilma said, "No, can't say I've met God. Though my dear old mammy did take me to church every Sunday for the tryin'. That thing out there is not God, Mr…"

Hugh took a long sigh, and for a moment he felt like a school child reporting to the office for some misunderstanding on the playground. His arms sank and he said, "Flemm."

"Oh, my… You poor thing. I'm so sorry. What's your first name?"

Hugh leveled the blunderbuss in his right hand at the woman's blue eyes and pulled the trigger. He could see, just before he squeezed, those blue eyes widening in disbelief. The bullet spray sank into the sand bags with a flat thump, and a fine rain of sand exploded back in his direction. At least fifty song birds took flight from the roof of the observatory in a twittering fluster, and there was a frantic scrambling sound. Then silence. Hugh began to reload his blunderbuss with the sulky attitude of a bully who knows he's done something wrong, but *would die* before admitting it.

"… What… The fuck!" The voice came from the roof of the hut. Two hands reached hesitantly over the edge of the concrete, and were followed by a pair of disgruntled hazel eyes. "Did you just… shoot at us?" the man asked.

"Did I?" asked Hugh, not even looking up from his reloading.

"You coulda really hurt someone, man. Not very diplomatic of you."

Hugh chuckled. "I'm a few things pal, but definitely not that."

Hugh finished reloading, put away his powder and once again raised the ridiculously large gun, this time bringing both of them to bear, one aimed at the entrance as before, and another up at the man on the roof, who promptly squeaked and ducked backwards out of sight.

"Now listen! I don't wanna hear any more about how I look like a penguin, or how shitty my last name is. I already know *aallll* about that, mkay? The only *things* I want to hear from now on are, '*yessir*,' and '*nossir*'. Now, come out of there with your hands raised and I won't have to –"

Suddenly there was a barrel poking out through the split in the sand bags, and two icy blue eyes behind it. Hugh's eyes widened, and then the old bag was firing. Hugh launched himself backwards and rolled. With the two oversized guns in his hands, he looked like some ungainly porcupine, or maybe a rolling pirate meatball. Several shots rang out, and Hugh felt hot chips of pavement stinging against his skin. Then he was on his hands and knees, scrambling backwards and out of the line of fire. When at last he'd made it to a point on the ramp where the old woman could no longer see him, he stopped and checked himself over for bullet holes.

Nothing. It must be a goddamn miracle. She must've fired six shots at least! The face of the Black Cat flashed in his mind like a crackle of heat lightning. *No. He wouldn't save me. Could he even do that? He'll say he did.*

Hugh gazed over the side of the concrete ramp down at his group of scantily clad commandos. They were pacing around like chickens without heads, looking up and shouting indecipherable nonsense. *My people*, Hugh thought bitterly. Then, a voice rang out in the silent aftermath of the gunshots. It was the hag. Hugh could almost see her in there, imagine her gizzard flapping to and fro under her bony chin.

"Now *you* listen here, Mr. Flemm! I ain't going to meet fur-ball out there, and neither are my associates here. If you knew what was best for ya, you'd stay put as well. I get the feeling your God ain't the most rewarding fella. If you wanna take me outta here by force, be my guest." The voice stopped, and was replaced with a wet cough, the sound of sucking through a straw at the last remains of a milkshake, and subsequently the faint slap of a loogie connecting with blacktop.

"But you should know, I got enough bullets for you, and every one of your friends down there. And an itchy trigger finger."

Hugh lifted himself up into a squatting position. He peeked back up the ramp and saw the barrel of the gun still sticking out of the barricade. He sighed deeply.

"I guess it's gonna be the *other way*, then, huh? Wilma?" asked Hugh.

There was silence for a moment, then, "I guess so, Flemm."

Chapter Thirty-Six

Stu Black

THE western sky was boiling.

A wall of black clouds, bubbling with green lightning and thundering with Godly fury. Stu was scared. Very scared. They'd said — *they*, being last folks Stu had talked to from the west coast — that the Pacific Ocean was drying up. *Just like that, lickety split, see ya later alligator, in a while crocodile, don't forget to write*. Like Poseidon had just decided to pull the bath plug. Stu'd had his doubts about that. *How could a whole ocean disappear?* Hadn't seemed likely at the time. But now, the answer to that question seemed to be running him down unceasingly.

The storm was slow. That little mercy had been welcome, though it wasn't nearly enough. *Not even close.* They'd been running from it for going on three days, but now it was upon them. In the next hour or so, they were sure to feel the full force of whatever shit was inside that horrible, roiling blackness. And there was surely some *shit* in there. It loomed over them like some tall, cruel school teacher. Stu had never felt so naked. *Not even a god damn tree to hold onto. Nothing at all.* The only thing they had any chance of holding onto was each other, and so that's what they were doing. Just shy of two hundred souls, strapped and bound together with arms, legs and anything else they had, which wasn't much.

Stu stood on a rolling dune above his huddled flock, with Sarah Bracken on his right, and Jim Quail and Billy Thompson on his left. They were all looking at the sky in silence with a hot, heavy wind blowing into their faces. A flash of green lighting splattered across the sky and struck ground not three miles away. The resulting thunderclap made Billy and Jim rush to cover their ears. Stu and Sarah stood still as stone. They'd both seen something in that green blackness. *A face. His face.* Two colossal, slitted green eyes in the clouds, gone as quickly as they had come.

"Jesus…" said Billy Thompson. "…Are we – are we gonna die? Are we about to drown in the *fucking desert –*"

"Quiet Bill. We're not gonna die. Not here, not now." But Jim Quail's voice sounded shaky and uncertain. They seemed words spoken more to reassure himself than for Billy's sake. Stu and Sarah remained quiet.

"It's not fair, man. For weeks, *weeks*, all I wanted was a few gulps of fuckin' water. Just a gulp or two. Maybe some to splash on my face, clean off this goddamn sand. I'm not greedy, I just wanted some water… just… and now… *here it is.* Here it is! What a joke."

Billy's voice was breaking. A few tears trailed down his cheeks, carving dirty brown lines.

"We go better go grab onto something, Billy," said Jim.

Billy laughed. It came out bitter and hard.

"Grab onto what, Jim? Didn't think I'd need a fuckin' floaty in the middle of the God damn desert! I'll be sure to put that on the list for next time."

He shook his head, turned and began walking down the dune to the human life raft assembling itself below. Jim gave Sarah and Stu one last searching glance, then turned and walked down himself.

Stu knew he ought to go join the others. Holding onto one another was the only chance they'd have, and it was still pretty slim. Alone, he'd have no shot at all. He'd be like a gnat caught in a washing machine. Still, he felt compelled to stand some kind of… vigil. Like his standing here would somehow protect the people below him. Even if it was only because he looked like he was thinking. Thinking up some plan, or calculating their next step. Except there was no thinking around this. No calculating and no way out. *No way out, but through.*

Stu turned to gaze at Sarah Bracken. She seemed to be radiating heat and light. Her beauty was stunning. She's what Stu imagined some kind of Martian goddess might look like. He had come to see her very differently in the recent weeks. As had others. She wasn't human, and it had become clear that she and the desert were one and the same. Hot and dry and *unfeeling.*

"Don't 'spose you have some desert fairy dust to help us out of this? That'd be… swell." Sarah kept looking into the storm, and gave no response. "I'm sorry I blamed you for what happened in Dallas," said Stu. "I… That was unfair. I appreciate all you've done. We wouldn't have made it out of the Phoenix city limits without you… Just wanted you to know."

Sarah turned her face just slightly, and shot her blue eyes over to meet Stu's. They were desert sky, endless and brisk and cloud-free. He saw a flicker of understanding there. Maybe pity. They held each other's gaze for a moment, then Sarah turned back to face the storm and started walking. Stu opened his mouth to protest, then found no voice would come.

Sarah glowed white and tan against the black of the oncoming storm. Her ragged white clothes rippled in the violent wind, twirling around her like doting angels. She'd kicked off her shoes, and so strode forth like a confident child into the maelstrom. Stu watched her go, and the sky seemed to pull her into the storm like a pair of eager black hands. In minutes, she was gone, swallowed by rapidly approaching sheets of rain.

Stu watched this as if in a dream, but as the roar of the storm grew louder, and the first spittles of rain began to smack against his face, reality came rushing back to him in violent color. Then he was running down the hill toward the huddle of terrified people he had convinced to follow him into… *what? Into this.*

He barely had time to think before the rain came crashing against his back like a thousand hammers. He realized then it wasn't rain, but a *wave.* The water was crashing down from the sky so rapidly the ground, even the thirsty desert sand, couldn't absorb it quickly enough. It was filling the desert up like a bucket.

A three foot wave of water came tumbling over the dune and hit Stu in the back just as he reached the huddle. He slammed into a woman with the full force of his weight, and their skulls collided with a sickening crack. It took a moment to regain his bearings, but in his star-speckled vision, Stu realized just how hopelessly doomed they were.

The group had already split apart into several islands of floating people. There was screaming, terrible human screaming, and Stu glimpsed a few people floating facedown, bobbing in the frothing water like lifeless planks of wood. Already the water was forcing them apart and carrying them away from one another.

A lightning strike, *green,* froze the scene in a burst of light. In that moment, he could feel the loss. Time came to a stop. Then the sound of thunder, like God burping into a megaphone. The last thing Stu saw was another wave, this one at least five feet tall, breaching the top of the dune like the frothing jaws of a Doberman. Then the blackness came and he was lost at sea.

When at last Stu woke, it was to the smiling face of a man with green eyes, and a twisted arm.

Chapter Thirty-Seven

Fred Windsley

FRED Windsley sat back in his polyboard Cadillac, arms crossed behind his head, and marveled at the black tempest raging around him. He sat in the eye of doom, and might as well have been sipping a Piña Colada.

He thought back to the days he'd spent walking across the Texas desert, and how he'd envisioned Mark Cuban waiting for him under a many colored umbrella, extending a cold beer in welcome. This wasn't exactly what he'd had in mind, but it *was* a hell of a show. And the water was welcome.

His office workers had become rather unruly with thirst lately, and he'd begun to doubt their commitment to carrying out his will. *The Lord's will.* A few executions had done the trick well enough in the beginning, but that only goes so far. He'd grown quite attached to the 16th century hand canon he'd excavated from the antique weapons store in Dallas. It lay next to him now, long and straight, leaning on the seat between himself and the Yellow Woman.

"Whaddyah think, deary? A gift from the Lord? He parts the storm for us, like Jesus parting the Red Sea! Or wait, was it Moses that did that?"

Fred paused for a response from the masked woman, but of course, there came no reply. There never did, though she seemed just as taken by the show around them as Fred was. Her green eyes gazed up at the twisting walls of black rain and sparkled in wonder. Fred was impressed, but all the same, a little bored. He reached across the Cadillac bench seat, an office couch, and brushed one of the wild strands of hair that fell out from behind the woman's mask. She stiffened noticeably when she felt Fred's hand near her.

"Why do you insist on that mask, hun? Ya don't need it. I've seen your face… but you're still not comfortable with me. I can tell." Fred let out a big sigh, like a disappointed and weary father. "I'm indebted to you. I would've died on that Dallas main street, like a *dog*. You nursed me back to health, splinted my arm…" Fred raised his still severely twisted arm, as if in evidence. "And for that, I'm grateful. Reeal grateful, babe. But at some point we'll need to move on from all that, and you'll have to stop holding it over my head like a god damn bowling ball."

The Yellow Woman turned to face Fred, and said nothing. She just peered out of her construction paper slit with those shimmering green emeralds.

"And now that I'm reminded of it. Where the fuck are you getting more construction paper for that mask of yers? It like you've got a first grade art supply closet hidden in your ass somewhere. I know you've got to be replacing it… I just never see you do it. It's… a little freaky actually, to tell you the truth."

Fred retracted his hand from the woman's hair and rested it on the strangely out of place weapon that lay between them like a misplaced piece of time. Fred's face darkened, and whatever playfulness had been in his voice fled like the last breath of spring before a winter gale.

"I want you to understand something. You can keep your silence, though I know you *can* talk, I really, *really* don't mind, *might be preferred actually*, but what I *do* mind, is disobedience.

And... what's the word I'm looking for- *inauthenticity*? I don't like the way you look at me. *Fix it.* I was chosen. *Me.* He chose *me*! And your job, same as all *you people,* is to serve his will. That means keeping *me* satisfied. And I expect you to do it with a *genuine* smile. Por favor. K? K."

The black violence swirling behind Fred seemed to swell, and a bolt of green lighting slashed its way across the sky above his head like a neon crown. Out of the hum of the rain and wind, the sound of deep rumbling laughter came bubbling free and seemed to put a period on Fred's sentence.

A wide grin spread across Fred's face, and he squinted his eyes amiably. "Good talkin'." At this, Fred stood and raised his arms, assuming the pose of the profit.

"HEAR ME."

Fred's voice strummed through the crack and buzz of the storm like a major chord played on a church organ. His small army of office workers were in a crying stupor. They stood at the edges of the storm, sucking greedily at the sky for the blessed moisture it brought. Small laps of water had come drifting into the dry oasis in three inch waves, and the naked subjects sucked at them like neglected dogs at puddles of rain water. They all turned at the sound of Fred's thunderous voice.

"DON'T EVER FORGET THE GOODNESS OF THE LORD! HE HOLDS ALL IN HIS GREEN EYES, AND HE CARRIES THE DESERT ON HIS BACK. HE IS JUST. AND HE IS MERCIFUL. YOU ASKED FOR WATER, CRIED OUT FOR IT WITH YOUR SOULS... AND HE PROVIDED!"

The office people cheered, their voices mingling with the rumble of the storm to make a hellish choir. Fred resumed his seat, and stretched back. *Sermon for the day, done. Gah-lee being a prophet is easy.*

It was nearly a full twenty-four hours of lashing rain and lightning before the storm passed, and the desert was once again a dry sea instead of a wet one. The sun turned the damp brown sand into an earthly sauna, hot and vaporous. Fred pressed his people forward. They were close. He could feel it. He could only hope that his general was more capable than he suspected he was, that Hugh was adequately prepared to receive Fred and the rest of his people.

It was around noon on the day following the storm that they found the first body. It was a middle-aged man, with a 'country stoic' sort of look to him. He lay in the damp sand on his back and his arms splayed out wide. A few of the office workers at the front of the parade poked at him with rulers and yardsticks. He looked pale and dead, like a beached fish. It wasn't until Fred dismounted his human powered Cadillac and came over to see what the commotion was that the man woke.

"Hey there, friend. Welcome to the party!"

Chapter Thirty-Eight

Stu Black

THE man was dressed in a strange combination of office attire, construction paper, and plain nakedness. He wore a tie over his bare chest and neck, and a crown of sorts; a multi-colored array of construction paper behind his head, like an elementary school student celebrating Columbus Day. His arm was a horror. The twisted mark of some foul accident, hooked and turned around, but still pliable and somewhat operational. His eyes were glittering with cruelty. Behind the human face, Stu Black saw the eyes of the black cat staring out at him. Smiling. *Uh-oh.*

"Hey there, friend. Welcome to the party!"

All this hit Stu Black in the first second of bright consciousness, registering in his brain before he'd even had a chance to breathe. And when he did, at last, try to take in a breath, he instead sent a sputter of water into the man's smiling face.

Stu tried again to breathe and found his lungs felt like sandbags. More water came gurgling out and it was all he could do to turn over onto his side to let it drain out. It was hot water, and acrid with the taste of stomach. It was fresh, though. Stu remembered the dry fire of thirst well, and even in this state, his mind cried out to hold it in, to keep that shit *down*. He couldn't.

The man with the twisted arm rose back in disgust at the spatter of water against his face, and wiped at it with his bare arm. "My goodness. Bit'a water in the gullet, eh? Get it *alll* out fella. What's your name, pal?"

Through gasps and coughs, he said, "– Stu – Black."

"Stu… Black. Now why does that sound so familiar." The man put his twisted arm up under his chin in a look of exaggerated concentration. Then with a gleam of understanding, he tried to snap the fingers of his mangled arm. It ended up looking more like some strange spasm than a snap. "I know you, man! You're the one my ol' pal Hugh told me about. The one who ran him out of Phoenix. Yeah! What a trip." The man shook his head in wonder. "Small World."

Stu was still focusing on clearing the last dregs of water from his lungs, but all the same, he felt his stomach drop. *Old pal? Not good. Nice job, Stu. Reeal nice job. Giving out your name to strangers, just like that. Shit.* He hadn't considered that he might be desert famous.

Then, for the first time since he'd awoken, Stu remembered what had happened to him. *The storm. Oh God…* He felt like he would be ill, and he wondered if he was the only one to have survived.

He'd held on to the woman he'd slammed against for as long as he could, but she'd stopped paddling and become a lead ball just moments after the waves began to crash against their little human raft. There'd been no choice then. *Let her go or drown. That was it.* After that, all he could remember was blackness and lightning. He shivered. Still coughing, but clear headed enough to speak, Stu began to rise onto his hands and knees.

"I think you might be confus –"

The man with the twisted arm struck his foot out, quick as a cat, and put the heel of his boot into Stu's chest, *hard*, pinning him back to the ground.

"Oh, no, man. No confusion. I see it now. Even if you hadn't told me your name. I saw it before you even woke up, buddy. You serve the other. The hag with the moron grandson."

"Huh –"

""Or maybe…" and then there was twinkle of fear and, maybe… *doubt* in the strange man's eyes. It was quickly snuffed by anger. *Fury.* And when he spoke, his voice seemed to be underlined with another, deeper tone, like a voice rising from under the earth and sand itself. "Where is she? The *woman.*"

Stu didn't need any clarification. It was Sarah Bracken he was asking about. Though Stu wasn't really sure if she had a name anymore. Or if she was even alive. He lay his head back in the sand and let the man press his foot into his chest, not that he had the power to stop him anyway. He was utterly exhausted. A limp noodle.

Stu took a moment and wondered how things had come to this. He thought about his life just a few years ago, back in Colorado. *Trees. And normal shit. Fuckin'… mailboxes… and Walmart.* He was just a man. And all this voo-doo-desert-God shit was really beginning to grate on his nerves. A beer sounded good. *A miller.*

Then the heel in his chest became a hammer.

"Where!" the man shouted. "Where is the Blue-eyed bitch!"

The sharp pain in his chest brought Stu zipping back to reality, and though he'd yet to come face to face with the Black Cat, he realized that this man, and that *thing*, were one in the same. He might have once been his own man, but that time was long over. His head was hollowed out like a gourd, and the cat had made his nest in there. *That's what Gods do though, right? Especially the vengeful ones. Zeus and Hercules. Perseus, Achilles…*

"I don't know, tell ya the truth," said Stu, grabbing the man's boot with both hands to ease the pressure. "She disappeared in the storm. Along with all the other people I was with."

"Liar!" The man pressed his boot harder into Stu's chest.

"I'm no liar, *friend*. And how d'ya suppose I might *direct* you to someone out here anyway? Nothing but sand in every direction. Not like I have a God damn coordinate map."

The man looked down hard into Stu's eyes for a moment, then took his foot off Stu's chest with a grunt of disgust. He began to pace in an agitated loop. Stu looked at his surroundings for the first time since he'd awoken, and was met with the strange site of the Office Workers. They were looking at Stu curiously, and for a second, he thought he might *actually* be going insane.

They were dressed like characters out of a kindergartener's fever dream. With a little bit of office casual mixed in. He could see immediately how exhausted they were, as someone who actually cared about the well-being of others. Most were in varying degrees of nakedness, and the sun had done its job there. Some of the most scantily clad had bodies the color of lobster shell, with great flaps of peeling white skin.

There seemed to be a group carrying some kind of litter with a woman wearing a yellow mask. Stu judged they were about two hours from death by labor. There wasn't much time to consider all this before the man Stu had come to realize was their king, came rushing back at him.

"Not every direction is sand, little Stuart. *No.* I think I'll just bring you along for the ride, a gift for the Lord. Maybe we'll put you on a hook like a fat juicy worm. How's that sound? Think we'll get any bites?"

Chapter Thirty-Nine

Hugh Flemm

"…WE can't force them out of their hidey-hole without losing multiple men. And even then, it's not a sure thing. It would be…. bloody."

"I'm forgetting, *Flemm*, why I've let you live this long."

Hugh Flemm stood at the edge of the forest of Clingmans Dome, now shrunken to just a few square miles of earth amidst a swirling golden sea. Two nuclear eyes stared back at him, vibrating with anger.

God seemed to be losing interest in maintaining the shape of a cat, and his form now, standing before Hugh Flemm, was *almost* that familiar feline shape, but not quite. It was *off*. Still, the tail flicked back and forth like an angry eel, and his green eyes, *as ever*, shone, slitted black like a witch's familiar. But the definition of his fur was disappearing, becoming pure void, like a shadow with no corresponding caster. His body seemed to swallow the sun's light like a black hole, except, briefly, in just the right orientation, Hugh swore he could see thousands of twisting, inky worms where fur ought to be. It made him want to gag, to take a bath.

"I thought you'd be less *useless* than some of the other rats I might have chosen. But you've proved that judgment to be wrong several times over. ROOT THEM OUT, FLEMM. What did you think your soldiers were for? Their lives are inconsequential. The hag *must die*. BRING HER TO ME."

"…What about my life? Huh? Is that inconsequential?"

A stinking pair of jaws the size of a doorway slammed shut an inch from Hugh's face. He was too stunned to react and, after a moment, just fell hard on his ass. His arms flailed out like a baby demonstrating the Moro reflex. It took Hugh a moment to put together what had happened.

The cat, *God*, had swelled to monstrous size and launched a bite at Hugh so fast, he didn't even see it happen. Not until the yellow, slimy teeth had almost clamped down on his nose did he grasp what'd happened. *This… this forest is the only reason I'm alive right now*. It was. If Hugh had been standing just a few inches closer, over the edge and into the desert, those teeth would have separated his head from his body like nail clippers.

"You disgust me," said God.

And once again, he was the size of a tabby, but still not *quite* right. He licked his paw, like a house cat just finishing up dinner. Hugh sat on the soft earth, leaning back on his hands, staring at the thing that had almost killed him. He realized he felt nothing but fear for that black bastard, and nothing but gratitude for the soft dirt he sat on. The sand at the edge of the forest was shifting and swirling, it made a gritty buzzing sound, and Hugh pulled his legs back from the edge, almost unconsciously. Though there was no change of expression, Hugh felt a horrible smile creep across the black face of God, felt it like a goose walking over his grave.

"That forest just saved your life, Rat. I won't deny it. But the truth is, it *won't* for much longer. The sand will prevail and swallow this island whole. *Like a pill*. The battle is all but over. Just this little, *troublesome*, bit remains. You can feel the sand seething, can't you? You're not that incompetent. Soon, there will be nothing between us. Bring me the hag, and I may allow you to continue serving me."

Hugh forced himself to listen to these words, but all he could think about was getting away from here, *somewhere else, anywhere else,* away from this demon. But he knew the cat was right. The island was being swallowed. Slowly, but surely. They'd had to move their sleds and bikes further up the mountain within the first day of arriving here. There wasn't much longer. Which begged the question…

"Wh – why – why do you want her so bad?" The stutter in his voice was uncontrollable, though his sentence came out with more confidence than he'd thought he could muster. The cat stopped licking his paw and looked up at Hugh with those terrible eyes.

"IT'S A MATTER OF PRIDE. A penguin wouldn't understand."

God's voice reverberated in Hugh's head, an echo in a steel silo. It hurt and shook and rumbled. Hugh closed his eyes and put a hand on the shoulder of that small, scared child inside of him.

"I'll bring her to you."

Chapter Forty

Keith Lonnagan

HE could hear them drilling. A grinding, grating, sort of sound that sped up and slowed down with the rhythm of the hands cranking it. It made him queasy. Not so much the sound itself, but what it implied. *They have explosives. They're gonna bring the whole tower down. They*, being Hugh Flemm and his strange, mostly naked, cronies. And they did have explosives. Black powder, recovered from that same antique weapon shop where all their guns had come from. They were drilling a hole to fill it up with the stuff and blow the concrete support beam. Of which there was only one.

As Keith Lonnagan sat on the observatory roof doing his afternoon stretches, he couldn't see the group of strange office people working fifty feet below him, but the sense of doom was there all the same. *Just keep your mind clear, Keith. Clear mind, clear body. Clear body, clear mind.* But there was another thing bothering him. One, big, thing. The sky to the west was black.

It looked as though the horizon were being eaten by some all-consuming black mold. The wall of clouds was advancing at a slow pace, but something told Keith that didn't mean it was going to run out of steam before it got to them. And he'd seen what the word, *storm*, meant now. He didn't feel quite as safe as he had in his skyscraper back in Manhattan, or rather, hanging out of his skyscraper, but he was glad to be up in the concrete observatory barricaded with sandbags, and not down on the ground. And, strangely, even having seen the devastation these storms could wreak, he felt himself willing it to come a little faster. They were in a race against the Penguin and his plans to bring their little refuge tumbling down in a heap of rubble.

There was a small round hatch which allowed Keith, Wilma and Harold to travel between the roof and the inside of the observatory. It opened now to reveal the grinning face of Harold Nettlebee.

"Hey, Mr. Lonnagan. Nana's makin' Spaghetti-Os. You want a cup?"

Keith's face was between his knee pits in the Kardapinasana pose, commonly known as the ear pressure pose. He moved his eyes to Harold, upside down in his view, and stuck his tongue out. Harold laughed, a good belly laugh.

"Yea, I'll have a bit," said Keith, rolling his legs back over his head and stretching out. "Give me a few minutes."

"Okie. Best while it's hot." Harold dropped back down below into the observatory, closing the hatch behind him with a heavy metal clunk.

Keith turned his head back to the approaching blackness. To the North and South, the storm seemed to be growing arms, wrapping the whole world up in a stygian hug. Though it was too far off to see the rain and wind, Keith could imagine the violence swirling beneath those evil looking tufts of cloud. A few goosebumps tickled the back of his neck. He sighed and lay flat. Above him, Wilma's sun-brella flapped in an increasingly rude breeze.

After a minute of lying flat and looking up at the sky, a small shape came crashing down onto the umbrella. It landed with a gentle thump, bounced once, rolled off the side of the tarp and fell onto Keith's chest. It took him a moment to process this, and another moment to realize what the object was. *A dead bluebird.*

It was as if the bird had been struck with a heart attack mid-flight. Something barked in Keith's brain, and for a split second, he saw green eyes, that horrible, gaping mouth. The face of the black Cat flashed behind his eyes like a lightning strike, then vanished. *Uh.* Keith was no great reader of omens, but he supposed that wasn't a good sign, and perhaps his cue to return to the protection of the observatory. Which he did, promptly, finding Wilma and Harold huddled around dinner. He climbed down the rusty metal rungs and took a seat across from them.

"I'm gonna lose it if I have to listen to that goddamn drilling much longer," said Wilma Nettlebee.

The inside of the observatory hut was dark, lit a moody blue by the rapidly fading evening light that entered from gaps between the sandbags stacked at the entrance. The orange glow cast by the small flame on the Coleman camp burner that sat in the middle of the room made it feel like some primordial cave.

"Ma brain's aching like it's got arthritis… and my *actual* arthritis is actin' up, too. That storm's makin' my kneecaps pop."

"What are they doing down there?" asked Harold.

Wilma and Keith looked at each other quickly, then back down at the Coleman burner with a can of Spaghetti-Os on top. They didn't want to speak the truth they both knew into reality, didn't want to scare Harold any more than he was already. They let silence come in and take a seat before Keith finally cleared his throat.

"I think they're gonna try and blow up the tower, Harold."

"Bu-t, how? Do they have dynamite or something?"

"I dunno. Maybe not dynamite, but… definitely something that goes boom."

Harold looked disconcerted, but then turned up through one of the makeshift windows in the sandbag walls to the western sky.

"They won't make it in time, said Wilma confidently, as she rummaged through a little bag on the ground to her right. She finally found what she was looking for and pulled a bent cigarette out of a little package labeled 'Hillsborough.' "That storm is gonna wipe them out. *And maybe us too.*" She mumbled this last part. Wilma put the cigarette to her mouth, then realized she didn't have a lighter. She turned to her bag, then stopped and put the end of the cigarette to the little flame of the Coleman. "Oooh, shit, that's hot." She got it lit, brought it to her lips and took a big drag.

"I hate it when you smoke in here, nana," said Harold.

"Don't deny a dying old lady her pleasures. You wouldn't put me out in the storm wouldja?"

Harold pinched his nose and turned away. To Keith, who still didn't know these strangers all that well, though he certainly liked them better than the lunatic carrying two big guns around like some pirate-cowboy, they looked like two characters out of some white trash fairy tale.

Wilma, the crone, in a Walmart brand tank-top and ragged house slippers. Her skin was like cheesy leather. It hadn't surprised him that she was dying, though he was sorry about it. *Shoulda done yoga.* And Harold, the gentle giant. A humungous, corn-fed Tennessee boy in a stained gray XXL t-shirt and basketball shorts.

The orange glow from the camp stove cast strange shadows on their faces against the blue-black of the evening, and not for the first time, Keith wondered how the hell he'd ended up here.

And if this might be the last place he'd end up.

Chapter Forty-One

Hugh Flemm

THE wind raged around Hugh Flemm, brushing his thin black hair up into a comical tuft reminiscent of a rockhopper penguin. He stood twenty feet away from the entrance to the observatory, unarmed and staring hard into the gray barrel of the old bat's 22-caliber rifle that peeked out from over a wall of sandbags.

"I think you might wanna wait before you pull that trigger. I'm unarmed. And I apologize for my rudeness last time we spoke. It was unbecoming. Can we start over?"

"Fack no, hun. Never was good at forgetting and forgiving."

The old woman's voice was muffled by the small window she spoke through, but plenty shrill enough, even over the smoker's wheeze, for Hugh to hear it clearly.

"You heard the drilling? You know what it means?"

"I know what *you* think it means."

"We're gonna blow up the base of your tower. And the three of you in there will fall like Humpty-Dumpty off his wall. Might get a little banged up in the process I'd imagine."

The storm was picking up, and Hugh found he had to yell to make himself heard over the rush of the wind. Below him and all around, the pines were beginning to shiver and sway like great black-green dogs shaking off after a bath.

"How do we know you've got enough juice blow it? Eh?"

"I thought you might ask that. I had the boys whip up a little proof of concept."

Hugh reached into his pocket slowly and pulled out what looked like an M80 firecracker with a little fuse attached, and a pink BIC lighter. He held them out and looked at the old woman's gun as if to ask permission. He could see, just barely, tucked back in her cave, two pinched and shrewd eyes, peering out at him with razor sharp disgust.

He flicked the lighter and lit the short fuse. It caught immediately in a shower of sparks, and Hugh tossed it down in front of him, covering his ears. The fuse quickly burned down to the fat stump of the firecracker and disappeared. There was a loud BANG, and the DIY M80 exploded. A piece of shrapnel flew toward the old woman and went hurdling through her narrow window. He could see her flinch, and the gun barrel wavered slightly. He couldn't help but smile just a bit with satisfaction, and he whistled long and low, like an impressed dad.

"Pure black powder for ya," he said. The old lady was quiet. "Listen… *err*, I don't even know your name. Excuse my rudeness, I'm Hugh. People call me The Gambler." There was a moment of silence, and then came that incredibly grating voice.

"I don't think anyone calls you that."

Hugh felt the heat of anger rising in his throat and swallowed it. "Well, regardless, I –"

"I usually only give my name to friends, but I s'pose for convenience sake… I'm Wilma. Now, whaddyah want?"

"Well, *Wilma*, I'd like you to come out of your hut there, *unarmed* and real peaceful-like. As I said earlier, there's someone wants to talk to you."

"I got nothin' to say to furball, fatso."

This time Hugh couldn't swallow the anger. He felt a little offended at the jab at his weight, especially since he felt like he'd dropped a significant amount of poundage as of late.

"Listen up, *you old fuckin' sack*! I'm a dead man walking! I got nothing to lose! Now, you can shoot me right here and now, my guys will blow the powder you're sitting on and we can all take a trip to Disneyland together, *OORRR*, you can come out of there, and maybe, *just maybe*, your friends might live to see another day. And maybe me, too. *You*, I'm sorry to say… well, your prospects are pretty dismal either way. It's your call, *Wilma*."

There was a minute long silence, and Hugh could just make out the shapes of two other people in the gloom of the observatory hut. The barrel of the gun remained firmly aimed, but Hugh thought he could feel a softening of resolve somehow. The storm that was almost on top of them now had begun to spit angry rain. The wind was whipping the drizzle into swirling gray patterns in the sky. The cool dampness felt good on Hugh's skin, but the blackness of the sky was beginning to worry him. *The powder might get wet, and then…*

"I don't have all day here." Hugh had to yell to make himself heard over the growing roar of the wind. Those sharp black eyes peeked back through the window slot.

"You sayin' that if I come out there and have a little palaver with ol' Mittens, you'll let my two boys here alone?"

"As much as I can… *yes*. That's the deal. As long they don't cause any trouble."

Another brief silence, and then the barrel of the .22 was retracted through the barricade window. Hugh almost laughed.

He hadn't expected this plan to actually *work*. He'd supposed it was good enough, a compelling ultimatum, but some part of him deep down had said it wouldn't go this smoothly. *No way.* But it *was* working. *Maybe I will live. How 'bout that.*

There was a cry of protest from inside the hut, and then Hugh saw a skinny, wrinkled, jerky-slice of an old woman squirming out through the window in the barricade. *Head, torso, legs,* and then she was tumbling down to the concrete, outside and vulnerable. A new face appeared at the sandbag window, round and worried. Once again, the barrel of the .22 jutted out, but the hands that held it were nervous. The gun shook.

Wilma picked herself up off the concrete, patted her clothes off and turned back to the window. She spoke for a minute in a low, hushed voice that Hugh couldn't discern.

"Hey, Wilma!"

She turned to face Hugh. He held up his wrist, pointed to an imaginary watch, and then turned his eyes up to the sky. Wilma nodded, turned, and began to make her way down the ramp. She hobbled like a bicycle with a broken wheel. It was hard to watch, but Hugh didn't exactly feel inclined to help her. When she finally reached him, she stopped and patted her pockets, alarmed.

"Shit. Forgot my cigs. You wouldn't ha –"

Hugh had already reached in his pocket and pulled out a crisp clean pack of Hillsboroughs. He had a big smile as he handed her one.

Chapter Forty-Two

Wilma Nettlebee

WILMA felt her hand relax on the worn wooden butt of the .22 rifle she'd stolen from the Clingmans Dome park ranger shack. *More like, borrowed indefinitely.*

She let her grip loosen because she'd known what was coming before the words even came tumbling out of that walking lard sack's mouth. She'd recognized the necessity of the deal she'd have to make if she wanted Harold to have a chance. A chance at *anything*. Though she supposed that was a goal of debatable value considering the state of America. *Nevertheless…*

Wilma turned away from Hugh Flemm, who stood outside the observatory hut on the concrete ramp in an increasingly strong breeze. He looked like a penguin with a combover , in the middle of a radical weight loss diet. His clothes hung on him loosely, flapping in the wind. *Not very intimidating.* Though there was something in his brown eyes, something that stunk of a wild disregard for life.

"You heard the man," said Wilma.

"You can't be serious," said Keith Lonnagan.

"Nana!" yelped Harold.

"I sure am. I don't trust that fat sonova' bitch as far as I can throw him. But I know that if I don't go out there, he'll kill us all. Just like that." Wilma snapped her bony fingers with a hollow '*click*'. "I can see it in his eyes. At least this way, you got a chance at… somethin'."

"I'd rather not live with the thought of you getting ripped up by that –"

"Oh, shut it. Don't be such a sissy, Keith. I'm fuckin' dyin'. Might as well be interesting."

"Naana – Don't go out there and, and – let that… thing –"

"Hush, hush, Harold. I been tellin' you my time's comin' for a while now, right? Remember? You're gonna be just fine, hun. You got Keith here to help with things." Wilma flashed a glance at Keith and was gladdened to see total agreement in his eyes. He wouldn't abandon Harold. *That's good.* "And I'm sure you'll make new friends no problem. Whenever some nice folks show up, that is. At least I can do something useful for you boys before I go."

Wilma did not wait to hear any more protestations and shimmied out the barricade window. Keith and Harold sat in shock at the speed she managed to worm her way out the small viewport. It was a bit uncanny for such an elderly woman. After she was out and looking back through the window, Harold scrambled forward, grabbing the rifle and rose to speak to his grandmother for the last time.

"Now you listen to Mr. Lonnagan, n'K? I love you, baby. Take care of yourself."

The casualness in Wilma's voice was comforting, like she was getting off the phone instead of leaving to face certain death, though Harold was far too shaken to respond. His mouth hung open as he listened to Wilma's parting words. She kissed her three first fingers and quickly slapped his forehead, then turned and gave Keith a quick nod that said, *'don't you do anything fuckin' stupid now'*. With that, she whirled and began to hobble towards the Penguin out on the ramp. The grin on the bastard's face was ugly, though Wilma realized she probably didn't look like Ms. America in her bird-soiled, Faded Glory digs.

When finally she reached Hugh, an alarm bell went off in the back of Wilma's head like a mousetrap. That kind of instinct that only a forty year smoker can cultivate.

"Shit… Forgot my cigs. You wouldn't hap –" And then Hugh was holding out a Hillsborough and smiling madly.

"I just recently took up the habit myself."

Wilma didn't hesitate to take the crisp gasper. She'd smoked for far too long to turn down a freebie. From anyone. As she took it, he drew another from the pack for himself.

"Thankee," Wilma said, putting it to her lips. Hugh was there with the light, ready. He lit hers, then his own.

"No problemo, Ma'dam. Shall we take a walk?"

"I s'pose."

They began the trek down the three hundred and seventy-five foot spiraling concrete ramp, Hugh walking casually, taking small mouth puffs of his Hillsborough like a high school girl, and Wilma hobbling along, breathing deeply of those wonderful, smoky chemicals, like a champ. Around them, the weather was turning sour at an alarming rate. Leaves and pine needles were coming loose, mingling with the bullets of rain already swirling in the air to make for an unpleasant shower of debris.

Hugh paid the storm no mind. He looked like a man heading back to his private study to smoke his pipe, pet his Saint Bernard and watch the fireplace. A man confident and casual in his victory. Wilma wasn't convinced, however. As she gazed up at the angry sky, and out over the pines, she could see black, undulating sheets of rain coming on quick. They looked heavy, almost *solid*.

"Storm's lookin' bad," said Wilma, between drags on her Hillsborough.

"Yeah…" Hugh Felmm looked up, as if noticing the storm for the first time. "Hardly matters though. We're all dead, anyway. Now it's just who's gonna make it the longest…. Drowning actually might not be a bad way to go. I can tell ya, I won't be a finalist in this silly little competition. 'Bout the only person I can guarantee I'm gonna beat is the old bat walking next to me."

Wilma shot Hugh a funny look and commenced to have a half-wheeze-half-cackle fit.

"Feeling a little retrospective this evening, are we? Wuddn't life always that way?" said Wilma, still with a little laughter in her voice.

Hugh smiled, not unkindly, and said, "Yeah. You might be right about that."

"The cat not appreciating all your… hard work?" asked Wilma.

Hugh chuckled. "Not exactly. I thought at first that he was God. He was very… *compelling*. But now I know, he's not God. Not *the God*, at least. But it doesn't matter. He's gonna turn everything to dust. And I'm gonna help him. *Am helping him*."

"Never too late to turn it around."

"Oh, *faar* too late, granny. This ship we're standing on is going down. No doubt about it. And I plan to be the last one in the water. I'd rather not get played with before he kills me. So, if he wants me to bring you to him, that's what I'm gonna do."

Wilma turned her face back to the horizon and stole a final look before it was overtaken by the pines rising up around them. It was black.

"Well… you gotta do, whatcha gotta do."

*   *   *

SHE'D finished her first two cigarettes and was a good way through her third before they started down through the trees and towards the edge of the desert. She could already feel *him*. Feel those eyes prying eagerly at the tree line, trying to find her, like some kind of invisible heat seeking missile.

Hugh had escorted her down the ramp at a leisurely stroll, but once they'd reached the bottom, he'd decided Wilma's shambling pace wasn't going to cut it for going down the side of the mountain. What was left of the mountain, anyway.

All fine with Wilma. She enjoyed watching Hugh's strange, half-naked Mad Max — or Office Max? — goonies hop to follow his commands. In just a few minutes, they'd assembled a makeshift litter with some materials taken from a sled they'd brought with them up the mountain. Wilma climbed on and was almost giggly as two big, strapping, tan men picked her up like a toy poodle in a purse. It became somewhat less amusing when she reminded herself where they were headed. And *why*.

Still, she enjoyed her cigarette, maybe her last, as much as she could. Hugh had given her the pack and lighter after the first. He'd looked queasy by the time they'd made it down the ramp, and was coughing like an asthmatic.

"You need em' more than me," he'd said.

She did.

They walked in total silence through the bending and creaking trees. *Nothin' to talk about.* And the storm was its own kind of entertainment. It seemed like it couldn't possibly get any worse before exploding into some kind of hurricane, tornado, tsunami-death-smoothie. It was as if it were holding its breath, just for Wilma. The sky was now completely black, and the sprinkle of rain had become a heavy drizzle, though not yet the torrent she expected was on its way.

She could sense the hesitation of the men carrying her, and especially in Flemm, who walked grimly beside her queenly little platform. They were nervous. More nervous than she was. And as they approached the base of the mountain, all the nonchalant, '*I don't care what happens,*' attitude Hugh had shown her just a few minutes ago, drained from his face. Even through the rain, she could tell, he was sweating.

A short burst of laughter came up from her shriveled lungs and turned into a cough. Hugh looked up at her sharply, and the baby-ish, spoiled look she'd first seen on his face when she'd first met him returned in full. He really was a Penguin. *A rat with useless wings.* Though he looked thoroughly soured, he didn't say anything, just faced back ahead and regained that pale, worried look.

Finally, the procession came to a clearing in the trees where they could see the desert. It was *writhing* in the hard wind and rain. And in the middle of the approaching maelstrom… *Him.* A small, black, house cat with an unusually long tail. A penny-sized black void against the damp desert. He was small on the horizon, but his eyes shone like some terrible lighthouse, probing and buzzing with hot atomic energy. Wilma thought she had resigned herself to whatever fate awaited her, but at the sight of those eyes, her stomach dropped. It was impossible to say how she could tell, but something told her he was smiling.

As they moved closer to the desert's edge, the cat moved to meet them, keeping his eyes fixed on the party all the while. When they were within about forty feet of each other, she could see something was wrong. His fur wasn't really fur at all, but a thousand-thousand, wriggling, black worms, that seemed to devour color out of the very air around him. His eyes were slitted like a cat's, but were open much too wide. *Much too wide.* And they stared right at Wilma, seeming to salivate.

Finally, they approached the desert's edge. A small flat area backed up against the rise of the mountain, little more than a steep hill now. The men carrying the litter were shaking. Whether from exhaustion or the sight of their God, she couldn't tell. Regardless, they put her down about ten feet from the edge, then proceeded to bow down to the ground in the Islamic Sujood style, placing their foreheads in the dirt. Wilma would've laughed, but the burning gaze of the demon in front of her was like some great bathtub drain, sucking her eyes in and holding them there, making her dizzy.

"Hello, Hag," said the cat, though his mouth did not move. "I've been waiting… OH, SO PATIENTLY."

His voice was like thunder. It rang inside Wilma's head so violently, she thought she might go deaf. The office workers behind her mumbled and whimpered, still facing down into the dirt. Hugh stood beside Wilma, and she saw his legs begin to shake, then buckle. He fell to his knees, eyes locked on the cat.

Wilma somehow managed to keep her feet, though the butt end of her thoroughly dampened cigarette fell from her fingers. Trembling, she reached into her pocket for another. Feeling the familiar cardboard of the pack gave her courage, and she shuffled forward to the very edge of the desert, where sand lapped against the soft dirt of the forest in twisting waves. The cat — *the thing* — sat in front of her primly, its velvety tail whipping back and forth like a strand of Medusa's hair.

"Hey, fur ball," said Wilma.

Her voice was more confident than she felt. *Stronger* than it had been in a long time. She surprised herself, and was amused to see a flicker of agitation in the cat's gleaming eyes. She pulled the pack of Hillsboroughs from her pocket and tapped one free.

The rain was getting heavier, but the black demon seemed to be emitting heat, and the drizzle blew around them, as if traveling over some invisible dome. She was thankful for the protection, if only to get her cigarette lit. The cat's eyes flicked briefly away from Wilma, over to Hugh. She heard him gulp.

"You did well, Flemm. Though I sense you still haven't killed the other two rats hiding in their concrete cage. As per my instructions."

Hugh tried to respond, but could only get out a small gasp before the cat spoke again.

"It doesn't matter. The storm will take care of that. And you, I think." His eyes returned to Wilma. "Now, to the main course." Those wide eyes flicked up at down, scanning her with green contempt. "You really are an ugly one, aren't you? I think you're going to taste dreadful."

Wilma laughed as she let out a breath of smoke. "Oh, you bet. It's mostly ash in here," and she touched her fist to her chest. "I imagine I'll go down about as smooth as a piece of bark."

"Where are your bird friends? Abandoned you? Right at the end, too. What a shame."

"I'm sure they're kickin' around somewhere. Cats and songbirds don't mix too well, practically speakin'."

The cat seemed to smile, though nothing on his inky face changed. "I believe you're right. The cat usually comes away full, and the birds, well… *dead.*"

Wilma took another pull on her cigarette and squinted out into the storm-blanketed desert. She looked like someone just off the night shift at the BP, havin' a smoke out by the dumpster, shootin' the shit with a co-worker.

"What's your 'grand-plan' here, Mittens? I mean, after you gobble up all of this, of course." Wilma gestured to herself like an overly confident high schooler at the prom. "It seems like you're a little angry now days. Ever consider retirement?"

The cat was silent for a moment, and a flicker of laughing anger ran across those wide eyes. "I was born of *your* hubris and greed. Human pride. I seek what once your kind did. *More.*"

"Huh. Ain't that somethin'." Wilma took a moment, then cocked her head like a puppy. "Wouldn't that make you kinda like us, poor, stupid humans? Greedy, and whatnot?"

Though still his mouth made no movement, the cat sighed and said, "I'm getting bored of this conversation. Shall we wrap it up? Do I need to get Hugh to push you out here, or will you come willingly?"

"No, no. I can walk out muhself. I can still do that much. Let me light another ciggy. Just wanna… feel it one last time." And she did.

The crisp pack of Hillsboroughs that Hugh had given to her was already warping from her iron grip, and she wrestled one last clean, white stick out of the package. She tossed the box to the ground, and brought the cigarette to her mouth. Looking down her nose at the last lighter flame she would ever see, it seemed to whisper to her, comfort her, like an old friend. Then that wonderful thick air was in her lungs, filling her up like warm milk. She closed her eyes, reveling in the oddly quiet breeze, and then stepped forward.

She felt, almost instantly, a sharp pain in her thigh. He was biting her. And then she was in the air, and the pain was gone. She opened her eyes and got one last glimpse of the world in slow motion. The pain was gone because her leg was gone, in its place, a leaking red stump. She was at least twenty feet in the air, thrown like a mouse, a mouse caught by a particularly cruel cat.

Below her was a giant black *thing,* though his shape was kind of fuzzy… *wrong.* One thing was clear, below two terrible green eyes, a huge mouth was wide open, slimy and purple with rows of gums and jagged, haphazard teeth.

Wilma exhaled and smelled the wonderful aroma of Hillsborough tobacco, and fell.

Chapter Forty-Three

Keith Lonnagan

HAROLD was rocking himself back and forth in the corner of the observatory hut, gripping the .22 rifle so hard Keith thought he might snap a tendon. Keith himself sat in the middle of the room, criss-cross applesauce, thinking. Not well, but *thinking*.

Outside, the world had become a toilet, mid-flush. The sprinkle had turned to drizzle, the drizzle to shower, the shower to torrent, and now, it was a straight up *flood*. Water was starting to pour through the cracks in the sandbag wall like someone was on the other side pumping it in. Keith hadn't known rain could be so *thick*. And now his ass was all wet from the growing puddle inside the observatory.

He'd kept his eye on Wilma for as long as he could, even going up on the roof to watch them carry her off on some kind of crude stretcher. He'd lost sight of them after they'd entered the forest, but he'd remained on the roof, waiting. *Waiting for what?* He'd known, but just didn't want to believe it.

Watching the trees had made him feel less like he was doing nothing at all. Though that was the truth of it. *I'm a pacifist. There was nothing I could've done. And it was Wilma's call anyway. She makes her own decisions, made her own decisions...* Yet, the events of the last couple of hours made him feel sick. He'd liked Wilma, even having only known her for a few days. And Harold surely hadn't taken her *departure* very well, the very large, very *strong*, child Keith now found himself appointed guardian to.

After about half an hour of watching the trees wag, Keith had thought he'd heard some kind of *crunching* sound. Though he hadn't been sure. A few moments after the sound had come rolling up the mountain, a flurry of birds had taken to the sky, *it seemed to Keith*, out of *panic*.

The wind had taken the little birds by the wings and flung them in all directions like candy wrappers in a tornado. It was hard to watch. And it made him uneasy. It was then that he'd heard the terrible, deep laughter. He had been *very sure* that time. It'd rumbled up the mountain side and shaken the very foundation of the observatory. A genial laugh. Like Santa Claus. It'd chilled Keith to the bone. He'd gone back inside then, to escape the rain. *It's done*, he knew then.

He thought the half-naked office people who served Hugh Flemm would've tried to storm the observation tower to get out of the rain by now. But no one had come. There really wasn't much to be done. *About anything*. Keith had stacked some of their boxes of canned food inside the observatory to try to keep them dry, as well as the camp stove, but he saw now that was hopeless. The rain was like an ocean falling from the sky. They might as well be in a stone dinghy.

Keith thought about Jeff Bridges. Or, rather, *the spirit of Jeff Bridges*? He wondered if he'd made his acupuncture appointment, if he was still roaming out there in the desert somewhere. Or if maybe he'd hallucinated the whole encounter. *Maybe it's both at the same time.*

Keith thought it was ironic and terrible that this much water should be dumped on one place when there were surely people out in the wasteland dying of thirst. Though he couldn't imagine there were *too many* people left out there. The Black Cat was making sure of that.

Without warning, Keith was knocked — literally — out of his thoughtful meditation by an explosion that rocked the whole observatory. The explosion was *loud*: *BANG!* Followed by the faint titter of falling debris. Harold, still terrified, sprung up into a frantic, standing position. He gripped the rifle like a life preserver as rain water flowed in over the sandbags and through the window gaps. And then, the room began to tilt.

"Harold!" yelled Keith, but his voice was lost in the roar of the rain and the moan of twisting rebar in concrete. It wouldn't have done much anyway.

Harold was screaming and wrestling with a sand bag at the doorway, frantically trying to escape the hut like a trapped animal. At that moment, something gave in the structure of the observatory tower and the room fell to a deep lean. Keith was thrown violently against the wall, hitting his head on hard concrete.

He had time to think, *Oh, no*, and then it was blackness.

*   *   *

WHEN he woke, the sun was once again supreme ruler of the sky. Harsh beams of white, desert light shot down through the long windows and smacked his face like a hundred hot little hands. His head hurt bad, like someone had whacked him with a baseball bat. He slowly lifted his hand to his temple and felt congealed blood there. *Woof.*

Lifting his head, an effort that made him queasy, Keith saw that the observatory had not totally collapsed, but rather, taken a bit of a drunken dive. Whatever the explosion had been, almost certainly the black powder Hugh Flemm had threatened them with earlier, it had brought the tower to a steep cant, but hadn't quite finished the job. Though Keith wasn't sure how much longer it would hold. Things felt a wee bit *tipsy.*

"Harold?" asked Keith. His voice came out hungover. Drooly.

There was a baking silence, and then a groan from under Keith's right thigh, which was itself, buried under a large pile of sandbags and rubble. He lifted his leg, as much as he could manage, to find the scrunched face of Harold under his calf. His eyes were shut tight and his nose was bleeding, just a little. The intricate game of twister they found themselves in was a comical sight. This was the second time since meeting the Nettlebees Keith had managed to entangled himself with the big lunk. He would have laughed, but thought his head might explode if he tried.

It took the better part of an hour to free themselves from the rubble and get their aching heads under control, but when Keith and Harold finally managed to right themselves and take stock of their situation, what they saw was bad. *Very not good. No bueno.*

They were still attached to the ramp, and suspended forty or so feet above the ground, as Keith had seen, but the whole apparatus was badly twisted. It looked like a giant toddler had come along and decided he didn't like this toy. *Stomp-stomp, throw-throw.*

The trees were all but gone, ripped from the ground, roots and all, by the violence of the storm. Only a few, shrimpy saplings remained. But what was more alarming was how very little of the mountain remained. Now that there were no trees to obscure the view, it was plain just how close the desert was to completely devouring what remained of Appalachia.

There was, at best, a square mile of earth left, the observatory tower springing drunkenly up in the middle of the patch like a flagstick on the world's last green. And circling their patch of dirt was a huge… black… cat. *Uh-oh.*

Chapter Forty-Four

Fred Windsley

LONG distance information give me Memphis Tennessee… help me find the PArTy! LA-da-tA-daDa-daDadaTa…

He was good and thoroughly insane now. Or maybe, more sane than he'd ever been. He felt himself merging with the great black one. *The CAT, BABY!* He wondered why he felt so elated this morning. He had this wonderful feeling of *fullness*. And he couldn't help but think that some kind of victory had been won, some kind of old grudge settled. *Somewhere.*

Despite the inexplicable joy he felt, Fred was rather tired of humming songs to himself and waddling through this endless desert. There's only so much boredom a king can take. Even from the front seat of a poly-board Cadillac.

He felt that they should have arrived at their destination by now, yet the sand stretched on and on, golden and featureless. It was mind-numbing. There had been, however, little treats on their path over the last couple of days that had kept him somewhat entertained. The first had been Stu Black, who now walked behind Fred's Cadillac litter, bound and gagged. The second had been a woman, though, in slightly worse shape than Stu had been.

Fred had never seen a drowned body in the desert. It was a bit unsettling, even for him. She had been a middle-aged woman, with mid-length blonde hair and, *well,* it had been hard to tell much else. The sun had blown her up like a deer on the side of the highway. The stink was awful. They didn't stick around to found out what would happen when she burst, an event which seemed inevitable. And imminent.

"Friend a yours?"

Stu had just lowered his head.

After that, they'd come across more and more survivors of the storm that'd scattered Stu Black's followers. It was almost as if the storm had dropped them in a line, like little bread crumbs. *Foul* bread crumbs. Some had been found alive by the end of that first day, a good twenty or so, but more had been dead. Bloated monstrosities, like the blonde woman.

"Gah-lee, Stu. It's like a little trail of sugar cubes, 'idn'it'? That storm must've been a real bastard. I wonder if it hit ahead of us as hard as it hit you and your lil' gang."

Fred fancied leaning back over the trunk of his Cadillac litter and talking to Stu. Of course, his gag wouldn't allow him to answer, but Fred didn't mind. He was a good *conversational backboard*, as it were.

Behind Stu, the growing number of survivors trailed out in a line, bound together with phone cords and salvaged electrical wire, carried all the way from Dallas. Watching them stumble along was as good a way as any of passing the time. *They sure are a ragged bunch*, Fred thought, though he hadn't considered the state of his Office Workers in comparison. Some had even lost their clothes in the storm and were nearly naked. Their skin looked like it might cook right off their bones. The relief of the cold rain several days ago made the sun's heat feel all the more potent, and it shone down like God's heat lamp once more.

…My uncle took the message and he wrote it on the walL… Dee dee de dedeeE…

Fred leaned backwards over the trunk of his trundling Cadillac and gazed up at the sky. He sighed.

"…Oh Stu, Stu, Stu… I think I may die of boredom if we don't find something besides another bloated corpse soon."

The rainbow umbrella mounted in the middle of the Cadillac cast multi-colored shadows across Fred's face. His paper crown fluttered in a brief, hot wind. He looked like some psychedelic king of kindergarten. But his eyes…

"huhynonduugommnownerehmmalgden…"

"What?"

"huhynonduugommno…"

"I can't understand you when you mumble, Stu."

Fred gestured to one of the men carrying his litter to break off and remove Stu's gag. The man dropped out from under the weight of the litter, gratefully, and went to Stu. The Cadillac dipped heavily, and there were groans from the other men underneath it. The man that had broken off had a huge divot in his shoulder where he'd been supporting the construction. It looked painful. When he managed to get the gag untied, Stu sighed with relief and stretched his jaw.

"…I said, why don't you come down here and walk then. Might help with your boredom," said Stu, looking up at Fred.

"Mmmm… no, I don't think so. Looks about the same, honestly. Just hotter. And, uh, more *walky.*" Fred leaned his head backwards over the trunk and gestured to the man to get back under the litter. He clicked his tongue. For a split second, Fred thought he saw defiance in those eyes. *Anger.* But the Office Worker went quickly back to his post and lifted up his corner.

"Nah, Fred. Ya got it all wrong. It's great exercise. I'm sure you'd just love it." Stu raised his bound hands, bleeding from cords tied too tightly around his wrists, in a mocking appeal to friendship.

Fred laughed. It was short and sharp. "Whaddhya think, hun?" Fred sat up and turned to the Yellow Woman in the passenger seat next to him. Before she could respond, Fred waved his hand at her and leaned back over the trunk. "Oh, that's right. I forgot. You don't have anything to say. *About anything.*" What Fred failed to see, were faint dark streaks running down her mask. *Tears*, wetting yellow paper. "Pretty shitty pitch there, Stuart. I might have been tempted to join you a couple of days ago. Just for the conversation. But we're so close now. *So very close.* And I think it might make a better impression on any would-be subjects if I rolled up in a Cadillac, rather than trudging along beside my prisoners. Yeah?"

"We're your prisoners, huh?"

"What else?"

"Well… I was just wondering what the difference between your *subjects* and your *prisoners* is. I know the mighty Fred needn't concern himself with the struggles of the poor, but your *subjects* are dying, *friend…* almost as fast as your prisoners. You've lost two today already. *Two people.* And nobody stops for them. No one even seems to give a damn. They're human for Christ's sake. Real people."

"Mmmm… And that's where you're wrong. These are the Office Workers. Laborers. Born in the old world, wiped clean by God, and reborn to a great new purpose! I, uh… didn't notice about the dying, though, to tell ya the truth. Two today? Really?"

Stu looked disgustedly up at Fred's upside-down face, split down the middle with green and yellow light like a cut squash.

"That's right," said Stu.

"That is unfortunate. Maybe I should start taking roll…"

"What are you?" asked Stu, a slight tremble in his voice.

Fred smiled, and his upside-down teeth shone jagged in the yellow-green of the umbrella. He looked like a mangled alley cat. He raised his crooked arm up in salutation of the sky.

"I'm the prophet, babe! And a *king*. Ain't that right, hun?" Fred did not look at the woman sitting beside him. She did not look at him, though, in her hand, she gripped a sharpened pencil. With white knuckles.

"I hope, *for your sake*, we're as close to… *whatever it is* that's brought us to this wasteland, as you say we are, because your *car* won't last through tomorrow. Maybe not even the rest of today."

"What are you talkin' about? My men are –"

And then, when threatened with the prospect of having to walk, Fred looked around at the state of his people, *really looked*, for the first time. It was a sad sight. There were still those that looked strong enough, tan and lean, and walking upright. But many more were bent husks of people. They were terribly under equipped for the desert they were crossing. Their exposed bodies were white and red with untreated boils and dead, cooked skin.

It made Fred a little sick to his stomach. Just a little.

And more than the state of his office workers, their numbers were shocking. Perhaps Stu was right. *Maybe I should give them a rest… But we're so close. I can feel it*. When he'd started out from Dallas, they had numbered around three hundred. He couldn't fathom how it had happened, but around him now, he could only count about eighty. And of those, half were knocking on the black door, as they say. *NO. It doesn't matter. We push o –*

There came a sharp pain in Fred's chest.

It was a queer kind of *tingling* sensation. It made a quick slithering sound, and then a *POP*, like opening a coke can, and Fred felt his breastplate jump with disapproval. He turned away from his people to look down at his chest. There was a hand there, gripping a pencil. A yellow, number two pencil, buried in the center of his chest up to the halfway point. He felt dizzy as his eyes followed the arm up to the face who owned the hand. It was a good face. Mask free. Kind and normal, wet with tears. And angry. *So angry.*

The shock was strong, and Fred knew in the back of his mind that his injury was serious, maybe fatal, but as he gazed into the face of the woman who had saved him from the desert, nursed him back to health, he felt himself filling with rage.

"You… BITCH."

Fred reached out and gripped the Yellow Woman's wrist, hard. She tried to press the pencil further into his chest, but Fred was stronger. Much stronger, even with his twisted arm. He slowly began to unsheathe the pencil from his breastplate. Gripping with his other hand, he pulled at the pencil like reverse seppuku. It made a horrible grinding sound as it slid free, wood on cartilage. The pain was setting in, and Fred growled with the effort. At first, there was no blood, but as the final bit of pencil came free of his chest, Fred felt a warm kind of *peeing* sensation, and a red leak sprang from the hole.

"Oh. Goodness…" Fred's voice was low and calm, but his arms still strained against the woman's frantic pushing. He looked down at the wound in confused disbelief. *But I – I'm his prophet. I'm his man… I can't – This can't…*

Despite the airy feeling in his head, and the growing black fuzz around his vision, that anger filled him up again like a diesel engine, and he flipped it on the woman beside him. His grip turned to cold iron, and the woman cried out in pain. He began to bend her own hands against her, turning the sharp pencil towards her throat. The Yellow Woman's eyes widened in fear, and she started to kick at Fred. She screamed. Fred sat up and used his weight against her, pinning her body to the seat. The blood was pulsing from Fred's chest now in nice little, round spurts. It splashed onto their entwined hands, making a slippery red finger bolognese.

"CUNT!"

Then the Cadillac was falling, and everything turned sideways.

He lost his vision for a moment, but when Fred regained his senses, he found himself on top of the Yellow Woman, sprawled on her back in the sand. *I don't even know her name. Good thing I don't need it to kill her*. He was smiling uncontrollably as he pushed the pencil down towards her unprotected neck. She was struggling against his weight, and losing, their hands slipped against one another in a tangle of blood and nails.

The tip of the pencil, honed to a terrible point, pressed up against the woman's neck. She gasped as it broke the skin and began to plunge into her windpipe. Then, Fred felt something slip over his head and down around his neck. *A wire?* He was being pulled backwards by his head, *strangled*. He tried to push the pencil just one more inch, *to finish the job,* but the wire pulling him was too strong and he had to turn away from his quarry.

"AGGH..." Fred howled in anger. Somewhere, the baritone of the Black Cat's voice came rumbling up through the sand to emphasize his pain. Fred twisted and lashed out wildly with the pencil. It struck something fleshy and sunk in deep. He heard a pained scream, and the wire relaxed. He slipped free and stood up, reeling in anger and shock. The sand felt slippery under his feet.

He'd hit Stu. The pencil was sticking out of his thigh, having buried itself an inch into the flesh of his leg. Stu and the Yellow Woman were both on the ground, bloody and wounded, but neither of them dead. Around the duo, the Office Workers had gathered and were watching in blank-faced silence.

Fred swayed in the desert sand, legs apart like a sailor looking for balance on a sinking ship. *That hot breeze again.* He swayed. From the center of his naked chest, a red circle spouted black blood in wet, steaming pulsations. The sand gulped it down eagerly.

"YOU – HOW DARE YOU… STRike… me…"

Fred looked down at his chest again. Slowly he raised his twisted arm and stuck his pointer finger in the hole.

"I'm… Leaking."

He looked up to catch Stu's eyes one last time, then fell backwards into the sand.

Thud.

Chapter Forty-Five

Stu Black

FOR a few minutes, they all sat together as one. The only sound, the rise and fall of their breathing, and the gentle whistle of wind rolling over sand.

"Well," said Stu Black.

The woman he'd saved narrowly from having a pencil thrust through her neck turned to look at him. She was crying, fat tears sliding down her dusty face in brown squiggles. But she made no sound, nor did she seem in distress. She simply looked *through* Stu, and then back to the unmoving body of Fred Windsley. Silence settled again. Around Stu and the woman, crowded the remains of Fred Windsley's Office Workers, as well as the twenty or so ragged and bound storm survivors. They were all gazing at Fred's body, wondering, *what now?*

Stu let the silence linger for another minute, though he knew soon the talking would have to start. They had a lot to discuss. But just as he was about to say his first word, Fred Windsley sprang bolt upright. He sat up like a kid in a sandbox, his legs in a bowed circle, his back straight as a board. There was an audible gasp, and the crowd moved backwards together in alarm. Fred looked around at the faces staring at him, then down at his hands.

"No, I'm looking for *Petunias. Petunias.* Not – pansie…" The words came out of Fred in the same way a child might speak them, Confused and dreamy. As his sentence trailed off, he looked down to see the neat hole in his chest, now slowly oozing thick, brown blood. "Oh. Right." Fred fell backwards and lay still. For the second time.

The crowd watched on in silent horror, as if they suspected he might get up again and start asking where he could find the garden center. Stu moved to get back on his feet, and was painfully reminded of the foreign object protruding from his right thigh. He tapped the eraser sticking out of his leg with his pointer finger. It sent a small thrum up through his bones. *Weird. Not good.* When he tried to curl his right leg underneath him, he found it would obey, but with a great amount of pain and a terrible tremble. A wave of nausea hit him, but he pushed through and somehow managed to get into a standing position. His leg was on fire, and he thought he might go insane if he didn't get the wire restraints off his wrists soon.

Wobbly, and practically hopping on his left leg, Stu made his way over to Fred's body as a hundred ragged people watched on in silence. When he got to Fred, he stopped and looked down at his face. His eyes were wide open, staring up into the sun. They'd be like boiled eggs in a couple hours. His chest wound had stopped bleeding, and already the blood had begun to thicken and congeal like fig jam. Fred was dead. *Fred's dead, baby. Fred's dead.* Stu turned around to address the crowd, gazing gravely at the pitiful crowd.

"Fred is dead. No doubt." And, as if emphasis were needed, Stu kicked Fred's ribcage clumsily with his good foot. Fred did *not* get up and start talking about Petunias this time. "Anybody have wire cutters?"

There was a moment of palpable tension. The office workers, just as exhausted and brutalized as Stu's storm survivors, clearly didn't have any idea what to do. They looked at one another in strained silence, and then, all eyes settled on the Yellow Woman. She seemed to feel the weight of their gaze, and she rose to her feet and wiped her eyes.

Without answering Stu, she walked over to the fallen Cadillac and began digging through a half-split bag of various tools and items. *Bottle of Jameson's, Hammer, jar of dirt…* and then, a pair of handheld wire cutters. She strode over to Stu and gestured for him to hold his hands out. Stu did, but slowly. She slipped the edge of the cutters between Stu's wrists, cold metal against his vital arteries, and cut. It took several squeezes to fully sever the braided wires, but she eventually got through, with a very satisfying '*SNIP*'.

The relief that flooded through Stu's wrists was Godly, *and not in the green-eyed cat sense of the word*. He rubbed the deep red rivets where the wires had dug into his skin and exhaled in relief and pain. The woman watched Stu thoughtfully for a moment, and then gestured down to his leg. Stu looked down and found that he'd forgotten, *again*, that he had a pencil sticking out of his thigh.

"Yeah… *shit*. That's gonna be a problem, 'idn'it'."

Stu reached down, grasped the pencil and yanked it free of his leg. He saw that the wound wasn't as bad as he'd first thought, but that nausea hit him again all the same.

"Think I… need to sit down for a minute."

He did.

*   *   *

IT was deep night when they found the body, and the young man sitting next to it, with his head hung between his knees. It was lying in a heap on the sand, arms slung just so one could mistake it for a sleeping child. But it was too still. Too bloated. It was Jim Quail, and the young man was Billy Thompson.

At first, Billy had been frightened of the approaching band of survivors. The Office Workers were an incredibly strange sight, especially in moonlight, and, of course, *stranger danger* still applied in the apocalypse.

Billy'd started to run, but had stopped at the calls of Stu Black, limping down the face of a blue dune, hands cupped around his mouth. They came together in a fierce hug. It occurred to Stu then, that he didn't really know Billy that well. Just that he was from Connecticut, really. He'd become much closer with Jim once they'd busted out of Phoenix, but sometimes a shared hardship is enough to call someone *friend*. And they did now.

Billy recalled his experience in the flood that had whisked him and Jim away into the desert like little rubber ducks, helpless. Billy was young and strong, a good swimmer. Jim had been neither of those things, and although Billy hadn't wanted to abandon the older man, his *friend*, he'd had to make a decision. Stu grimaced at the retelling. Pictures from that terrible night, highlighted in green lightning, flashed in his mind like frames in a slideshow. He saw the woman he'd tried to keep afloat, saw her slip beneath the black water. He clenched his jaw.

When finally the storm had ceased, Billy'd found himself washed up on hot sand, utterly alone. He'd wandered for a day, keeping to the general easterly path they'd been on, more dazed than hopeful of finding anyone. At the end of that first day he'd come across Jim's body. He'd just sat down then. Sat down with no intention of getting up. *Where was there to go?*

"I'm sorry, Stu. I – I wish I could have saved him… I know he was your frie –"

"There's *nothing* to apologize for, son. ***Nothing.*** I know he'd be glad you're alright. *I know it.* We didn't meet before all *this…*" Stu gestured to the emptiness around them. "Whatever *this* is. I'm not sure if we would've gotten along. I think so… *even with his politics.* But from what he told me, I think he had a good run. A good life. And he was your friend as much as mine, Bill."

Stu and Billy stood together, looking over at Jim's body, neither of them laughing, but both wearing faint, sad smiles.

"We should bury him," said Billy.

"No. Not bury. We can do him better than a shallow grave in this empty place."

"What other choice do we…"

Billy turned to see the crowd of people gathering behind him and Stu, just noticing them again. They were an absolutely ragged bunch. Even in the blue dark of the night, it was apparent that many were on the brink of total exhaustion. The few that had some strength left were hauling a sledge of some kind. It seemed to be a collection of random office materials, and enough bits of wood for a small, but serviceable fire.

Nothing else needed to be discussed. It seemed to Stu, and to Billy, that a fire would be the right way. And so they arranged the scraps of Fred Windsley's poly-board Cadillac into a pyre for a fallen friend. Some of the survivors who'd known Jim pitched in, though many were too starved and dehydrated to help. Mostly, they sat and watched as Stu and Billy stacked and arranged the scraps. The woman who'd formerly worn the yellow mask did not help, but when the monument was complete, she rose and brought Stu a BIC grill lighter. They looked at one another for a moment, before she returned to her seat.

"We still have to…" said Billy.

"Yeah. I know. I have a strip of jeans we can use to… cover his face," said Stu.

The pyre was complete, but the body of Jim Quail still needed to be hoisted up to lie on top of it. Both Stu Black and Billy Thompson had experience with death. Billy had been a prison guard under the employ of Hugh Flemm for a short period, and he'd seen a number of hangings in that time. Stu had now led hundreds of innocents to their deaths, a thing which he would be forever incapable of forgetting, but *handling* the bloated body of a friend was something different. More personal.

Billy and Stu looked at one another grimly and made their way over to where Jim's body lay. His face was turned down into the sand. Stu gently pulled at his shoulder to roll him on his back. It took more force than Stu had anticipated, and Jim's body made a terrible sloshing sound as it rolled onto its back. It was still Jim's face, though horribly mangled by the sun's heat. It made Stu sick, but he bit down hard and got on with it.

"I'll take the head, Billy. On the count of three, alright?"

"Alright."

"One, Two, Three –"

They hoisted the body between them, Billy lifting by the legs, Stu, the arms. They'd built the pyre close, so it wasn't a long journey. Stu was glad of that. He wasn't sure he could've carried Jim much farther, and not because he felt like he might collapse from hunger, though he did feel that way, but because of the way Jim's head had rolled when they'd picked him up. Something in the movement had made Stu's stomach fall out from beneath him. His mind flooded with images of Fred Windsley, and the shadow that had seemed to loom behind him. *The cat.* That shadow was hopelessness and despair. It screamed, *what's the point?*

Even wading in those thoughts, Stu managed to get Jim to lie nicely, *peacefully,* on top of the three-foot mound of wood. He pulled a strip of denim from his back pocket, a thing he could not recall ever saving or even *having* in the first place, and placed it over Jim's bloated eyes.

They sprinkled the pyre with gasoline, another useful leftover from king Fred Windsley, and as soon as Stu sparked the grill lighter, the pile was blazing. It cast its orange light out into the night like a star in a dark and lonely universe. Stu stepped back from the heat and wiped his brow. He turned to Billy and saw he was weeping silently. Stu put a hand on his shoulder and looked back at the fire. Behind him, a hundred beaten humans gazed into the marmalade of the fire and were warmed against the chill of the desert night.

*   *   *

THE first silky orange strands of dawn began to weave their way across the blue-black of morning, as if thrown by some galactic spider working on a bit of cosmic embroidery.

Stu Black watched as the sky lightened, ray, by orange ray. He was tired. But he knew that walking overnight had saved them some of the simmering pain that was surely awaiting them today. This was *it*. If they found nothing by the end of the day, that would be the end. *The end, okie-dokie artichoke, ba-bab-ba-dee that's all folks!* The last of the food and water brought by the office workers from the bones of Dallas was nearly gone, and everyone needed a rest. *A good, long, rest.* It didn't seem likely that they would get it. Stu was starting, not for the first time, to miss his jail cell back in Phoenix.

"Not much gas left in the tank, Stu," said Billy.

"Yeah… I know. I got a… *well*, not a *good* feeling, but *a feeling*. A hunch our trip ain't over just yet."

Stu squinted at the rapidly brightening eastern horizon once more and thought he may have seen something, a black silhouette jutting crookedly out of the sand. Then it was lost again in the haze of the morning. He took a big breath and began to walk. Billy followed.

As the day warmed, and the sweat began to flow, Stu's thoughts turned towards the woman who'd killed Fred Windsley. Their interests had aligned when it came to the straight up murder of that psycho who'd called himself a prophet, though Stu had acted more out of self-interest than anything else. Regardless, he was glad he'd helped. It was one of the few times in his life he'd picked the winning side.

Although, looking at them now, you wouldn't have guessed they were winners. Of the three hundred or so people who had left Phoenix as followers of Stu Black and Sarah Bracken, now only thirty remained. Ragged, hunched, and scorched husks of people. Stu himself felt the weight of their grueling journey as well. He'd lost what he guessed was nearly twenty-five pounds since his time in Phoenix jail, and he hadn't been particularly overweight when he'd started out. The days had merged together, and Stu realized he couldn't even say how long he'd been out in this God forsaken desert. It was like the screw of time had loosened along with his brain. *Doesn't matter.* It didn't.

The Office Workers weren't fairing much better. Stu had marveled at them when first he'd been captured by Fred Windsley, and his curiosity hadn't waned. It was as if some great hand had passed over their minds and turned them into children again. *Big, hapless, naked, children.* Stu suspected that was exactly what had happened, though he shuddered at the idea that one's mind could be altered that way, and again, at the fact that he knew who had done it.

Regardless, they were still *people*, and they still had needs. Fred had ignored that fact, and in his error had killed hundreds of the poor souls, not to mention ensuring his own downfall. The ones who remained now were the lucky, and the strong. Though, the 'strong' was a relative term, and the 'lucky' certainly wouldn't count themselves as such. And now, brought together through the turning gears of an unpredictable world, they were all together.

There was another feather tickling the back of Stu's mind as well: Sarah Bracken. *She's not gone.* He felt it in his stomach. Still, he wondered how anyone could survive a storm as violent and terrible as the one she'd walked into without some kind of divine intervention, wondered if her *child* could've survived. That thought led his mind back to the Black Cat. Fred Windsley was dead, but if he hadn't lied, and Stu thought he hadn't, Hugh Flemm was alive. And *ahead* of them. *There's a final showdown coming.* As fantastically western as that sounded, Stu knew it was true. One final laugh before the last bit of America really, *truly* died. It might be the difference between a planted seed, and a patch of scorched earth. Stu was almost sure Sarah Bracken's role in this final play might not be concluded just yet.

Overhead, gray against the now bright blue sky, a bluebird sped by. A few of the desert travelers stopped and gazed up at the bird. It gave a sweet little chirp as it flapped off into the east. It had been a long time since he'd heard that sound, and Stu smiled. Just a bit. Fred had mentioned something about an old woman and a moron. He hadn't known at the time, but Stu felt now that whoever they were, they were somehow connected to the birds. The song birds, anyway.

As this flashed in his mind, another shadow appeared in the sky above Stu and his ragged band. *Black* on blue. Wide wings with a featherless red head. *Vultures.* At least ten sailed overhead, straight and silent. The smile vanished from Stu's face as he watched them go, gliding on unseen currents of air. They looked like death.

Suddenly, the office woman was beside Stu. She looked serious. Concerned. She put a hand on Stu's shoulder, turned to the horizon and pointed. Stu squinted, and at first saw nothing, and then… *yes. A squiggly tower,* some kind of structure. It was unmistakable. Around the tower, there seemed to be some sort of raised platform… *dirt?* It was too far away to tell, but it was surely something. Something besides sand.

"Well," said Stu, looking back up at the vultures. "Guess that's it. Point B, right? Looks like a golf flag."

The woman beside him didn't smile.

Chapter Forty-Six

Hugh Flemm

HUGH Flemm was sitting with his back against a cracked piece of concrete at the bottom of the Clingmans Dome ramp, one Blunderbuss propped up on his knee, when the fat kid and the guru came limping hesitantly into view. When they caught sight of Hugh, they backed up the ramp the way they'd come.

"Oh lookie- you made it. 'Magine that. I ain't gonna shoot ya," called Hugh weakly, though he did shift the end of his oversized gun towards them. More out of habit than anything else.

"No? That sure is a big gun you've got there… No urge to pull the trigger again? You seemed plenty eager to fire off a round or two when we first met," shouted the toga man.

"Oh, urges a-plenty, son. But my powder's wet. Unfortunately." Hugh lifted the gun up above his head with his right arm, grunting against the weight, and pulled the trigger. The gun clicked. Metal on wet metal.

Silence greeted this display, and then the two bunker dwellers hobbled cautiously back into sight. Hugh raised a hand and smiled.

"Well, howdy boys. Seems we've come to the end of the road. Hellava a storm, that was. *Hell of a storm.*"

"Where's my Nana?" asked the fat boy.

"Your nana? Oh – you mean the old lady… uh, sorry to break it to you, but she got a little bit, well, she got eaten," said Hugh.

"*Eaten?*" the two asked in unison.

The fat boy was on the verge of tears. Hugh almost felt bad, but something about the sight of them leaning on one another was just too funny. He laughed, and once the first giggle came tumbling out, he found that he couldn't stop. It came like a flood. It was all he could do to point with his blunderbuss and gasp.

"By – that –"

Toga man and the fat boy turned to follow the line of Hugh's gun. They saw a half mile of trashed earth, and then the desert, baking under a hot sun. Sitting on the edge of their patch of dirt was a small black shape. A cat, *the cat,* sitting primly, tail waving back and forth like a lava lamp. The green eyes shone like emeralds under the sun. Somehow, he seemed to be smiling. The sight of the cat brought Hugh's giggling to a stop. He felt cold under those eyes.

"YOU – MONSTER! I'm gonna kill you!" yelled the fat boy.

"Woah, Harold, woah," said the Guru. He held Harold back from running down the hill towards the black thing, and certain death. Hugh laughed again, this time he was able to keep it under control.

"That your name, bud? Harold?" asked Hugh.

"No! You don't get to know my name! Only friends get 'to know my name'!" screamed Harold, turning his fury on Hugh.

"Hey – alright. I get it," said Hugh. "What about you, Ghandi?"

"I'm Keith. Keith Lonnagan."

"Bond. *James* Bond," Hugh replied, then chuckled.

Keith looked at Hugh curiously, his brow furrowed.

"Say, Mr. Flemm. You, uh, doin' alright? Your leg is lookin' a little…" asked Keith.

"You from New York, Keith? I hear it in your accent. I forget that we used to have a country. Accents, *cities*… Kind of strange, thinking about it now… Oh, uh, thank you for noticing. Yeah, I took a little tumble in the storm. Seems I may have hurt myself, just a tad."

Hugh bent his left leg and grunted in sudden pain. Under his ragged black pants, something jutted out from above his knee. *Bone,* where no bone should be. That is, *outside the body.* Keith looked like he might throw up, and he turned away quickly. Harold wasn't paying attention, his gaze still fixed on the Black Cat waiting patiently at the desert's edge. Keith gathered himself, and turned back to Hugh.

"Where are your goons? There were like twelve of them. The naked guys."

"Thirteen," replied Hugh, looking down at the ground. "They're gone. The storm washed em' out to the desert, just swept em' up, easy as pie. They got those explosives off before they went though," Hugh said bitterly, smiling faintly. "I'm not sure how or why I'm still here and they're gone. Maybe 'cause I was the fattest. As your *nana* so kindly pointed out. Could be they're alive out there, but… I doubt it. I think he'd make sure they didn't get far," Hugh said, nodding towards the black speck. "Not the most forgiving one, him."

"Isn't he, like… Aren't you two on the same side?" asked Keith hesitantly. Harold had turned to pay attention to the conversation now, though he kept one eye on the monster at the bottom of the hill.

Hugh chuckled, and thought about how he'd ended up here. Deep in the well of his mind, that little child was screaming in confusion. *Yeah, I thought we were.*

"Well, not exactly. He ain't on *anyone's side*. I… I – He was so – I just wanted…" Hugh stuttered. And he realized that he didn't know what to say to these fellow humans. He was as lost as a puppy in a gutter. Maybe he'd always been like that, maybe the cat had nothing to do with it. Keith saw the struggling look on Hugh's face, and began to walk over to him. Hugh raised the blunderbuss, now scared.

"You – you stay back!" he shouted. Keith didn't stop. "Stay away!"

"Mr. Lonnagan! Don't go near that guy!" shouted Harold.

Hugh cocked the hammer back on his gun and pulled the trigger. Nothing came but a wet clicking sound. He repeated this again and again until Keith was kneeling at the end of the barrel, looking piteously down at him. He reached up and gently lifted the gun from Hugh's hands.

"Look around, man. There's nothing left. It's just us. Just the three of us. Whatever he said to you, whatever he *promised,* you won't get it. There's nothing left for him to give, except what you already had. *Sand.* He wants to bring everything down. That's all."

"I know," said Hugh, trembling. "I know it. And I helped him anyway. I just wanted to be the last one on the sinking ship."

"Well. You might be. No need to be a dick about it though." Keith reached up and flicked Hugh's forehead. Hugh's mouth fell open in confusion.

"What about…" asked Hugh.

"What about what?" asked Keith, taking a seat next to Hugh. He closed his eyes, and Hugh saw he was bleeding pretty bad from his temple.

"Well… aren't you going to… *fight* or something?"

"Fight the cat?" Keith scrunched his face in thought and let out a short laugh. "I'm sure that strategy went swimmingly for the ones who tried it. I'm actually a pacifist. But *maybe*. We'll see. Don't think we'd have much of a chance, though. No, there's not much to do but wait. I'm gonna meditate. Wanna join?"

"Mr. Lonnagan?" cried Harold from over on the ramp. He looked concerned and anxious. Kind of like he had to pee, but couldn't decide where to go. "Don't trust that guy!"

"Uhh… *no*. I'm good," said Hugh.

"Suit yourself." Then Keith put his hands on his crossed knees and steadied his breathing.

Hugh Flemm looked over at this New Yorker wrapped in a dirty bedsheet and shook his head in wonder. He turned to face Harold and shrugged. The horizon grabbed his attention once again, and he met the gaze of those gleaming emeralds. *That invisible smile.* But this time, he thought he felt a little bit of doubt in that malicious gaze. A twist of fear in the fury.

Chapter Forty-Seven

Sarah Bracken

SHE'D thought, based on some unexplainable feeling, that she might be protected from the storm when she'd decided to walk headfirst into it. She'd thought she was *different*. But as the water filled her lungs, as she sank below the writhing waves, alight with bursts of brilliant green lighting, she panicked. Panicked like anyone would. Panicked like a woman scared for her unborn child. The waves bated her around like giant unrelenting cat paws, and between frantic gasps of air, she swore she heard laughing. *Or thunder?* She screamed, and cold water rushed to take the air's place.

She thought back to when the Penguin had almost hung her, hung her, Stu Black and Jim Quail on those makeshift gallows in the middle of Chase Field. How they'd come together in that Phoenix jail cell, almost like they'd known each other long before then. And now she would die *here*. Away from both of them. And of all things… *Drowning*. It was not what she had expected.

What did I expect? She wasn't sure. Maybe some heavenly light to shine down and give her superpowers. Or God to lift her up through the storm and make her goddess supreme of the desert. *Something. Not this. Not cold, black, wet death.* But no light came. God did not appear. And as the waves crashed above her, and the immense pressure of the water pushed down on her chest, blackness crept over her vision. She felt herself hit the sandy desert floor and come to rest. Her closing eyes saw the last bubbles float from her mouth and up towards the electric light show overhead. *So… far away…* She raised a hand to her stomach.

Then… there was a face. A warm arm looped under her back, lifting her up through the black water and towards air. A terrible crashing sound rushed towards her, and then she was above the surface again. The sound of the storm was like a million planetary hammers being slammed down on wet steel.

Lightning crackled unceasingly in everything direction, a thousand-thousand jagged green fingers across the black sky. Sarah coughed, threw up what felt like a gallon of water, and took a deep, gasping breath. She looked in the darkness to her savior. The woman's face was outlined in green crescents. She was scared, and yelling something, though Sarah couldn't make out a single word. She recognized this person. A middle-aged woman who had been traveling with them since Phoenix. *Debra? No… Dana?* She couldn't remember her name, and all at once she felt like some kind of terrible fraud. Even in the bowels of a world devouring storm like this.

*I was the one who told them to come. Stu told them the risks. I just told them to follow. What was I **thinking**? Exactly the same thing you thought before you walked into a hurricane: I'm special.*

Then there were tears mixing with the rain of the storm, and Sarah held onto Debra, or *Dana,* for dear life. They paddled together, but the effort was like trying to pedal up Niagara Falls in a duck boat. The waves slammed against their two-person life raft, and boiled around them like living things. Sarah had heard laughter as she sank below the waves, now she heard anger. The wind howled, and somewhere in its deep whistle was a roar of disapproval. It was like the storm was angry that she hadn't drowned, *frustrated.*

Maybe it is. Maybe He is. Good.

The thought that the Black Cat was controlling the storm —
No, was the storm — was a scary one. But then Sarah realized,
she'd known that from the beginning. She'd known it when she
walked into its black depths. It made her want to fold, to fall back
to the sandy floor of this flash-ocean and let the darkness have
her. Then she saw her rescuer's face. Saw the fear, and the
hope. No. We'll live. We'll fight, and we'll live. So they fought.
Fought with and for their lives, paddling and holding onto each
other like two fleas in a washing machine. Time disappeared, and
the world became a black roil.

*   *   *

WHEN she came to, everything was white. The sand was still
damp, but drying quickly. Steam rose from the ground all around
her, the world's largest sauna. Sarah was lying on her back,
staring up at the blue sky through heavy mist. She felt like she'd
been run through a rock tumbler. She opened her mouth to call
out to her storm partner, *to Dana,* but when she tried to speak, all
that came out was water. Then she was bent over, coughing and
coughing and coughing…

When finally all the water was out, and she could breathe
easily, she tried again to call out. Her voice was haggard, hoarse
from exhaustion and choking up water.

"Hey… Dana? Hello?" she whispered to the white walls of
steam around her.

Nothing.

Sarah rose unsteadily to her feet, peeled the wet hair off her
face and threw it over her shoulders, swaying in the process.

"Hey." She'd found a little more confidence in her voice
now, and she began to walk. She couldn't see more than ten feet

in any direction, the steam was so thick. It was making a hissing sound as the sun drew it from the sand, and she could feel the ground shifting under her feet, *deflating* almost. And that familiar heat from above, the hot, heavy hand of the sun on her shoulder again.

"Dana?"

Nothing but that hissing sound.

Sarah wandered aimlessly in the fizzing whiteness for another fifteen minutes before she saw the gray lump in the sand. A human shaped lump.

"Hey!" Sarah cried, rushing towards the shape in the mist. She couldn't believe she'd actually found something in this unending white maze. *What kind of luck.* Approaching the bundle in the sand, she could see it was indeed her storm companion. She was heaped on her side, face turned to the sand. Sarah fell to her knees and rolled the body over.

She couldn't help but shriek. The face was bloated and disfigured. As if someone had pumped water below her skin and then hit it with a heat gun.

Her eyes were open, but milky and bloated. Sarah fell back onto her butt. She didn't cry, just looked at the woman who had saved her life, and felt worthless for not having been able to return the favor. She stayed this way for a long while. She couldn't have said how long, but by the time she stood, the sun was out in full force and the mist was gone. Without a trace.

The desert felt good. Like a worn pair of shoes. And when she lifted her head, she heard the wind whisper in her ear, as it had since she'd left Phoenix. It said…

East.

Chapter Forty-Eight

The Black Cat

THE old bitch tasted about as good as she'd looked. *Ashy. Just like she said.* The flavor was still lingering in the back of his throat, old and bitter. It was glorious. *Victory.* It tasted like victory. Very soon now, everything would be coming together. Everything would be one. *One desert. One God. Me.*

The anger that had been driving him mad during the past weeks had subsided, but also replaced with a sort of unease. Even after the death of the old woman, something felt *wrong*. He'd thought she would be the last piece holding things together, the final crumble, but still, his work wasn't complete, and he knew it. There was still *dirt*.

There's nothing to be concerned about. No one is left to oppose me. The woman is broken. The storm broke her. She will come to me. A new agent for my will, perhaps. Stu Black is captured. And yet, somewhere in the blackness of his mind, he didn't believe it. He felt *eyes* on him. It made him itchy, like the king of an empty kingdom, except it wasn't *really empty*. This frustration and strange anxiety was mounting, though watching the old hag's fat grandchild squirm was helping ease his mind tremendously. *Relaxing.*

He sat on the edge of what remained of the rats' little refuge, sending his will across the hot air. *They feel my smile. Good.* Still, the earth repelled him, like some invisible electric fence, a patch of hot fire. It wouldn't matter soon. The desert was winning, as it always had and always would. *Three sailors on a sinking ship.* He laughed, a deep rumbling thing, like thunder over open plains. He couldn't help it. The fat boy was pacing around, rubbing his face and talking to himself. It was just *too good. My favorite show.*

At the sound of the laughter, Harold turned to meet the Black Cat's gazing eyes. They shimmered green behind the heat lines rising from the desert floor. He opened them wide and poured his malice into the invisible tension there. He watched with satisfaction as a dark gray stain began to grow from Harold's crotch. He couldn't help but laugh again.

He turned his attention to the other two. *That one annoys me. The yogi. What does he think to accomplish, meditating? Now? Go ahead and pray to the emptiness, fool. You'll be praying to me soon enough. And – ah, dear Hugh. My captain. You don't look so good.* He locked eyes with the Penguin. There was a growing pool of red coming from under his right leg, and his skin was turning ever more pallid. *Have you decided to switch sides, dear boy? You did so well bringing the hag to me. I haven't forgotten that… though I don't really have any use for a lame duck, do I? Or a broken penguin.* At the sight of the Black Cat's twinkling eyes, Hugh seemed to slump. *If defeat had a face. HAhah…*

Then… a sound. *Vibrations.* Across the desert, behind him. *That must be Freddy now, my… wait – NO. Something's **wrong**. I… remember – Yes – Fred is dead! Stabbed in the heart! How could I have forgotten? Murdered by that yellow masked WHORE! And that one who refuses to die, STU BLACK. They dare cross my desert without permission?*

Before he knew what he was doing, he had wheeled away from the shrinking island and was galloping towards the rippling vibrations in the sand, a monstrous black void silently racing across a golden sea. He'd grown his size without thinking, and he towered in the desert like a black, feline Clifford.

The black one felt his form slipping as he bounded across the dunes. His fever was up again, and his fur had begun to turn to inky, wiggling worms. His eyes burned like nuclear headlights. *I'll tear them to shreds, just like I did that old piece of jerky. My blanks, my Office People, will break at the first sight of me. They'll regret their disobedience as soon as their 'fearless leaders' are turned to red pulp.*

He sprang over a dune, and was mid-air before he realized what he was looking at. A group of fifteen people or so, arranged in a tight square. From his right, he heard a voice shout,

"*Now!*"

He had enough time to clock the voice as Stu Black, and the anger bubbled up in him like an over-boiling pot of oatmeal. His eyes turned down to the group of blanks and ragged survivors below him, and he saw they all held weapons: *muskets, pistols, hand cannons, slingshots...* Then there was a terrible boom and a white pain in his eyes. He screamed — *roared* — a howl fit to bring the sky crashing down to earth. Yet, it did not restore his sight. He hit the ground hard and blind. He heard shouting voices around him as he scrambled to regain his composure.

*Guns? Bullets should not pain me so! Unless – but – Earth? Did they fire **dirt** out of those barrels? How could they know? How – how, HOW?*

"YOU RATS! WHAT DID YOU DO? I'M GOING TO RIP YOUR GUTS OUT AND FEED THEM TO YOU! YOU'RE ALL DEAD!"

But the sound of voices was getting farther away. A sliver of vision had returned to him, and then he realized what was happening. *They were a distraction. It was to lure me away from the island!*

"ARGGHG- NO!"

The squirming mass of black worms moaned. Then he was on his feet. One eye had fully returned to him, and he held it open. It hurt, *stung,* a new feeling for him, and he reeled in its wake. But there was no time to wallow in his pain. He steadied himself and crawled back up the low dune he'd come flying over just moments before.

Across the field of sand, a line of people were running towards the little island of dirt. Running *hard.* Even with one eye, he could see the specks of Harold and Keith, up on their feet and shouting at the runners in encouragement. He knew then, that he wouldn't get all of them. The ones in the back of the line, the ones who had stayed behind to blind him however… *They're mine.*

He sprang forward in pursuit, blinking open his other eye. His vision was blurry, and he roared in fury again as the wind blew against his bruised pupils. About fifty yards away from the edge of the dirt island, he caught up to the runner in last place.

It was an Office Worker. A blank. A big man without a shirt, and red lines on his arms like some samoan warrior, drawn in red sharpie. He looked up behind him as he heard the cat approaching and screamed. It was cut short as the huge cat leaned down and bit him in half without even breaking stride. It happened so fast, the man's legs kept running for a step or two before they realized their upper half was gone.

Next in line was a young woman. Not a blank, but a survivor, all the way from Phoenix. She turned at the crunchy wet sound of the office man being chomped behind her. When she saw the black shadow approaching, with those furious green eyes, she simply stopped and stood still. She was gazing up like a child when a paw came crashing down on her head and reduced her to a red smear on sand.

By the time he'd made it to the island's edge, the field of desert behind him was smattered with red like a toddler's food tray after meatballs. He'd gotten all the ones who'd stayed behind to shoot him, plus maybe fifteen more. To his dismay, Stu Black was not amongst them. The island was crowded now. Maybe fifty people on a square mile of dirt… *less*. From the crowd emerged Stu and the woman who had once worn the yellow mask.

The Black Cat writhed and paced in agitated, jagged motions. His body was no longer cat-shaped, his eyes no longer eyes, but pits of toxic green madness. He was a demon, *in full*.

"Hey there, kitty-kitty," said Stu Black, standing on the edge of the dirt island with his hands on his knees, breathing hard. He was bleeding from a small round wound on his thigh. "You like our little trick? We practiced real hard."

The black shadow continued to pace in silence, and then in a deafening voice that seemed to come from everywhere, he said, "YOU ACT UNBOTHERED, BLACK. BUT I SEE YOUR PAIN. I TOOK MANY FROM YOU TODAY. I WILL TAKE MORE TOMORROW. AND THE NEXT DAY. UNTIL NONE REMAIN. YOU KNOW THIS."

"You're right about some of that, I'll grant… They were brave folks you just murdered. And they deserved better. *Much better*. But I'm gonna have to disagree with you about that future forecast. I don't know anything of the sort."

The demon was silent. Then, he began to arch his back in a wave motion. There came a terrible growling, like hot, bubbling mud and rusty, grinding gears in a wet bag. Then the pulsing shadow was vomiting red liquid high into the air, raining chunks of flesh and hot blood onto the group of survivors. There was a piercing scream as a torso came crashing down into the crowd.

The wormy shadow looked to Stu Black. They locked eyes as the red rain dripped down through his hair.

We'll see.

Chapter Forty-Nine

Stu Black

THE dirt was a good idea. *The only idea, really.* Of course, there'd been no guarantee it would work. But it *had*. And that was good news. *Good news*, bought for the price of thirty-three human lives. He wasn't sure how much longer he could handle all this. How much more death and despair he could be party to. Though, the cat really wasn't giving him much *wiggle-room* on that front.

Stu Black sat with his arms laid over his knees, staring out over the purple desert evening. He was about ten feet from the edge of their little island refuge and he could hear the sand buzzing, shifting and swirling like waves lapping at a shore. *Maybe the last bit of American soil.* That was a funny thought. In that way, maybe they were like those poor saps who'd defended the Alamo. *Died at the Alamo.* All holed up and trapped like mice at the center of a yard being slowly mowed over, *around and around.* And they *were* trapped.

The cat was gone. For the moment, at least. The desert was going to bed, and slowly fading into the blue black of night, the last slices of purple and orange sunset being sucked into the horizon. Stu had to admit, it was a good view — *beautiful* — and especially so without those green eyes staring back out of the darkness. But the feeling of dried blood in his hair made everything feel a little more gray. *Darker.*

It'd been two days since they'd made their daring run across the dunes. When first they'd spotted the crooked tower jutting out of the sand, Stu had wanted to just run for it. Something in his mind had screamed at him then, *that's what you've been looking for!* But the Yellow Woman, who he'd since learned was actually named M. *Or maybe Emma? Emily? Emmabilia?*

She still hadn't spoken, and Stu wasn't sure if she was actually capable of it, but her non-verbal communication was impressive, he had to admit. He'd asked her before, just after they'd, sort of, tag-team murdered Fred Windsley. Perhaps it had been a lack of trust, but she hadn't given her name then. Stu supposed that the prospect of trying to outrun a giant bloodthirsty cat was enough to finally push her over the edge. She'd made an M sign with her fingers and mouthed the sound, along with something else he couldn't quite understand. He'd pressed her for a bit more, maybe a last name, or even just the rest of her first, but she'd just looked at him like he was speaking Russian. *Okay then.*

Despite all the name business, she'd had a good plan. *A hard plan.* But maybe the best, and only, option they had. When Stu had started walking off towards the crooked tower, just as carefree as a toddler, she'd stopped him, along with the rest of their strange caravan. She'd taken Stu and pointed out something that he never would have seen without her help. *A black speck* at the edge of the little mound of dirt that the tower jutted from. When he'd seen it, his blood had gone cold. *No doubt. Him.* From their vantage, the speck looked small, insignificant. But Stu's gut told him that *speck* would be anything but. Something about that far away pinprick of ink screamed of danger. He'd actually felt uncomfortable looking at it. Somehow it had felt like… *a smile.*

"Oh, Jeebus Crisco, "he'd whispered. "What do we do?"

He'd felt like a child then. Helpless and tired, looking to his mom for a box of raisins. It was the same thing he'd been doing since Phoenix, and all at once he was reminded of his total uselessness. First it had been Sarah Bracken, and now it was this *M*. Still, he was grateful for her being there. They likely would've been human catnip without her caution.

M had taken a moment, bitten her lip and then proceeded to explain her plan by drawing in the sand. She'd also gone into a small sledge where the Office Workers had been carrying the most essential of their goods, what remained of their water, their food, some tools, and… *a jar of dirt*.

Stu had laughed then. He couldn't help it. It was too ridiculous.

"Why'dja have them carrying a useless jar a…"

Then she'd slapped him. He'd stopped laughing after that. She'd pointed across the dunes to the plot of dirt with the crooked tower, and after a few minutes of strained miming and guessing, Stu had figured her meaning.

"It's… the dirt. He can't walk on the dirt."

It'd been Stu's idea to load it into what was left of their weaponry, which hadn't been much. They would likely lose any weapons they used, *along with the people who were firing them*, but Stu had felt strongly that any volunteers willing to stay behind and face the demon ought have the absolute best chance possible for escape. Guns would help.

The choosing had been hard. In the end, over thirty people had volunteered to stay behind. Stu had whittled them down to fifteen, which he'd judged would be enough to make an effective firing squad. They'd all known what would happen to them, but seeing the twinkle of hope in their eyes had given Stu strength. Of course, that wishful feeling had vanished less than an hour later, as soon as he'd turned to see the first one of the office people being eaten alive.

The night was getting cold. Stu sat, gazing into the darkness, and wondered what came now. He wished then for Jim Quail. He'd always been the smart one. The guy with real wisdom, and enough of a sense of humor to make you listen. But Jim was gone. Stu had burned him on a pile of cubicle dividers and couch cushions.

The sound of foot steps behind him, turned Stu's attention. It was Billy Thompson. He plopped down beside Stu, brought his knees up and laid his arms over them. Stu looked at him for a moment, then turned back to the desert.

"Hey, Billy," he said.

"Hey, Stu."

"What's on your mind?" asked Stu.

"What's on yours?" asked Billy.

Stu paused and took a deep breath. "Well... to be honest, Bill... I'm thinkin' we're screwed. Screwed bad. I don't know what to do. Except what I'm doin' right now. Wait. Look out at nothing."

Billy didn't respond for a moment, then turned to face Stu. "If that's all you can do, that's all you can do. No more to it. We're all just trying our best. And plus, *well,* maybe I'm too much of an optimist, but I think we can take him."

Stu chuckled and said, "Yeah, could be you're right."

There was more to say. So much more. But their talk was cut short by the sight of a lone figure walking out of the dark pool of night. A figure in the shape of a woman.

Chapter Fifty

Keith Lonnagan

KEITH Lonnagan lay like a starfish on the roof of the now decidedly bent, Clingmans Dome observatory tower. The stars were coming out slowly, emerging like dollar store stick-on-gems against a purple-pink cushion of evening sky. Keith was tired. It'd been quite a busy couple of days and, he was almost longing for those, at the time seemingly endless, days of solitude he'd had in the desert between New York and here. Not the *almost dying of dehydration* part, though.

There were only about fifty people on their little island of dirt, but that was fifty more people than Keith had been expecting. Of course, he'd welcomed the company, but it had gotten a little… *crowded.* And it was getting more so, as the desert continued to eat away at their remaining patch of land. *Inch by inch.*

He'd been meditating against the wall next to Hugh Flemm when Harold had started screaming like a maniac. Though he hadn't opened his eyes to check, he'd felt the presence of the Black Cat leave. It was like lifting a rhino off his chest, that horrible, evil gaze. Then there had come an echoing **BOOM** from over one of the far dunes. Keith didn't think he'd ever forget what had followed, *a suicide sprint.* Eighty people running across a field of soft sand, fleeing what looked like Satan himself, a gigantic writhing, twisting ball of black and green fury. *With teeth.*

When finally Harold's screaming had pulled Keith out of his meditation, he'd just stared. It took his brain a second to understand what it was he'd been looking at.

"Well… look at that," Hugh Flemm had muttered.

Before he'd even known what he was doing, Keith had been on his feet and screaming along with Harold, cheering them forward out of the jaws of death. *Literally*. That'd been the easy part, cheering for the human spirit. He'd welcomed them in, one by one, patting them on the back and offering words of hurried greeting. *Good Fucking job! C'mon! Run! Run, bastards! Over here!*

Afterwards had been hard. *The blood rain*, had been hard.

*   *   *

IT came down, as it always had, and always would, to resources. Stu Black's Phoenicians and the strange group of people dressed in office supplies, who had now apparently changed allegiances, to Hugh Flemm's dismay, had come only with what they could carry, a few back-backs and pocket items. Some of them, not even that much. They had barely any water, and no food. They were skinny, sunburned, exhausted things that looked more like pieces of jerky than healthy humans. Not that Keith was in all that much better shape himself.

The only edible, and or potable, supplies left *anywhere*, as far as anyone knew, were those that Harold and Wilma Nettlebee had stocked in the dome observatory. What they'd gathered back before the waves of sand had come like a thousand tsunamis and buried Tennessee in sand. It was several crates of water, enough for fifty people for a week, at best, if they rationed, and a veritable mountain of Campbell's canned soup. *We're all gonna get scurvy.*

It had also occurred to Keith that the immediate survival of the last fifty people left in the southern United States had come to hinge on the dietary habits of a large teenager from Gatlinburg.

Harold Nettlebee. He thought it was funny, but the mood didn't seem like one that would be very receptive of his ironic observations, so he'd kept it to himself.

Of course, a few people, including Hugh Flemm, were injured. Some were doing their best to tend to them, but the fact was that nobody here was a doctor. Hugh's condition was especially perilous, and though he was receiving some water and food, no one was really all that invested in his well being, *understandably so,* but it still made Keith's hippocratic Buddha-bone tingle with pity.

The meeting between Hugh Flemm and Stu Black had been particularly intriguing to watch. Apparently Hugh, who Stu called *the Penguin,* had tried to hang him back in Phoenix. Keith thought that was pretty on-brand for the guy, but it was Stu's cool head that had been something to mark.

Hugh hadn't been in too much pain to drag himself to the desert's edge to watch the world's shittiest 5k, and so had been rather bemused to look up and find Stu Black standing over him, covered in blood. Hugh had smiled and said,

"Oh, hi there Stuart. Long time, no see. You're looking a bit, uh- bloody."

Stu hadn't smiled then. His eyes had been hard as chips of flint, and for a moment, Keith had thought he might kill Flemm. But he hadn't. He hadn't said anything, just glanced at the limp, broken leg, then moved on to tend to other injured people.

Keith's own introduction to Stu Black had been similarly brief. Stu had held out his blood soaked hand and given both Keith and Harold firm shakes. He'd said,

"Howdy. Name's Stu. Stu Black. I'm sorry to barge in on your party, but it seems like you might be sitting on the last bit of America here. I hope you don't mind if we join you."

"Hey, free country, isn't it? I'm Keith, this is Harold," Keith had replied.

Stu had laughed a little at that, and replied, "Yeah... well, s'pose we'll see how long that lasts. Nice to meet'chu boys."

"Yeah, guess we will. Nice to meet ya."

"Hi, Mr. Black," said Harold.

"Hi, Harold. Hey, this might be a little strange, but you two wouldn't happen to be keeping a bunch of blue birds around somewhere, would you? I've sort of been expecting to... see some."

Keith and Harold had looked at each other then, and Harold had begun to weep.

"It was his grandmother, Wilma. She was the one with the birds," explained Keith. "They're all gone now, though. Couldn't say where... scattered. Storm took the last bit of forest, and now the desert is coming for the rest. As you can see."

Stu had bowed his head at that news and said, "I'm real sorry for your loss, Harold."

After that, the conversation had turned away from magical blue birds and devil cats to more practical things: *food, water, time.* Stu *had* commented on Keith's monk getup, though. Keith had subsequently explained about his quest to become a yoga instructor... *briefly.* Stu had nodded and coughed, uncomfortably.

They'd distributed an equal amount of food and water to everyone on the island. Dinner that first night had been cold and quiet, fifty beaten people gazing out at nothing, and all thinking the same thing. *What now?*

The next days were meeting new people, portioning out supplies and waiting to see who might die from exposure. There was the observatory, but besides that, no other shade remained on the island. The days were just as hot as they'd ever been, despite being on a patch of earth rather than sand. There was nowhere to hide. People crowded up at the base of the tower, inside the observatory and underneath what remained of the ramp, but inevitably, some remained in the glare of the sun, setting up improvised lean-tos and bivouacs from ripped clothes and backpack canvas. It was a sad sight. And the prospect of facing the black cat again made the mad, heroic dash they'd braved seem pointless. *The sand is going to swallow this place. And the shark is circling.*

All this played in Keith's mind like a scratched record as he gazed up at the darkening night sky. He wondered how he'd come here. *Why.* Stu had asked about the blue birds and it'd reminded Keith of how important they'd seemed back in New York, how *imperative.* They'd called out to Keith, and apparently, to Stu Black, whispered: *come south.*

Maybe there were others out there as well, making their way over empty sands. But they would find no pot of gold at the end of the rainbow, as both Keith and Stu knew. The old woman, *Wilma,* had been something special, some kind of beacon, or lightning rod, or maybe the birds had just really liked the way she smelled. Whatever the case, she was gone. She was gone, and they weren't. But, the question came again… *Now what?*

An answer, not one that Keith liked, came as the last bits of purple sky fell into the abyss of horizon, and a green fire lit up the night.

Chapter Fifty-One
Stu Black

IT was Sarah Bracken who walked out of that black night. She looked more *human* than Stu remembered. Her clothes were ragged and brown. Her hair stuck to her face and shoulders in sweaty strands, and she was limping slightly. As she walked out of the desert darkness into the dim of star light, Stu and Billy could only sit speechless at the edge of the sand. Finally, Stu was able to shake off his daze and stand up, followed by Billy Thompson.

"You!" said Billy.

"Sarah! I – you – made it," said Stu.

"I did," said Sarah. "Most weren't so lucky."

"No – No, they weren't," echoed Stu.

He wasn't sure what to make of this new Sarah. She seemed different than when she'd left. *Less magical*, he guessed. She didn't have the same *lightness*, that had been growing in her since Phoenix. He'd had the sense then that she was going to become some kind of desert angel, or wandering spirit, something beyond human struggles. *S'pose it didn't work out quite so easy.*

The woman standing before him now looked like a ferret trudging out of a rain storm. *Alive, breathing, dirty.* It was almost comforting to see her this way. It proved she was, *in fact*, human. Or at least, it helped her case. And another thing was adding to the effect... *her stomach.* It had been easy to forget that she was pregnant when they were crossing the Texas desert, but now, away from the fantastical, on a normal womanly frame, it showed. She looked tired. Sore. Round.

"I'm glad you're alright," said Stu. "We don't have much here, but at least there's some water and a bit of soup. Come on over and we'll…"

The night exploded in green fire.

It was as if two garage doors straight to hell had been opened out of the blackness. For a moment, it was so bright, Stu had to look away. It took a second for his eyes to adjust, but he didn't need them to know what the source of the light was. *He'd come.*

The brilliant green disks shone in the night like a million nuclear reactions folding in on one another, and at their hearts, two slits of black. The desert came to life, the sand vibrating and buzzing like the whole world had been set on top of some unfathomably large speaker. A sound like a fog horn, a deep bellowing brass, began to play out of the nothingness, from everywhere and nowhere.

Sarah had also seemingly been taken by surprise. She turned to face the light, and in the process, fell in the sand. Understanding dawned on her face, she'd begun to scramble backwards towards the safety of the earthen island, flailing in the soft, vibrating sand. She was just six feet or so from Stu when a massive paw came clawing out of the blackness and closed on her back foot. She screamed as one of the claws went clean through her calf. Stu, without thinking, ran out into the desert and grabbed Sarah by her arms. He began to pull frantically. Billy, finally shaking off some of his own shock, rushed out to help. It made no difference.

Sarah, breathed heavily in pain, looked up at Stu and mouthed the words, "Let me go."

"No! We can pull you back!" screamed Stu.

But the cat was too strong, and before Stu could even react, the paw reeled her into the darkness. She was gone. Stu and Billy stood in the sand gazing up at giant green eyes. Then came a laugh. A rumble that made Billy Thompson's bladder let go. A chuckle so deep and dripping with amusement, that it was thick in the air.

In the blackness, Stu and Billy watched helplessly as the huge green eyes turned upwards like headlights and illuminated the body of Sarah Bracken. She was hanging upside down by her pierced calf, lifeless. Below her, a yawning, many layered mouth, the mouth of a kraken, was opened wide. The appendage that held her up, which could no longer truthfully be called a paw, twisted, and then Sarah was falling into that gaping mouth.

The sound was like a fish on a slip 'n slide. Then she was swallowed, and the eyes were turned back on Stu and Billy, still sitting stunned on their asses. Realizing their peril, they turned and scrambled back to the safety of the island.

"YES. RUN. I LIKE IT WHEN YOU SCUTTLE LIKE RATS. IT'S JUST SO… FITTING. I'M TIRED OF THIS LITTLE GAME WE'VE BEEN PLAYING. I THINK IT'S TIME WE END IT. WHADDYAH SAY?"

\#

"YES. I'M QUITE BORED OF THIS DIRT, *AND THE LITTLE THINGS CRAWLING ON IT*. LET'S SEE IF WE CAN'T DO A LITTLE STOMPING."

The Black Cat emerged out of the darkness of the desert into the cold starlight as if he could control the very night itself. The blackness swirled and coiled around those two great green eyes like ink suspended in water. His voice was crooning and deep. *A father's voice*, thought Stu Black, *but not my father*. It froze Stu in place at the edge of the desert, and as the black shape sauntered forward, he could only gaze in terror.

A fifty-foot ball of slinking, wet black eels, turning in on one another endlessly, the sound of wet, fleshy friction, and bass. A vaguely animal shaped, black-wormed monstrosity. It was headed by two nuclear fog-lights, which themselves seemed to be doors into a terrible green underworld, and a veined, bony mouth. The horrible jagged grin stretched from ear to ear. *Unnatural. Unholy. This was that feeling, the feeling of being smiled at. This is what he was hiding. What he **is**.*

"COME MR. BLACK, DON'T LOOK SO FRIGHTENED. IS IT MY SMILE? I'VE BEEN TOLD IT CAN BE A LITTLE OFF PUTTING."

That laugh again. A rumble that shook the very ground.

Everyone on the island was awake now, stirred by the pervasive voice that played inside their heads. Although some were stumbling backwards, away from the advancing black horror, most stood still as statues, awed.

A paw, cloaked in smoke, formed of a thousand wiggling black worms, glistened under the starlight as it slammed into the sand. He was at the edge of the island now, looking down at the last doomed dregs of humanity. Stu had gathered his courage, and now spoke back to the demon in a voice that surprised even himself, though there was still a faint tremble in it.

"Hey there putty-tat. You know, *someday*, you're gonna pay for all you've done. You'll *die*, just like the rest of us. And suffer. For all the people you've killed and all the pain you've caused. It may not be today, but…"

The cat laughed, and it was all Stu could do to not clasp his hands against his ears. It was too painful to listen to.

"I DOUBT IT. BUT EVEN IF I DID *DIE*, IT WOULDN'T BE FOR THE THINGS I'VE DONE. NO, I CAN NO MORE DIE THAN THE DESERT ITSELF. PERHAPS SOMEDAY I WILL

CEASE TO EXIST. BUT NOT TODAY, STU BLACK. AND NOT BECAUSE OF ANYTHING YOU CAN DO. I PROMISE."

"Well. I guess we'll just see about that," replied Stu.

Another skull shaking chuckle.

"WE WILL."

With that, the cat roared. It was the sound of a thousand out of tune tuba players and hissing fire. One of those terrible wet paws sprang forward and landed on the dirt next to Stu and Billy Thompson. It hissed and burned like an egg dropped on a hot skillet, but the cat did not pull back. The sand vibrated and pulsed like a living creature. It began to rise like water in a jacuzzi. For a moment, the demon stopped and grunted in effort, but then the terrible smile was back, and he took another step onto the dirt. It hissed and burned black in the night, but he did not turn away.

Stu, stunned, was pulled backwards by Billy.

"Stu! C'mon! We have to move!" screamed Billy, as the second paw came crashing down into the dirt.

"There's nowhere to go…" Stu whispered back, but he let himself get pulled anyway, and then they were running towards the leaning tower at the center of the island. Behind them, the ground shook with the impact of heavy footfalls. All around them people were screaming, running. Running towards… *a mass grave*.

"AHHH-HAHHA… OH MY, THAT TINGLES! I THINK I SEE THE APPEAL. IT'S VERY FIRM UNDER THE TOES, ISN'T IT? A LITTLE HOT FOR MY TASTE THOUGH, I *PREFER* SAND, OH. HELLO THERE."

Stu turned and stole a glance over his shoulder as he ran towards the observatory tower. He saw a middle-aged woman standing still in front of the smoking black monster, whether out of fear or defiance, he couldn't tell. She was trembling though, Stu could see that much.

"WHAT'S YOUR NAME, MA'DAM?"

The cat's green eyes focused their wide beams down onto the poor woman like stage lights. She looked like a child then, at the mercy of an unforgiving god.

"Sh-sh-she…" the woman stuttered.

"NO NEED TO BE SHY NOW. SPIT IT OUT."

"She-Sherril."

"OH, WHAT A BORING NAME, *SHERRIL*. BUT I THINK YOU'LL TASTE FINE ALL THE SAME. NOW I WANT YOU TO HOLD VERY STILL, SHERRIL."

Stu turned away in horror as the demon opened its gaping mouth, like the unhinged jaw of a snake, and a dripping purple tongue came lolling out. It hit the ground next to the woman, and then curled around her waist. She didn't begin screaming until she was in the air and being pulled into that reeking abyss of teeth and gums. Her scream didn't last long. It was punctuated with the sound of snapping bones.

"A BIT OVER RIPE. BUT WITH A PLEASANT NUTTINESS. SIX OUT OF TEN."

Chapter Fifty-Two

Keith Lonnagan

IN one minute flat, the night had turned from a sad, but peaceful star gazing session, to a bloody, green hellscape.

People were running and screaming. Somehow a fire had broken out and the few small patches of grass that remained on the island were burning green in the night. And last, but *definitely* not least, a giant smoking demon was marching across the dirt with a slow, shimmering wave of sand following close behind him.

Keith sat up and hung his legs over the edge of the observatory roof. For a few moments, he just stared. It was like some far away dream, and suddenly the demon was just a house cat, and the fleeing people were little mice. It was almost funny. He heard Stu Black's voice shouting,

"To the tower! Everyone, up the ramp!"

Hey, that's where I am. I'm on the tower… Oh. And then it was a human flood, fifty people all rushing to the base of the long crooked concrete ramp at once, and then up. A small herd of scared two-legged mammals. The tower began to shake and trembled under Keith's bony ass. *Oh, goodness.*

The storm, combined with Hugh Flemm's explosives, had left the tower bent and broken, but not dead. Still, it was in a very precarious condition, and the sudden, jolting weight of fifty bodies rushing up its ramp was causing a lot of unsettling shaking. Keith thought *a quick drop and sudden stop* might be preferable to death by giant demon cat, though neither options were really that enticing.

What was all this for? Why did I come here? Just to die? So lame. He didn't know it, but Keith Lonnagan was having the same crisis of character that Sarah Bracken had experienced just a few days prior. *I thought I was… **different**. Guess not. Even though I met Jeff Bridges's spirit animal or whatever. And crossed a thousand miles of desert. And got my yoga license in two and a half months. And I'm a New Yorker, God damnit!* But all this in the face of living, breathing evil meant little and less. He had no super powers. Just a clear mind. And a purple yoga mat.

"Oh man…" Keith mumbled.

Suddenly, Harold Nettlebee was sticking his head up through the hatch in the observatory roof.

"Mr. Lonnagan! Come inside! It's not safe, the big monster is –"

"I don't think being inside is gonna help much with that, Harold."

"But Mr. Lon –"

'W'you hand up my mat? I'm gonna go down for a session."

"But Mr. Lonnagan!"

"I'll be alright, Harold. Now hand it to me, would'ja?"

Harold looked pleadingly at Keith for another few seconds, and then retreated back down into the hut. A moment later he returned with Keith's worn, purple and yellow yoga mat. He handed it up through the hatch.

"Thank you. Now listen, I'm gonna be fine, *Just fine*. But in case… I'm *not*. I want you to remember everything your nana told you, mm? You're a good kid, and all grown up. You don't need my help to get along. Just keep doing what you've been doing and you'll be fine. K?"

Keith didn't wait for a response, and turned to the edge of the observatory which overlooked the ramp. The whole thing was swaying now as the crowd of people surged forward towards the top of the tower. Keith looked up for moment to see a little black shape come darting out of the night. It was a bluebird. It did a little loop around his head, then flew back into the night from which it'd come. *Mmm.*

Keith lowered himself over the edge of the roof and dropped down onto the ramp clumsily. The crowd of people was almost on him now, and he held his mat out in front of him to part the human sea. Some ignored him as they rushed past, while others tried to drag him back towards the observatory. But he was confident, and he slipped through the crowd like a salmon swimming upstream. Stu Black's voice came spiraling out of the chaos.

"Keith! Keith Lonnagan! What are you doing?"

Keith didn't respond. He kept pushing until he was free and the ramp lay empty before him. He started walking. *Keep it casual. It's important to keep a calm, relaxed body. Don't want any shoulder knots. Ugh.* And before he knew it, he was at the base of the ramp and in the soft earth. He reached down and grabbed a handful. Bits of dried pine needles and forest detritus littered the moist soil. He rubbed it between his fingers. *Mmm.* He shoved a handful into a fold of his bedsheet robe. Then another and another.

Satisfied with his collection of dirt, he unrolled his yoga mat onto the uneven ground and smoothed it out. He'd used it so frequently that the yellow word cloud on the front had worn almost completely off. The only half-legible word remaining was *Leisure,* but the *lei* had worn off, and now it just looked like *sure.*

And that's what Keith thought. *Sure. sure, sure, sure. One stick, two stick, red stick, blue stick, I got a downward dog that'll make you sick. Look at that. I'm basically Robert Frost.*

Then he was praising the sun and folding down *into plank- upward dog- downward dog. Oooh… yeah…* He let a little fart out. *Oop.* Not loud enough for those at the top of the ramp to hear, but loud enough to reach the ears of the giant black demon, who was now looming just feet above him, rows of gnarled teeth smiling down like the Cheshire cat after a few bad years of crack abuse. His green eyes glittered with amusement.

"YOU WERE THERE WHEN THE OLD LADY DID SOMETHING LIKE THAT, WEREN'T YOU? THAT DRIED UP BITCH TASTED JUST LIKE SHE SMELLED. STALE. YOU… WELL, YOU LOOK A LITTLE BONY, BUT MAYBE MORE FLAVORFUL? WHADDA'YAH THINK?"

Keith finished his pose and stood to face the demon straight on. Bearded, still in the ragged white bedsheet stolen from the Hilton hotel in New York, and thirty pounds lighter than when he'd begun his journey from Manhattan, Keith Lonnagan finally felt that he was beginning to look the part of the wandering yogi. He smiled up at the cat and breathed in. It smelled like death and rotting fish. Like burning oil and trash.

"Dunno man. I haven't tried *myself*, to be honest. No salt around either I don't think   "

"I CAN MAKE DO."

Then that gaping mouth was open wide, the long, purple tongue lolling free and wrapping around Keith's thin body.

"Weird," he said, as if he'd just tried pickle flavored soda for the first time.

The purple tongue pulled him into the air, past the rows of yellow teeth, and then the mouth shut. *GULP*. The black Cat licked his bloody lips.

"MMM. NO. NOT A FAN. NEEDS MORE MEAT. 4 OUT OF 10."

Chapter Fifty-Three

THE crowd of dirty, tired and dying survivors pushed past Stu Black, shoving him roughly left and right, like a rag doll in a human river, all fighting for a spot inside the concrete observatory. *The badly swaying observatory.* They were packed tight against the entrance to the small room. *This is bad.* Stu wondered if it might have been a mistake to call them all up here. *Better a quick fall than teeth.* That, at least, was a comfort, though something in the back of his brain told him that was not how this would end.

That terrible voice again. It sounded casual, and someone was talking back. Stu finally managed to shove free of the crowd and gaze down the long winding ramp, just in time to watch Keith Lonnagan get swallowed whole. Stu couldn't speak. His mouth dropped open without permission, and then, the black cat looked up at him. Those green headlights locked onto Stu's like lasers.

"OH, STUAAART," the Black Cat called.

All Stu could think was, *what the hell was Keith doing? He just decided to exit the party early? What the fuck.* The thought bombed through his brain at a hundred miles an hour, and was replaced with the imminency of death via cat.

A giant paw, twitching all over with black worms, stepped onto the concrete ramp. The observatory tower shook with the impact. That laugh again.

"OH MY, HAVE I REALLY GAINED THAT MUCH? I NEED TO WATCH MY CARBS."

Stu was now out in front of the crowd, standing still, legs braced like he was getting ready to absorb the impact of some great wave. His brain raced, searching for anything that might help. Anything at all. *Explosives? Gone in the storm. Guns? Left in the desert, plus, we played that trick already. It won't work again. Sarah… eaten.* In the end, as the Black Cat took another step onto the ramp, Stu arrived at the final option, and the only one remaining to him. *Just fight. Use your fists. Fight!*

The ramp was shaking terribly, but Stu paid it no mind. He began to turn red, and shiver. His breathing became quick and strained. Then he finally let it go: a scream. A howl of anger and anguish and everything else inside him. It came flying out of his throat with an unexpected resonance, as if some unseen hand had helped it along, given it a little lift.

It lasted ten seconds, and for a few ticks of the universal clock, everything was quiet. Stu kept his eyes on the cat, and for a brief moment, he thought he'd seen fear there. It was replaced quickly by that wide, dripping smile. *Amusement.*

"What are we doing here?" Stu shouted. "I mean, what, THE FUCK, are we DOING HERE? If you want me, come and get me! I'll shred your insides like a cheese grater, you Goddamn cat! Come fuckin' TRY ME!"

The last words came out with such venom, Stu didn't even recognize his own voice. He ran forward, picking up loose pieces of concrete from the ramp and throwing them at the cat.

"HAHAHA – OH STUART! WHAT SPIRIT!"

Behind Stu, a quiet had grown among the tightly packed crowd. Then, Billy Thompson was there, running down the ramp beside Stu and screaming like some Mongolian war chief. He held a can of beeferoni in each hand and lobbed one like a professional pitcher. It struck the eye of the cat and was instantly vaporized in a meaty red mist. The cat laughed, but Billy didn't notice. He had his eyes closed. And neither did the crowd behind him pay any attention to the futility of the attack. They'd all come to the same conclusion as Stu Black. *Die quiet, or die fighting.*

It was a rush down the ramp, like the last ride out of the gates at Helm's Deep. Fifty shrieking people, who just minutes earlier had been running the opposite direction and screaming out of fear rather than courage. The black cat watched this pitiful charge with malevolent giddiness. His tongue flicked out of his wide mouth and slapped against his lips hungrily. Thick saliva dripped down in long purple strands from the horror of his mouth.

"OH BOY, OH BOY – ALL THIS FOR LIL' OL' ME? YOU SHOULDN'T HAVE, REALLY."

Then he was bounding up the ramp, causing the whole structure to crack and crumble violently. Some of the charging people tripped and fell, but most kept their feet and continued their battle cries. They kept up the barrage of stones, but the cat paid it no mind. He was smoking. *Hot.* The pieces of thrown rubble sizzled off him like oil off a hot pan.

The black demon and the crowd of humans met each other halfway down the ramp. Picture a black bowling ball, with a mouth, rolling over a crowd of little miniature pins.

The crowd's fierce cries turned to shouts of pain and horror. In a split second, the cat had crashed through their lines and sent ten people flying. Two went over the edge of the ramp. One screamed. One was already dead. A woman lay against the edge of the concrete ramp silently looking down at her legs. One foot was facing the wrong direction. The other was laying loosely by her side, as if the bones inside had been put through a blender.

Stu, who himself had been at the front of the charge was thrown nearly fifteen feet in the air. He landed hard on his back and the air left his body — *air say, 'fuckit'*. He still had enough brain left to think: *Well, we gave it our best. We did all we could. It wasn't enough, but it was what we had.*

Suddenly, those green, dinner table sized eyes were hanging in the air above him, shimmering and smiling. They were deep doors into a virulent hell.

"STU. STU, STU, STU. SHALL WE WRAP THIS UP?"

*   *   *

THOSE terrible jaws clicked open with the crackling sound of breaking bones. The Black Cat's head was all mouth. Kaleidoscopic rows of yellow teeth dripped viscous saliva. Purple veined gums stretched tight over tendon and cartilage. The smell made Stu's eyes water. *Roadkill. Decay. Sewage.* And from the deep throat, a twisting purple beast, a *tongue*, came wiggling free, unrolling itself like a fleshy snake. Stu could only watch, the cries of the wounded people all around him fading into his periphery.

The pale purple tongue, reeking like a band room floor of old spit and metal, came flopping onto the ground next to Stu. It curled underneath his back, and then it was lifting him up, into the air, *into the jaws*. Stu exhaled and closed his eyes. *Alright.* In that moment, he made his peace. Even in the act of eating, the cat managed to speak in that omnidirectional voice.

"GOODBYE STUART. SAY HELLO TO YOUR FRIENDS FOR ME –"

Abruptly, the cat stopped. Suddenly, the tongue was retreating. It dropped Stu hard onto his back. The purple snake curled back into its cave, and the horrible mouth snapped shut like a clamshell. The look in those noxious green eyes was one of confusion. And then… *fear*.

There came a deep groaning sound, like God got the tummy-rumbles. The Black Cat's eyes widened in surprise, and then he was screaming, howling in pain and fury.

"NNNOOO – YOU, STOP THAT! STOP IT IMMEDIATELY! BITCH! HOW DARE YOU! HOW DARE YOU!"

Stu lay still, watching the spectacle like a child in front of a TV set. Around him, the cries had stopped. Everyone was watching. The cat backed away from Stu with panicked, erratic footsteps. His spine was arched high in pain, and the black worms on his skin were vibrating madly, like streamers in a strong wind.

Then Stu saw it, a pointed bulge growing out of the cat's side, through his ribcage. It punched forward, stretching the skin, and the demon howled in pain. He twirled around and batted the air with his gigantic paws. His eyes shone so hotly, Stu thought they might catch fire.

"YOU FUCKING RATS! DIRTY CUNTS! I'LL KILL YOU! SHRED YOU ALL UP LIKE –"

That bulge came jutting out from the beast's side again, and it looked to Stu as if it might break the skin. Just before he thought it would punch through, it retreated again. The Black Cat let out a determined growl of anger, and then leaped over the side of the ramp. The force from his jump made the tower sway, and Stu thought for sure it would fall, but somehow it held. It took him and the other survivors a moment to comprehend what was happening, but after a few stunned seconds, they all ran to the ramp's edge to watch.

Below the tower, almost no dirt remained. The desert had crept up behind the black monster, and had left little more than a football field's worth of earth. Still, the sand glittered and shook with energy, as if it were electrified, though its rapid advance had halted, seemingly because of the sudden pain its master was in. The cat was running, off the dirt and into the sand. That bulge came again, like a knife poking out from his insides, and he lurched sideways. Stu thought he'd seen something come free. *A… foot?*

The beast kept his feet, but wandered drunkenly to the right, like a plane missing a wing. Stu could hear his stream of expletives, but that God-like quality had faded from the voice. It sounded *small*, far away.

"You… bastards… can't kill me… I am the DESERT!"

Then, at last, he fell. A little cloud of dust puffed up around his fallen body. The survivors on the ramp were silent, all of them only half believing what they were seeing. Stu could still see the heavy rise and fall of the cat's frame, and it seemed like his body was shrinking, just slightly.

Again, that bulge came, except this time it didn't retreat. It poked out like a skewer through a piece of raw meat. A red, bloody arm, and then a face. The face of Sarah Bracken. Stu turned and began to run down the ramp. He almost toppled over from a sharp pain in his back-,a reminder that he'd just been vaulted fifteen feet in the air. His thigh also sent him a sharp reminder that he'd had a pencil stuck into his leg a few days ago. Still, he descended the ramp as quickly as he could.

By the time he got to the body, Sarah had both her arms free of the reeking bloody corpse, but the skin was still gripping tightly around her torso, like a birth gone terribly wrong. Picture the chest burster scene from *Alien*, but a giant cat and a pregnant woman instead of an alien and that one dude. She was grunting with effort and frustration. The cat was still breathing, but slower and shallower. His eyes were closed. *Thank Christ.*

Stu limped over to the huge black body and began to climb, gripping the wormy fur between his fingers. He didn't pause to talk, only scrambled over to Sarah, grabbed both her arms circus style and began to hoist her out.

It took their combined strength to yank her free. When finally her stomach was through the gap, it made a sound like a drain being unplugged, and the whole corpse sank like a punctured floaty. The smell was overwhelming, thick with rotting meat. For a few seconds, Stu and Sarah sat together, covered in blood and fleshy pink viscera. Breathing. Looking at one another. Stu chuckled.

"We… Someone else is in there."

And suddenly, a muffled cry came up through the bloody porthole.

"Euyyy… ahmmma… helmmnm!"

Stu gathered himself and lowered his upper body down into the hole. He felt around, his hands and arms sliding over slick bloody sacks until, finally, his fingers found a foot. He grasped the ankle and tried to pull himself up. The weight was too much, and he kicked in distress, then he felt Sarah's hands, pulling him up. And other hands too. Five minutes of grunting and finagling later, Keith was out, and free of the carcass.

"My, that was unpleasant," Keith said, spitting out a glob of red, and running his hands through his long, bloody hair.

Stu, now covered himself almost completely in chunky blood, could only look at the two of them and smile stupidly. Around the cat's body, which was no longer breathing, gathered the rest of the survivors who could walk. Some of them were prodding the body or had crawled on top. Others kept their distance.

"I don't understand…" said Stu. "Was this your plan? How? I thought he couldn't be killed," said Stu.

Sarah looked at Stu tiredly. "No plan, Stu. Just lucky. This guy –"

Cough. "Keith," said Keith.

"*Keith*, had the bright idea to bring some dirt in with him when he got swallowed." Keith reached into a fold of his robe and pulled out a blood-soaked handful of moist earth. "I think that's what saved us from being digested," said Sarah.

"Bit and clawed our way out. I don't think he liked us messing with his insides. Honestly, I didn't think that was gonna kill him. Sometimes you just get lucky, eh?" Keith shrugged and grinned.

"You're insane, " said Stu, smiling. "How did you know he wouldn't chew you up before he swallowed?"

"I didn't." Stu could only shake his head in disbelief. "Not like we had a whole lot of other options, man," said Keith.

Quiet descended over the trio, as well as the survivors around the great black body decaying in the sand. The wind blew gently, and something smelled fresh to Stu, as if over one of the sand dunes somewhere was a hidden field of flowers. *A green meadow, instead of green eyes.* The sand was no longer moving like it had been. It was still and quiet. And to Stu, it almost seemed to be receding. *Like a tide*. The electricity was gone out of it. The Black Cat, too.

And though these things made him feel good, hopeful even, when Stu Black stood and scanned the horizon, he saw only a broken tower, and empty sand.

Chapter Fifty-Four

Keith Lonnagan

JUST as Keith Lonnagan thought he might lose his flippin' mind if he had to go one more second without a shower, it began to rain. And this time, it didn't come in some biblical flood. It started slowly. A gentle sprinkle, and then a smooth turning up of the dial into a steady downpour. There was no wind and no lightning, just the cool air and the fuzzy sound of rain on earth. And even a bit of shelter to hide underneath afterwards.

The two-day old blood was hard and crusted on his skin and in his hair, but the cool water turned it into liquid again easy enough. The Cat stunk even when he was living, and the stench of his congealing blood two days out was *potent*.

Keith had thought after a while he might become nose blind to it, but it seemed to have just gotten worse. It was heaven, scrubbing himself down, and even getting to wash his clothes, though it was less of a robe now, and more like a loose collection of rags. Someone had lent him a pair of boxers for the interim, but he would've gone naked just as quickly. He didn't think anyone would really mind. Not anymore.

Two days after the unexpected death of the Black Cat, no one was really sure what to do. It seemed the only thing people *could do,* was rest. Not to say they didn't deserve it. A grand total of thirty-eight people remained — as far as anyone could confirm — in the United States. Not exactly a diverse gene pool, but just right for a hot yoga class. *I suppose most classes from now on will be hot.*

Of the thirty-eight survivors, six remained in critical condition, a result of the charge they had mounted against the black demon. And with their lack of supplies, it was looking more dire everyday. Keith thought it a somewhat cruel joke to have survived such a horror as that hideous black monster, just be knocked out by an infection. Or, more likely, *starvation*, though it wasn't *all* over yet.

M, the woman Stu black had come in with, was proving to be a remarkably capable doctor. *Or, doctor proxy, I guess.* Stu Black, Sarah Bracken and Billy Thompson were also performing quite well as stand-out leaders, though Stu's injured back and leg were slowing him down quite a bit. Keith had been trying his best to help, but he found that he mostly just got in the way. He felt at his best with Harold, and lately, Ms. Bracken.

Aside from the general feeling of anxiety surrounding the topic of food and water, the other event that loomed on the horizon was the birth of Sarah's child. She still had quite a ways to go, maybe four months or more, but it seemed like her stomach was growing daily, and the awareness that they lacked a real doctor was becoming painfully acute.

Keith had met Sarah Bracken for the first time inside of a demon cat's stomach, *hey, that's something you don't hear everyday.* And he supposed that experience had brought them together in a special way. He found that though he barely knew her, he was becoming rather invested in her wellbeing, beyond the level of concern a new acquaintance might warrant. Other people in the pool of survivors were feeling similarly, Keith judged. Maybe it was the fact that she just might be the last pregnant person any of them would see. Or maybe it just felt good to care about someone again. He couldn't say.

Despite all that, Keith got the feeling that there was much more to Sarah Bracken than he knew. *Or could know.* He'd asked Stu Black about her and gotten a rather curt few sentences about how she'd helped him cross the desert from Phoenix. *Wonder what happened there…*

Aside from all these worries, Keith was feeling good. And the rain was improving his mood by the second. The small island of dirt that remained, punctuated by the slanted tower, was no longer being consumed by the desert. Keith thought it might even be growing. *Maybe… Just a little.* Some sparse patches of grass, and even a couple of little weeds had begun to grow. The sun no longer seemed as harsh as it had been, and the sand had lost that electric, *slithering* feeling. It was as if the death of the Black Cat had put the world at ease again, at least for the moment. Though, Keith did have his doubts that the cat was actually *dead, dead.* It had all been far too easy. *Far too easy. We got lucky. Very lucky. But we might as well enjoy the spoils. Aaallll thiisss sand!*

He sat in the rain until he began to prune. Finally, he rose from his criss-cross spot on the desert's edge and walked back to the base of the tower wearing his borrowed underwear. He sat down next to Harold Nettlebee, who was leaning against the warm concrete, gazing into the gray mist of the rain.

"Whaddya say Harold?" asked Keith, about nothing in particular.

"Mmm… I miss nana."

"Me too. I didn't know her like you, but she certainly had a… charm to her."

"You think *He's gone, gone?*"

Keith paused and put his fingers to his temples in a telepathic power pose. "Hmhmmhhmmhhhmmmmmmm-woowooowowahhaa… Let me check my psychic link with the spirits of the underworld and cosmic bread loaf… *survey says…* No. Prolly not. But he's not here now, so no use in worrying about it."

Harold giggled at this. Keith smiled. They looked out over the soft damp dunes of the desert and listened to the zizz of rain.

Chapter Fifty-Five

Sarah Bracken

THE concrete of the crooked tower, warm against her back, made Sarah Bracken think of Phoenix, and the cell she'd occupied across from Stu Black and Jim Quail. She'd been upset by the news of Jim's death. Stu had told her the day after the showdown with the Black Cat, almost reluctantly.

She understood Stu still harbored a bit of that coldness towards her, and she couldn't blame him. She felt the same, almost like all the things she'd done between Phoenix and here had been some kind of chilly, waking dream, a fuzzy movie playing on a faraway screen. The storm, and the brush with death she'd experienced there, had wiped away whatever desert power had been taking control of her mind and body. Now she felt kinda like a used rag. Though perhaps it was partly the growing strain of pregnancy that was returning her to the grits and aches of humanity. Her back hurt. *Human. I'm human.*

The death of the black shadow had changed things. She could feel it in the air. Everyone could. The *strangeness* was fading, and it was time to start picking up the pieces of reality. *At least until He shows up again… And he will.* She'd even begun to get some memories back. *Green* memories. Not the terrible green of the demons cat's eyes, but the green of grass and backyards and life. They were comforting, though still vague and mostly shapeless. It was good to know they were still there at least, tucked away somewhere in her brain. It made her feel like things might just turn out alright. *Just… maybe.*

Sarah sat in the rain, letting the two-day-old dried blood roll off her in grapefruit colored streams. It was glorious. Keith Lonnagan was doing the same at the desert's edge twenty or so feet in front of her. Both of them were quiet. Meditative. This rain had none of the malice or violence that the last storm had brought. This was healing. *Gray, not black.* And it had come at the perfect time.

She and Stu had been trying to keep panic among the survivors to a minimum, all while they both knew how little bottled water remained from Wilma's stockpile. This shower was exactly what they needed. Water traps littered the earth around the tower, fashioned from just about anything and everything that was available; clothes, pieces of plastic, wood, shoes, everything except the dirt they stood on. Sarah had even put up some makeshift gutters at the end of the big concrete ramp to funnel as much of the rain water into bottles as possible. It wasn't the answer to all their problems, but it was certainly a start. *And isn't that always the hardest part?*

Keith rose and began to make his way back to the shelter of the tower. He looked ridiculous with his lengthening beard and dirty boxers. When he passed by, she chuckled, and Keith shot her a good humored smile. He walked on, and the fizz of the rain slowly drew her attention back out to the gray desert and sky before her.

So what now? It seemed to be the question that never really went away. *What do you do after surviving a battle to the death with a giant demon cat, and find yourself more or less stranded in the middle of a desert of unknown size?* She had a feeling there was no handbook with an answer to that question. No *For Dummies* book.

As she gazed into that soft grayness, Sarah Bracken half expected to see the Black Cat, green-eyed and smiling, emerge from the rain, laughing.

"THOUGHT YOU GOT ME, EH? *HAA-AAHAH-AAH –*"

But he didn't. And though the fight was finished for the moment, there was still much to be done. And even more uncertainty than before. Were there others out there in that American vastness? Were they dealing with their own demon cats? *Were they losing?* Too many questions to answer. *Too many to answer just sitting on my ass anyway. Let's worry about food first. And maybe dig up a pharmacy somewhere.*

Sarah rose from her criss-cross and did another scrub down, relishing the cool hands of the rain, and flushed away the last remains of blood that still stained her skin. The blood ran down into eager soil, giving life and nutrients to plants yet un-sprouted, but lying in wait.

As she made her way back to the shelter of the observatory tower, Sarah got a view of nearly everyone on the island. *Everyone left in my world.* Most of them were sitting, just as she had been, gazing out at the rain in silent contemplation. Some slept, others nursed wounds that would likely never heal completely, or at all. They were a sad bunch. But they were survivors. And she was one of them.

Chapter Fifty-Six

Epilogue - Hugh Flemm

THAT staring, dead face flashed against the back of his eyeballs like a hot iron. The lolling tongue. The wide green eyes. The way steam had risen out of his mouth when finally he'd keeled over. Like there'd been some kind of hellish furnace deep down in his gullet. *The black cat is gone. He's gone. I saw him die.* But Hugh Flemm knew better than just about anyone else, that was a load of bologna. The cat wasn't any more dead than Jim Morrison — Hugh Flemm, an avid Morrison conspiracist. And no matter how many times he told himself, *he's gone,* a deep, *fatherly* voice at the bottom of his brain stem kept whispering, *no… Not yet.* **Not yet.**

He was two-days north into the desert. He doubted anyone back on that shitty little spot of dirt would even notice he was gone. When the cat — *not God, no, not God* — had come, Hugh Flemm had watched the slaughter with disinterest. As the people around him had begun to scream and flee, he had remained sitting. Too comfortable, and too weak to move. It wasn't like he could've run anyway. His thigh bone was snapped like a toothpick. No doctor was likely to come strolling along and fix it, either. They were more apt to hang him from that damn tower, than spend their time fixing him up. *That fuckin' Stu Black. Glib Bastard.*

He'd decided then that there were worse ways to go than being eaten. He would accept the Black Cat's judgement and hope for a swift death. By that time, the pain in his leg had become near unbearable. His wound was infected, and that blood-heat was rising up through his body like poison. He'd known then that it would only be a matter of time. *Better to get it over with quick.*

But just when he'd expected the end, something surprising had happened. *They actually pulled it off. They killed the bastard.* Hugh had watched with astonishment as the scene played out. No one noticed him, sitting quietly away from the action. No one cared. Even the Black Cat had failed to note his existence. That is, until Sarah Bracken had sprung out of his ribcage like some alien parasite. The cat had fallen just so, in his dying moments, his big green eyes had been staring right at Hugh. Hugh couldn't help but let his jaw drop in fear. They were looking into one another. Those green eyes, big as gongs, flashed with a sort of hateful *amusement.*

They'd stared at each other in silence while Stu Black had helped pull Sarah Bracken free of the cat's stinking body. And they'd *spoken.* Or, perhaps it would be more accurate to say, the cat had spoken to Hugh. For him, the voice had been as loud as thunder. Louder even. It had come from everywhere. It was a voice he knew well, but it seemed that time, he was the only one who had been able to hear it.

"MY GENERAL… I'M GLAD TO SEE YOU," the cat had said, though he did not move his mouth. "I HOPE YOU HAVEN'T HAD A CHANGE OF HEART. THESE RATS GOT LUCKY, I WON'T DENY IT. BUT YOU KNOW WHICH IS STILL THE WINNING SIDE, EH? *GAMBLER.*"

Hugh had nodded, just slightly at this. The cat had no longer been moving, and now Keith Lonnagan was being pulled free of his bloody stomach. *That hippy, smart ass.*

"I ALSO HAVE A DISTASTE FOR THAT ONE… FOR ALL OF THEM, REALLY. I KNOW YOU FEEL THE SAME. WHAT DO YOU SAY WE ERASE THEM FROM THIS PLANET? YOU

AND ME? IT MAY TAKE SOME TIME… BUT THAT'S REALLY ALL YOU HAVE, ISN'T IT, FLEMM? CERTAINLY NO FRIENDS. NOT HERE."

Hugh had actually replied out loud to this. The sound of his own voice had startled him.

"I do have friends – you – you feline fuck."

"OHH, HAHHAA – I'M SORRY. DID I HURT YOUR FEELINGS? WOULD YOU LIKE ME TO LEAVE? IT'S A SHAME… I MIGHT HAVE BEEN ABLE TO DO SOMETHING ABOUT THAT LEG OF YOURS. LOOKS LIKE IT MIGHT BE A BIT OF A SLOW BLEEDER. I DO HOPE YOU FIND A DOCTOR AROUND SOMEWHERE."

"No! Wait – I… I – I – You can fix me?" This time, Hugh had replied in his thoughts, which, it seemed, was all that was necessary.

"WELL…"

And then the contract had been struck. Though there had been a moment, perhaps when the old hag had bitten it, no pun intended, that Hugh Flemm might have become someone else. Maybe not a good man, but something more than what he was. That opportunity for change was gone. He had taken the bargain. *My life for you.*

His leg had healed in front of his very eyes. Like shaking an etch-a-sketch, his bone had returned to its proper place, and the flesh had mended. *Lickety-split, just like that.* That hot feeling in his blood had subsided as well. Hugh had smiled widely. He had been about to jump up and start dancing with joy, when the pain had come flooding back in a hot, sick rush.

"THIS IS NO FREE LUNCH, FLEMM. THERE'S A PRICE… A SMALL PRICE. JUST A FEW WORDS REALLY. *YOUR LIFE FOR ME…* SAY IT."

The pain had been so awful. So hot and nauseating. There had been no *real* choice.

"My… My life for you!"

The desert sun was beating down like a hammer. Hugh's flesh was as red as lobster shell, and scabbing over with white flakes of peeling skin. But he was walking. And that, at least was something. *Something miraculous.*

He raised the plastic Aquafina bottle to his lips, only to get one final, tantalizing droplet of spitty water. *That's it.* It hit his lips like a single raindrop on August concrete. But there was no fear. He knew he was protected. At least… *insured.*

There came a soft purring. The feeling of fur against his leg.

*My life… **for you.***

Roll Looney Tunes Outro.

* * *

Acknowledgements

The Desert Daily started out as a daily reminder of what I want to do with my life. I want to tell stories (let's just ignore the cliché for now). But telling stories is difficult, especially when you don't know where to start. I certainly didn't. In the end, you have to just begin.

It will be bad, and it will be hard, but it will be worth it.

I was in Okinawa Japan when I wrote this book, squeezing in paragraphs between teaching English classes. My co-workers there were the ones who supported me, even though I hadn't known them longer than half a year. Their kindness truly made all the difference. I was determined to write something- no matter what- but it was their interest and encouragement that made this book what it is, I have no doubt.

I'd like to thank all the teachers and administrators at Ginoza High School, as well as the ALT's of Okinawa, who were all so kind and welcoming, and who had more confidence in my abilities than I did. I'd also be remiss not to mention Ayva Dorris, who read as I wrote, and kept me going through the whole process.

A special thanks to Masami Miyazaki, Shinako Vessels, Sawako Kurane and Ayva Dorris.